T012031

TIP
COUNTY

A STORY OF LOYALTY, PATRIOTISM, AND HEROISM

GEORGE V. WARREN

TIP COUNTY
A STORY OF LOYALTY, PATRIOTISM, AND HEROISM

iUniverse books may be ordered through booksellers or by contacting:

iUniverse
1663 Liberty Drive
Bloomington, IN 47403
www.iuniverse.com
1-800-Authors (1-800-288-4677)

Because of the dynamic nature of the Internet, any web addresses or links contained in this book may have changed since publication and may no longer be valid. The views expressed in this work are solely those of the author and do not necessarily reflect the views of the publisher, and the publisher hereby disclaims any responsibility for them.

Any people depicted in stock imagery provided by Thinkstock are models, and such images are being used for illustrative purposes only. Certain stock imagery © Thinkstock.

ISBN: 978-1-4502-9996-1 (sc)
ISBN: 978-1-5320-2103-9 (hc)
ISBN: 978-1-4502-9997-8 (e)

Print information available on the last page.

iUniverse rev. date: 04/07/2017

To Nancy and Ray, who left us too soon.

Also to my three children and seven grandchildren.

1

TIP COUNTY

Tippecanoe County sits in central western Indiana. This story is about the people of Tip County, as the residents call the place, and about one man in particular, James Elroy "Roy" Emerson, whom his friends call Roy or Roy E., the newly elected county prosecuting attorney.

Interstate 70 out of Indianapolis going west to Saint Louis, Missouri, bisects Tippecanoe County. High school students say North Tip is the sophisticated part of the county, running from the interstate north to the Crawford County Line. South Tip, on the other side of the interstate, is mostly rural—good farmland and lowland running through the Eel River country to the White River. South Tip people resent the airs of North Tip residents.

Tippecanoe County is home to some 220,000 souls, give or take a few hundred. James Elroy Emerson (hereafter referred to in our story as Roy) knows this to be a fact because he's just run for prosecutor there—it's a bigger county than meets the eye. The voting rolls carry many fewer residents than people, and there are still many hundreds on the city, village, and township clerks' election rolls who don't vote in Tip County anymore, having previously taken off for Terre Haute and points west.

Industry has come to Tippecanoe County within the past decade, recent additions being a vehicle assembly plant and a large steel plant to supply steel plating to the vehicle assembly factory. The auto company bought up a huge chunk of farmland east of

Terre Haute, built a truck-and-bus plant there, and brought in a few thousand auto workers to staff the productions lines. The steel company, in building its factory to supply sheet metal to the auto plant, took another hunk of farmland out of production and set up a sheet-metal-and-rolled-steel manufacturing facility within a short commute to the auto factory.

The industrial complexes are in Tippecanoe County and in Terre Haute's county, Monroe. A political compromise brought them there—the elected boards of county commissioners from both counties got into a bidding war for the plants and offered so many tax abatements that the state's governor became alarmed, got into the act, cracked a few heads, and forced a compromise between the county boards. So that's why the auto company's plant is in Monroe County and the steel company's facilities are in Tippecanoe County.

Following the construction of the steel plant, an influx of workers came into the area. Line workers and craft people from the mills of Youngstown and Pittsburg were glad to get steady work in Tip County, even though they were far away from relatives and friends in their beloved Allegheny Mountains. Jobs at both factories drew unemployed people and underemployed individuals from throughout Indiana and Illinois, and a goodly portion of the new hires migrated from the upper southern states of Kentucky, Tennessee, and Arkansas.

As a result of the infusion of newcomers, there was a distinctly southern flavor in and around the auto and steel plants, and many an old Rebel battle flag could be seen fluttering from radio antennae of trucks in factory parking lots. Country and western is the music of choice, and Walmart (built in a minimall at the Decatur exit from Interstate 70) does a booming business in work shirts and blue jeans. Chevy and Ford trucks are the most popular means of conveyance, and God help anyone who parks a Japanese car in a plant employee parking lot. It'll get keyed or have tires flattened quicker than the owner can say *Toyota*.

2

TIP'S POLITICS

One would think from all this building that Tippecanoe County would vote Democratic, influenced by the labor unions and the new workers. But it doesn't; Tip County is solidly Republican, and it has been for as long as anybody can remember.

Up in the county seat, Decatur in North Tip, the country reapportionment boards have done their jobs well over the years, crafting and gerrymandering the voting districts so that Republican control was assured. The county legislative body—called the County Board of Commissioners—has been solidly Republican for decades, except for one session in President Franklin D. Roosevelt's first term, when the voters took out their Depression-bred frustrations on the Republican farmer-legislators in the old county board of supervisors and voted in some union people.

But the union people lasted only one term, and pretty soon it was back to business as usual at the courthouse, with the Republican old guard in control. This political oligarchy changed when James Elroy Emerson was elected as county prosecutor.

As industry began to remold the countryside, more minorities began to appear—members of labor unions with money in their pockets and middle-class values in their minds. There had always been African Americans in Tippecanoe County because one of the many termini of the prior century's underground slave railroad ended in nearby Vincennes, and church people in Tippecanoe County made welcome the escaped slaves and their families in Decatur and the surrounding communities.

Many former slaves were given small pieces of land to work, and they farmed them until they got legal titles. They and their offspring stayed on the land, generally maintaining low profiles, except for those few who migrated into the cities and villages of Tippecanoe and took the menial jobs to which they were consigned by racial segregation.

Mexican American migrants worked the fields of Tippecanoe County to bring in the crops, but this was a seasonal group, and only a few got off the migrant trail and settled down. Those who did so generally put down their roots close to Decatur, although a few hundred permanent Mexican American residents located in and around Dansville, a large village in South Tip.

Making steel is *hot* business, and some hardy Eastern Europeans (Croats, Romanians, Bulgars, and Ukrainians) came down to the steel company from Chicago and took jobs as puddlers and ladle operators. None but these seemed to be able to stand the intense heat around the furnaces.

Irish immigrant farmers had worked the fields for many generations as tenants, and some got titles to their own land. Most of the Irish, though, worked for German titleholders, and the Irish children didn't want to do tenant farming as their parents had. Instead, when the Irish kids finished high school or dropped out before graduation, they migrated away to get trade and vocational education; if they returned to Tippecanoe County, they generally settled in the cities and villages.

There were merchant families of English origin and Jewish refugees from the pogroms of Russia and Eastern Europe who came to Decatur and, after years of hard work, acquired their own grocery, drug goods, and laundry businesses. There were just a few Asian Pacific Islander Americans.

3

Roy's Family

Mother and Father Emerson were a mixture of several nationalities, so it isn't possible to say they were German, Irish, or Scandinavian. As far as Mother and Father Emerson were concerned, they were just Americans and spoke only the English language.

Both of Roy's parents were educated through grade school but had very little high school education. They came from poor families in Pittsburg and had to go to work to help their parents, who were not in the best of health. Paul Emerson, Roy's father, was a hulk of a man who worked in a steel mill in Pittsburg and met Mary Emerson, Roy's mother, who worked in the factory cafeteria. They fell in love, and little Roy was conceived prior to nuptials.

Being decent people, the Emersons married before Roy's birth so that he would have both a mother's name and a father's name on his birth certificate. A couple of years later, the Emersons gave birth to a pretty little girl, Emily, who was the apple of their eye. Roy was a kinda mischievous child; he had a pretty good build, favoring his father, but he was a little on the short side, favoring his mother. His sister, Emily, favored Roy's mother, who had been a beauty in her early years but whose good looks had been worn down by years of hard work and poverty.

When the family moved from Pittsburg to Tippecanoe County so that Father Emerson could take a job in the steel mill, the family had very little money. They could not afford housing in North Tip, so they settled in a mobile home park in South Tip, and Roy and

Emily grew up in the park, much to their chagrin, as the kids in school taunted them, calling them trailer trash.

Roy was good with his fists, and although he was of short stature, he was extremely strong. Roy usually made short work of anyone challenging him or Emily or calling them names, and the offender didn't repeat those mistakes again. Roy was not a very good student, but he tried. Emily was a much better student and helped Roy with his homework and his tests. Roy's mother, Mary, although not formally educated, was an intelligent woman, and she pitched in with Emily to see to it that Roy got through grade school.

4

ROY'S SCHOOLING
AND TALENTS

Roy attended Tippecanoe County Grade School No. 1, which gave an elementary education from kindergarten through eighth grade. Roy passed all his grades but was certainly not at the head of his class. Tippecanoe No. 1, however, had athletics for boys and girls in the seventh and eighth grades—football, basketball, and baseball for boys, and basketball and swimming for girls. As soon as Roy reached seventh grade, he tried out for the football team.

Watching him tackle and block, the coaches decided he was the ideal man for the offensive and defensive lines. His blocking and tackling were so good—although he was slow as molasses on pull plays—that he was assigned to the eighth grade team. For two years he played on the offensive and defensive lines of the eighth grade team. He was a tough blocker and could tackle and go after the quarterback if he could get though the opposition team's offensive linemen. A number of times his opponents took a swing at him; he held his own in any on-field altercations, although the officials and his own coaches told him repeatedly to behave himself and follow the rules. Yet he would just be reprimanded because his honest-looking face and believable lies would always convince the officials and his coaches that the other guys had started the trouble.

High school coaches scouted the teams from North Tip and South Tip, and Roy's play on offense and defense for Tippecanoe

No. 1 caught their eye. He was recruited to go to Calvin Coolidge High School in South Tip to play football, even though his grades coming out of elementary school were not exemplary. He completed his studies in eighth grade, and his mother and father enrolled him in Calvin Coolidge as a freshman. His sister, Emily, was still at Tippecanoe No. 1 and was a top student in all her classes there.

As a freshman, Roy was a tough customer on the football field. He was too rough to play freshman football; the coaches raised him up to the junior varsity team to play with sophomores and some juniors. The coaches, who were very supportive of Roy (knowing that he was poor kid from the trailer park in South Tip), played him as a starter on the JV football team, going both ways on the offensive line and as a "nose tackle" on defense.

Roy often got beaten up pretty badly in each game, but he didn't complain and was considered a tough kid. Nobody messed with him in high school. Unfortunately, because of his father's hours at the steel plan and his mother's hours working in the plant's cafeteria, they were not able to watch and cheer Roy along at many of his elementary and high school games.

Roy just barely passed his classes as a freshman. In the summer months, he worked out in the high school gym's weight room and became very strong. When the two-a-day practices started for football in August, Roy was in top shape. He was still aggressive in his play on the offensive and defensive lines, and when some of the seniors were injured in the early games of Roy's sophomore year, the coaches moved him from the JV to the varsity team. Even though he was a sophomore member of the varsity team, he soon became a starter and played very aggressively, going both ways. The coaches were pleased with his enthusiasm. He just barely got through his sophomore year, grade-wise, with tutoring from his mother and Emily.

Going into his junior year, he followed his same summer schedule: some work down at the grocery store as a bag boy but a maximum amount of time in the weight room at the high school gym. He appeared for his two-a-day practices in his junior year in top physical condition, and the coaches placed him as a starter at left tackle on the offensive line and nose tackle on the defensive line.

Roy wasn't much of a runner, but he was a punishing blocker and really fought his way through the opponents' offensive line to get to the opposing quarterback, halfback, or fullback carrying the ball. He was fearless and took on big guys without any hesitation. Once in a while he would get knocked down on the field, but after a short rest, he would always go back into the action and finish the game. The coaches were impressed. He just barely passed his junior year tests, but he was promoted after some summer schooling.

In his senior year, Roy was the starting left tackle and nose tackle. He played hard all season, and his team won the conference title but lost in the district playoffs. His team just couldn't seem to score against the team from Terre Haute. College coaches scouted Roy in his senior year when he was named All Conference, First Team, Offense and Defense. However, they saw that Roy was a slow runner, and his slowness (despite his aggressiveness and spirited play) was not in accord with the playbooks of Division I colleges in Indiana.

Nevertheless, Roy was given a shot at the team at Boyne College in Crawfordville, Indiana, where he was given a grant in aid. Boyne, an all-boys school (one of the last few in the United States), was one of the Indiana Ivy League colleges, and it had a pretty good football team and good coaching staff. But Boyne's administrators insisted on proper performance in the classroom and in one's own demeanor, as a representative of the college. A list of social rules was to be enforced with the student body, particularly those involved in the fraternities.

Roy worked out all summer in the weight room at Calvin Coolidge High School in preparation for his freshman year at Boyne. He showed up for August two-a-days at Boyne in top physical condition, in better shape than the upperclassmen who had been through spring practice but had gotten a little sloppy in the summer months. Watching Roy play, the coaches felt he was too strong and aggressive to play on the freshman or JV teams, and he was promoted to the varsity team even as a freshman (something that is very unusual for an offensive or defensive lineman with slow feet). In his first varsity game he was a backup, but both the offensive tackle and noseguard were injured early, and Roy was sent in to play. He did well for his first college varsity outings and remained a starter.

5

ROY'S BOYNE COLLEGE FRATERNITY CAREER

Roy would have had a moderately successful college career, and a powerful Boyne Alumni Association (very loyal to the college, its faculty, staff, alumni, and students) would have placed Roy after his graduation in a successful job—but it was not to be for Roy.

Roy's downfall was his drinking and his poor academic performance. Although he was a starting offensive player on the college's football team, most of the Boyne fraternities overlooked him. There was one fraternity, though, that paid particular attention to Roy. Its initials were TKD. Roy could never really behave himself at fraternity rush parties; his drink of choice was a half pint of peppermint schnapps, chased down with a large bag of corn nuts. He had few social skills around the ladies, who, although not enrolled at Boyne, were an important part of the social scene on campus. Only TKD offered Roy a bid to join as a pledge, and he accepted.

Roy could never memorize the Greek alphabet, so he never fully understood the meaning of the Greek letters TKD. Everyone else on campus knew the TKD fraternity by its nickname, Tap a Keg a Day. And that's pretty much what the fraternity did. When Roy joined as a pledge, TKD was already under strong social sanctions by the Dean of Students for repeated violations of the college's social rules for conduct at school fraternity parties. Roy got along fine with the members of the fraternity, but he was pretty antisocial toward the ladies who preferred the company of the other TKDs. By the end of Roy's freshman year, he had been elected the fraternity's social secretary, but the college's Dean of Students called in Roy and other officers of TKD and gave them a strict warning about infractions of the rules, mainly because the parents of young women who had attended the end-of-the-school-year TKD party and who had been fondled or otherwise mistreated called the college president and bitterly complained about disorder at TKD's parties.

One of the parents happened to be a Boyne College graduate, a generous contributor to the college, and a member of Boyne College's Board of Governors. His complaint against the behavior at the TKD party toward his daughter, a student at Indiana University, produced an immediate result in the Dean of Students' office: TKD was kept on social probation and given a warning that continued infractions in the coming school year would bring the end of TKD on Boyne's campus.

6

TKD's Death Kegger

Roy did his usual workouts during the summer, having been promoted at Boyne from freshman to sophomore status—but just barely! He came to the two-a-day practices in August in excellent physical condition, even in better shape than he had been in spring practice. He approached his duties as TKD's social secretary very casually, and he and his fellows generally ignored the Dean of Students' warnings about violations of the college's social rules.

The first semester went on with plenty of physical activity for Roy on the football field. He more than made up for his smaller stature with aggressiveness and fearless play. The team did well in the fall season. The last game of the year was with Martin University, another of the Indiana Ivy League schools, located down in Greencastle, Indiana. Martin had a pretty good football team, but Boyne got the best of the Martin Tigers in their Bell Trophy game (played that year on the Boyne field), and great joy broke out on the campus after the winning game.

Roy tackled the Martin running back, seriously setting back Martin's last-ditch effort to score a touchdown. Roy's helmet flew off with the violence of the tackle, and as he fell to the gridiron, he really slapped his head on the turf, suffering a concussion. Nevertheless, he walked off the field, showered, and went to the TKD house for the after-game party, which was a doozy. Roy had a couple of half pints of his beloved peppermint schnapps and a huge bag of corn nuts.

Having a severe headache, he passed out and slept on the couch in the frat house's living room after downing the schnapps. The crowd generally ignored him. There was gaiety and mirth going on all around him. There were two wet T-shirt contests, mud wrestling involving men, women, and mixed women-men teams, all sorts of fondling, and God-only-knows-what sexual activities going on in the members' rooms upstairs.

The next day, the father and mother of the Indiana University student who had been one of the sex attractions at the TKD party, winning a wet T-shirt contest and several mud-wrestling bouts, both individually and with a male partner (and goodness only knows what else she and other male partners did afterward), sharply questioned their daughter about the previous day's activities at the TKD house. Of course, she lied (fearing a sanction of removal from college by her parents) and put all the blame on the TKDs and none upon herself.

Her father made a fiery phone call to the president of Boyne, whom he knew personally, and the ball got started to remove the TKD house from the roll of campus fraternities. On Monday, all the officers of the fraternity were called into the dean's office, including Roy, and given the death sentence as a fraternity at Boyne. They were banned forever as a fraternity or as a dormitory for Boyne students. Any infractions would result in dire consequences for the members of the fraternity, particularly for the officers of TKD.

Roy was suffering persistent headaches from his concussion in last Saturday's Bell Trophy game with Martin, and after the meeting with the dean, he decided to take a medical leave from college for a week and go back to Decatur to rest at his parents' mobile home and to seek medical attention. He drove his beat-up Ford back home, rested for a day, and then was hospitalized for two days and instructed by hospital medical staff not to return to school until the following Monday. So Roy was not on campus for TKD's death kegger.

Now, the president of the House Committee, which owned the TKD house and grounds, was the father of the current TKD president. The house had long ago been paid off, and all improvements made to the house had been fully funded by the fraternity's alumni. The house was located at the end of a street near campus but separated from other structures by vacant lots all around, on which the members played touch football, threw Frisbees, and played catch with softballs.

The Saturday night death kegger was a particularly joyous one—beer from kegs flowed everywhere, and guys and girls were frolicking, some without tops and others without bottoms. There was drinking, dancing, carousing, and God knows what else. In the room where there was dancing, one guy from the fraternity got into a pushing contest with another fellow over a particular girl, and their affray knocked over some lit candles, which quickly caught the draperies and furniture on fire.

At first the fires were ignored, but when the walls began to burn and the paint was blistering on the ceiling, the police and fire departments were called. The revelers bailed out of the house, many trying to cover up their nudity or partial states of dress. The TKD house was engulfed in flames, and although everyone got out safely, the house was burned to the ground. The party had truly been a death kegger, and its tale is still told among Indiana college students.

On Monday morning (when Roy had returned from his home convalescence), all the officers were called into the Dean of Students' office, read the riot act, and suspended from Boyne College, to be considered individually for readmission after a semester's suspension on a case-by-case basis. Roy tried to protest that he wasn't even around for the death kegger, but his absence didn't matter to the dean; he was booted out with the other members of TKD.

Roy returned home rather dejectedly to tell his parents, but they understood that what happened was not his fault. Roy's father's call to the Dean of Students produced no favorable result for Roy. He was out for the remainder of the school year, and he would have to crawl and beg to be readmitted and, probably, excluded from the football team.

Not wishing to return to Boyne, Roy decided to follow in his father's footsteps. His father had been in the US Navy, where he served with the black gang in the bowels of an aircraft carrier, tending the boilers. Roy was all in favor of an enlistment, but he didn't want to follow his father into the boiler room of a large ship. Roy approached the navy recruiter, but he imposed a condition— he would enlist but only for training as a medic, with possible attachment to the US Marines as a navy medic. After all, he had been a pretty good football player, and he could easily master the rigors of navy and Marine Corps training. Roy was signed up for a four-year stint in the US Navy, with assignment after boot camp to the marines for instruction as a medic.

Roy's father drove Roy and his mother up to Lake Forest, Illinois, on the north shore of Chicago where the Great Lakes Regional Naval Training Command facilities were located. They dropped him off, with his mother crying over him, and he was billeted in the enlisted training detachment's quarters. Soon, Roy became immersed in his navy training.

7

ROY IN NAVY BOOT TRAINING

Roy was actually enthusiastic during his navy boot training, particularly the physical exercises. The training staff would arrange wrestling matches among the trainees, and Roy would always win. He was awkward in swimming, but the trainers knew that he was headed for marine medic instruction and would, undoubtedly, be assigned to Vietnam (which was really heating up), where there would not be much swimming inland.

Roy was doing poorly in his academic studies as a recruit, but he made a pal, an attractive Jewish girl from Waukegan named Becky Davidoff, who helped him with his tests and exercises.

Becky and Roy talked all the time, and they tried to get passes off the base to go to a bar whenever they could. Both had pretty good conduct and excellent attendance ratings, so they picked up a couple of passes. At the bar, Becky would load up on beer, but Roy stuck to his peppermint schnapps. He was always disturbed that he couldn't find corn nuts at the bar, like in Indiana, and he had to satisfy himself with beer nuts. Becky and he played pool; Becky was pretty good, and Roy was so-so.

Whenever they take a cab back to the base, Becky would snuggle up to him and want to make out. Roy wasn't much of a ladies' man, so his necking didn't really satisfy Becky. Once, she suggested that they get a motel room together, but Roy said he wasn't interested.

Becky found him to be a very different guy, not into chicks all that much, as their fellow recruits were. Becky and Roy liked each other very much.

The boot training ended; Becky went off with another trainee for a week's vacation to a hotel in Zion, but Roy decided to stay around his barracks for a couple of weeks until his navy medical training program began. He would spend some time in training at Great Lakes and then finish up his training with the marines at Camp Pendleton in California. As mentioned, things were heating up in Vietnam, and it was expected that the marines would be sent there to get into the fight. Roy expected to go into Vietnam with the marines.

For his time lolling around the barracks before his medic's training program began, Roy enjoyed on-base cooking; he was one of the few recruits who did not complain about the navy's food service. After chow, Roy would generally go to the weight room and lift for an hour or so. After a shower, he would take a light jog around the base and then go back to his barracks and read cowboy and western novels until his next meal.

He stayed away from the in-town bars and restaurants, trying to conserve his money (which wasn't all that plentiful). He pretty much followed this routine for the first ten days of his leave; there was no purpose in going home because his parents worked all the time and Emily was in school. His old buddies from the high school were spread all over the country. Some had enlisted, like him, in the military services. Some had tried to get jobs at the auto and steel plants.

One afternoon, toward the end of his leave, he followed his morning and noon routine—breakfast, lifting, jogging, a shower, lunch, and back to his bunk to resume his reading of his paperback novels. Unexpectedly, Becky Davidoff showed up at his barracks' bunk and gave him a kick with her athletic shoe; she was wearing civilian clothes. Roy had fallen asleep, and his paperback novel had fallen out of his hand and onto the floor of the barracks.

Roy woke up with a start and saw the pretty face of his friend

Becky, smiling at him. She looked great with a tight shirt showing some cleavage, tight blue jeans, athletic shoes and socks, and her lovely hair in a ponytail. She told him to get his fat a—up; she was taking him out to lovers lane, and they were going to neck for the rest of the afternoon and then have sex that night at the No-Tell Motel. Roy tried to ignore her, turning over in the bunk to pick up his dropped paperback. He retrieved it and started reading it once again.

Becky reached over, gave him a passionate kiss on his ear, and whispered quietly to him, "Guess what I have outside in my car?"

Roy growled, "Knowing you, it's probably a box of condoms!"

"No. Guess again."

"Okay, a *new* girlfriend for me, who is not searching for a girlfriend because *you* are my girlfriend, I think!"

"No, you fool, out in my car is a cold six-pack of Old Milwaukee Beer; five for me and one for you, as a chaser."

Roy was curious and asked, "A chaser to what?"

Becky replied, "To a half pint of peppermint schnapps and a huge bag of Indiana corn nuts."

With that, Roy put down his book, reared up in his bunk (striking his head on the top bunk), shook his head, and said to Becky, "Let's go. Why didn't you tell me that in the first place?"

"I wanted to get you all 'sexed-up' first. You're one of the few guys who respect me. The guy this past week also respected me, but he, like you, is foolish enough to go off to training, where he and you can get yourselves killed. And it would pi—me off to lose two very good friends to war."

Roy rolled out of his bunk, put on the top of his sailor suit, his shoes, and his sailor hat. He grabbed Becky by the hand, gave her a chaste kiss on the cheek, and went out to the car with her. There, sitting in the front seat, was the chilled six-pack of beer and his beloved schnapps and a big bag of Indiana corn nuts.

Roy let out a sigh, opened the door for Becky, and then settled into his passenger seat, holding the loot in his lap. Becky started driving off the base, having sweet-talked the patrolman at the entrance gate into giving her a short-term on-base pass for her civilian car. She told Roy how she had gotten his attention: she'd opened her car door when he'd begun questioning her, bent over to tie her shoe, and as she'd showed him her navy ID card, she'd given him a good long look down her shirt at her cleavage.

That trick had worked its magic on the shore patrolman. As they exited the base and she turned in the pass, they heard the shore patrolman say, "Lucky guy," about Roy. Becky wanted to go right to a motel, but Roy flatly refused. If she went there, he insisted, he wouldn't go in.

So Becky drove down to a picnic area where there were benches and a fine view of Lake Michigan and the skyline of Chicago in the distance. It was a balmy day. At night, the park served as a lovers' lane, particularly for the navy personnel from Great Lakes and their in-town girlfriends. The only people in the park this midafternoon were Becky and Roy.

They got out the loot and proceeded to enjoy it. With Becky's first bottle of beer and Roy's first good swallow of his peppermint schnapps, both began to relax. He put handful after handful of the corn nuts into his mouth and swooned like a man who had just had a sexual release. Remembering that he was supposed to be a gentleman, he offered the corn nuts to Becky, and she took a handful.

For the first time since they had met, they each had an opportunity to tell about their backgrounds. Becky had grown up on the north shore, been a swimmer in high school, dated sailors, and loved to ride on the back of their motorcycles, greatly aggravating her parents. She refused to go to a four-year college but got an associate's degree in recreation from Lake County Community College and defied her parents by enlisting in the US Navy. Becky said her parents had practically disowned her.

Roy told Becky the story of his life and upbringing, his football prowess in grade school and high school, his arrival at Boyne College, and his unceremonious suspension from the college for a fraternity party he did not even attend. So he joined the navy for four years and wanted to see combat, just as if it was a football game—he didn't want to sit on the bench.

Becky teared up when listening to Roy's story about his and his sister's growing up in a trailer park, his having to fight with kids who them trailer trash, and his wrongful expulsion from Boyne College. Surprisingly, Becky reached over, while Roy had a mouthful of corn nuts and had just taken a swig from his schnapps, and gave him a passionate kiss on the lips and felt down the outside of his pants, where there was a bulge in his groin. She stroked the bulge and asked him to go right away to a motel with her. Again, he said no, but he had enjoyed Becky's passionate embrace and the rubbing on his crotch.

Roy looked at Becky's tearful face and said, "Look, Becky, dear, I really respect and like you, but I'm like a man caught on a busy street between a walk and a don't-walk sign. I don't know where life is going to take me. To go with you to a motel, although I would like to do so very much, would just be for sex and not for love. I don't think you deserve that. You are a very fine lady and helped me to get through the paperwork involved in my boot training. I think if it hadn't been for your help, I would have flunked out, but I have to say the answer is still no."

For the rest of the afternoon, Becky and Roy just held hands at the picnic table, drank all the beers, and finished off the Indiana corn nuts, and Roy got Becky to take the last swig of peppermint schnapps from the half-pint bottle. On their way back to the base, they stopped at a seafood restaurant, and Roy bought them both a seafood dinner. At the base entrance, Roy asked Becky to drop him off; he needed to walk off or jog off his dinner, the corn nuts, the bottle of beer, and the half pint of peppermint schnapps. They necked in Becky's car for a couple of minutes, and then Roy exited and took a good long walk, with a little jogging, around the training base before returning to his barracks and hitting the sack in his bunk bed.

The next few days were uneventful. Finally, his short training period as a navy medic commenced. Once again, he had no trouble with the physical part, but he was all hands with the medical part and not too smart with the books and the written tests. Roy must have had a needy look about him because a pretty young member of the training class, Mary Best, who was headed for a hospital ship with the fleet, took him academically under her wing and gave him help so that he could master the books and pass his tests.

He enjoyed what he was learning but worried about his performance as a navy medic in the field with the marines and how he would function under enemy fire. He thought he would be okay because he had been kicked around so much in his football days. Also, he was not afraid of being involved in combat, although he would be an unarmed medic.

The training program took several weeks; Mary ended up at the top of the class, and Roy just scraped through, being "the goat," or the bottom performer, of the class. Both graduated and got their rank as a navy medic.

Mary was a bit of a protected girl, with a pretty face and a nice build, but she was a little on the heavier side. Roy owed her a lot, so he invited her to go out with him for dinner, drinks and maybe some dancing on the evening of their graduation ceremony. Both dressed in their cleanest navy garments and hailed a cab to go up to Waukegan to the hotel that had a bar, restaurant, and nightclub. Roy had his usual schnapps; Mary had a Bloody Mary, and each ate a good seafood dinner.

They went into the bar and had some more drinks, Roy sticking with his schnapps and Mary with vodka, as had been in her Bloody Mary—she knew better that to mix her liquors. They talked about their lives and where they might be stationed. Mary's mother had been a navy nurse, and her father, a navy enlisted man. She called herself a military brat. Unlike Becky's parents, Mary's mother and father supported her decision to join the navy and become a medic as an enlisted service member. Roy told Mary about his life and how he was heading out to Camp Pendleton to train with the marines and, probably, would be deployed with them overseas. As they danced in the nightclub to slow tunes, they held each other closely. Roy could smell Mary's scented shampoo and her alluring perfume. Mary could smell Roy's after shave and cologne and feel the bulge in his navy pants.

As it was getting late, Mary suggested that they get a room in the hotel and spend the night together—they would probably not see each other for some time. Roy turned Mary down (she cried a little), just as he had turned down Becky, but it made him feel pretty good that women thought enough of him to want to take him to their beds.

They took an expensive cab ride back to the Great Lakes facility, and Roy walked Mary from the gate to her barracks, kissed her passionately good night, and then jogged lightly to his barracks. The next day, Mary got her orders to report to the fleet. She sought out Roy and kissed him goodbye. She promised to write. It took a couple of days for Roy to get his orders for Camp Pendleton, but they came through as he had expected. Immediately, he departed in a navy plane for San Diego, where he was picked up by a marine sedan and delivered to the training center at Camp Pendleton.

8

ROY WITH THE MARINES

When Roy arrived at Pendleton, he was billeted with the marines and assigned to take appropriate marine training as a combat medic. One young marine was brazen enough to call him a "swabbie son-of-a-b—" because Roy was not going to be a combat marine. With a couple of swings, Roy flattened the mouthy marine, and thereafter the rest of his classmates left him alone. The other marines didn't know he had grown up fighting his way past guys who called him and his sister trailer trash. The marine training program flew by, and the marine noncommissioned officers finally accepted Roy as a valuable addition to their troops.

After the Gulf of Tonkin Resolution passed through the United States Congress, President Lyndon Johnson had Secretary of Defense McNamara order the marines into the affray in Vietnam, called the Vietnam Conflict because Congress had not declared war on the Viet Cong or the regular North Vietnamese government. Roy shipped out with the first load of marines headed for Da Nang in Vietnam, and he landed as a medic with the first contingent of marines to touch down on Vietnamese soil.

During the long trip by ship to Vietnam, Roy practiced his medical training, day in and day out. When the call of "medic, medic" finally came, he wanted to be fully prepared to do his best to treat and to save *his* combat marines.

After setting up their base at Da Nang, the marines were immediately sent into the field to come to grips with the enemy—Viet

Cong troops and North Vietnamese regulars. Roy was right up front in the thick of each battle and was subjected to injury from bullets, shrapnel, and fires caused by phosphorous rocket or mortar shells. Every time Roy went out with the troops, he suffered some sort of minor injury; he always treated himself and didn't report himself as wounded to the commanding officer, fearing that he would be held out of the next fight.

Roy became very proficient in treating injuries under enemy fire; when the cry "medic, medic" went out, Roy got to the injured soldiers as fast as his fat legs would carry him—remember, though, that he had *slow feet* on the football teams in grade school and high school and at Boyne College. He saved the lives and limbs of a lot of marines; some marines he carried on his shoulders back to the rear where an ambulance was waiting. Daily, he would return to his marine billet, treated his own wounds, and get as much shut-eye as he could.

The marine commander liked Roy because he exhibited no fear, even in the fiercest fire fight. The commander knew, although Roy never told him, that Roy was continuously being wounded, so in one report the commander put Roy in for a Purple Heart medal and a Bronze Star medal with V device. One morning, as the troops were assembled for inspection prior to departure into the field, there was a short awards ceremony; a number of the marines, including Roy (the navy medic) received the Purple Heart, and several marines were awarded the Silver Star medal. The commander pinned on Roy's fatigues a Bronze Star medal with V device.

As the marines and Roy saddled up to go into the field, Roy slipped both medals into the twin medic bags he strapped across his chest and climbed on the back of an M-48 tank to be in the lead of the attack column.

Sure enough, the enemy had laid an ambush for the attack column, but they had not expected an M-48 tank to be in the lead. They opened up on the tank and the marines following it. Bullets zinged off the tank turret around Roy. As soon as he heard cries of "medic, medic," he dismounted from the tank and ran to the downed marines. The fire fight was a hot one and lasted for several hours, during which Roy did his best to keep his marines from dying. Unfortunately, a couple of them did succumb to their wounds, and Roy felt very dejected.

He used up all his supplies. He ran to the rear and emptied all the medical supplies, particularly blood expanders, out of the ambulances at the rear of the column, and ran back as fast as his little legs could carry him to the downed marines. Eventually, the enemy broke off contact, and the marine column, with its wounded and dead, returned to base. After the ambulances drove off to the hospital, Roy went to see the unit commander; boldly, he confronted the officer, picked out his medals from his medic bags, and offered them back to the commander.

Tearfully, he said to the commander, "Here, sir. Please take these medals back. I couldn't save all *my* marines today, and I feel the dead deserve these medals and not me."

The marine commander looked fondly upon Roy, told him that he was a fine medic and that good men are wounded and die in combat. Roy had earned his medals, and they were for his personal sacrifices and to keep him working as hard as he was doing for his buddies in the Corps. Then the commander did a strange thing; noticing blood on the front and back of the sleeve of the left arm on Roy's fatigues, the commander put his finger into the hole, and Roy gave out a yowl.

The commander said, "Roy, you took a bullet through and through your left arm; don't give me any of your bull—. Get over to the hospital and get that wound sewed up before you get gas gangrene. We marines don't want to lose you. You seem to be the guys' favorite medic. Do you know why?"

"Yes, sir, I think I do! When the whistle blew when I played football both ways on the offensive and defensive lines, I went into the game. I feel the same way now, even though bullets, shrapnel, and rockets are flying around."

"Now get going over to that hospital, Emerson. *Semper fi.*"

Roy was pretty tired, so it took him a while to walk to the hospital. He saw some of his marines waiting to be treated, so he just sat down on a chair and fell asleep. He was probably sleeping for a couple of hours, still wearing his bloodstained fatigue shirt, with his crossed medical bags and his beat-up red cross on his helmet, when a lovely older nurse came over, looked at him, and asked him if he was hurt and if he was there for treatment.

Looking up at her through sleepy eyes, he thought he saw an angel. As he looked closer at her, he beheld a lovely nurse with short dark hair, a pleasing face, a nice figure, and a comforting smile. He said, "Yes, ma'am." She upbraided him for not speaking up sooner. He assured her, "My wounded marines come before me." She said that Roy was wounded too and that the others had already been treated. They had overlooked him because he was asleep. They had thought he was just their escort.

She hustled Roy into a treatment room and got him up on a gurney. She told him to take off his battle gear and strip down to the waist. He did as he was told, being surprised at the amount of blood on his fatigue jacket and medical bags and the dents in his Red Cross helmet from bullets and shrapnel. He was examining his helmet carefully when the older nurse came back to the door of the treatment room. She didn't enter right away but admired his upper body and his biceps. She saw the bloody fatigue shirt and the bloody medical bags and was amazed at the dents in his helmet. She stood there but shook herself away from her reverie and went into the room to help treat the bullet wound in his left arm.

She cleansed his wound, both front and back. It was clearly a through-and-through shot, but it had not hit a major bone or ruptured an important artery. There had been bleeding, but by now it had pretty well coagulated. As she bent over to pour sulfur into the wound, Roy could smell her fine hair shampoo and her alluring perfume.

As she bandaged his arm, without even knowing why, he reached over and kissed her on the cheek, saying, "Thank you, Nurse, for your fine care."

She didn't react right away but kept at her job, bandaging him up. He put on his bloody fatigue shirt. She told him to wait in that room for his discharge and went to get him two new medic kits and took his old kits away from him. Then she closed the door and sat down on a chair next to his gurney while he put back on his fatigue shirt.

She looked him right in the eye and said, "I am Lieutenant Commander Margaret Mary Bucher, the assistant superintendent of nurses here. It seems that you marines have eyes only for my young and pretty nurses, yet you just kissed me and thanked me for your care! What is your name and rank?"

Thinking that he was going to get court-martialed, Roy blurted out, "Navy Medic First Class James Elroy Emerson—called Roy by my friends—assigned to the marine detachment here in Da Nang, I go out into the field with the marines every day. This is the first time I have ever been to the hospital."

Nurse Bucher said to Roy, "As I was bandaging your arm, I think I saw other self-treated wounds on your body. Am I right?"

Roy replied, "Yes, ma'am."

"Okay, Medic Emerson, take off all your clothes, but keep on your skivvies."

"All of them, ma'am? How can you send me to the brig with no clothes on but my skivvies?"

"I'm not sending you anywhere; I want to examine you and treat those wounds!"

Roy undressed again, down to his skivvies. Nurse Bucher laid him down on the gurney and looked him over from top to bottom on the front. She found numerous self-treated wounds, dressed them, and reprimanded him harshly for not coming to the hospital.

She noticed that as she examined him, he got a bulge in his skivvies. This event made Margaret Mary Bucher feel pretty good because other men on base didn't seem to care for her one bit! On his back, the nurse found numerous self-treated wounds and even down on both legs. She cleansed all his wounds and applied ointments and dressings. She told him to turn over and get dressed. She watched him while he dressed. He was about ten years younger than she was, but she thought he was a hunk of a man and was a very brave navy medic.

She lectured him to come to the hospital when he was wounded again. She was about to pull away from his bed when Roy, unexpectedly, reached over, grabbed her, brought her into his arms, and gave her the most passionate hugs and kisses he had given any woman in his life.

His eyes filled with tears, and he murmured to her, "Thank you, my nurse angel."

After pulling away from his amorous advance, she stepped back, looked squarely at him, and then went over to him and gave him the most loving hugs and kisses she could. As she was leaving, she said, "Medic Roy Emerson, am I going to see you again?"

Roy responded, "Sure thing."

She left; he got finished dressing, put his twin medic bags across his chest, popped on his Red Cross helmet and walked out of the hospital to get chow and retire for the evening.

The next morning he was up with the troops. His unit commander came to him and showed him a communication from Lt. Cdr. Margaret Mary Bucher, RN, at the hospital, advising that he had been wounded, should be held out of combat for a day or two, and should receive a Purple Heart medal.

Roy said, "Unless you are giving me a direct order, I refuse to stay behind today, tomorrow, or the next day. My wounds are nothing compared to what happens to the others. You know I am one of your best medics. I belong with my marines, but the Purple Heart medal is up to you."

The commander looked at him sternly and said, "All right, saddle up!" Roy did exactly that; he went over to the motor pool and climbed up on the back of the lead M-48 tank, which was just pulling out to go into the field with two companies of marines on search-and-destroy missions. There were several bitter battles that day, the next day, and the day after. Roy tended the troops, used up all his medical supplies, and got injured several more times, but he kept going. He helped to carry out several severely wounded marines to the ambulances in the rear of the column.

Eventually, the enemy was overcome and broke off the fight. This time Roy rode back to the hospital in the ambulance with some of the wounded, and he treated them as they were returning to base. He didn't even realize that part of his Red Cross helmet had been blown apart, and he had received a superficial head wound. When the ambulance carrying Roy arrived at the hospital, he helped to carry all the guys in. He was pretty tired and a little woozy from the head wound. When he sat in the chair next to one of his wounded marines, he fell asleep.

He had been asleep for several hours when he felt someone kicking him in his combat boots. Coming out of sleep, he looked up and saw his angel, Lt. Cdr. Margaret Mary Bucher, RN.

Looking sternly at him, Margaret said, "I see you ignored my orders to your commander and have been going back into the field. Look at you. You are full of blood, and part of your helmet is torn wide open. You have a head wound that is untreated. Get into a treatment room."

"Ma'am, I will only go in there if all my marines have been cared for."

"Yes, they have; now get your ass in there, and let me have a look at you. When you go in there, take off that damn fatigue jacket that is full of blood, and take that battered helmet and those crossed medical bags off your body."

"Okay, I'm going."

Walking into the examining room, Roy nearly collapsed and was propped up and helped onto the gurney by Margaret Mary. He did as she told him in removing his things, but he was passed out on the examining table when she came in. Immediately, she called the doctor, who looked at his wound, found it superficial, and said that Nurse Margaret Mary could treat him.

While Roy slept, Margaret treated his head wound with cleansers, salves, dressings, and a tender kiss, which Roy did not feel. She gave him a poke, and he woke up. She told him that she was going off duty and would drive him to his barracks but only after she got him a good dinner. He looked undernourished.

Roy was surprised because he had always thought of himself as being a little chunky. He did as he was told, and together they walked to her sedan, which was assigned to her and to the nursing supervisor.

She drove him into the city, past a row of brothels, outside of which American troops were standing and eagerly awaiting the services of the ladies within, and stopped her vehicle at a clean Vietnamese restaurant. She came around and helped him out of the sedan and into the restaurant.

Inside, she ordered for both of them, with some Vietnamese rice wine to help him ward off any infection. They held hands over dinner and told each other the stories of their lives.

She was career navy from a military family. She had once been married but had a miscarriage, after which she and her husband divorced, and she had been single ever since. She had risen in rank but very much missed the company of a man.

"You, Roy, seem like a pretty nice and brave fellow. I like your company."

Roy repeated the story of his life and told Margaret Mary that he cared for her very much and couldn't help himself when he gave her that first kiss. It just seemed to happen, but, he admitted, he wanted to do it again and again and again.

She reminded Roy that she was older than him, and guys his age preferred her younger nurse charges.

He said, "That's not it. I generally like you. You are an angel."

With that remark, she came over to him and passionately kissed him. She could sense the bulge in his pants. "What do you do in your off time?" she asked.

"I don't take off time," he admitted.

"If I request off time for you, would you go with me for an R&R [rest and recreation] visit to Thailand?"

He replied, "Sure, I'd love to go with you. To tell you the truth, I would hope that we would have *one* room and *one* bed, but if you want two rooms and separate beds, that's okay with me. I have a little money saved up."

She looked back at him and said, "We'll see."

They finished their meals, and she drove him back to his barracks. As he was about to get out, he reached over to hug and kiss her passionately, and she reciprocated.

It looked like love had come for the first time into Roy's lonely existence. He blew a kiss to Margaret and said he hoped to see her again soon.

The next day it was business as usual in the field, but this time the location was changing to what the marines called Happy Valley, up north of the Que Son Mountains, and the marines were getting trained for helicopter assaults and landings. There were major battles in Happy Valley that lasted every day for nearly a month. Finally, the enemy decided his losses were too great and broke off combat with the marines.

By now, the marines were leap-frogging strong points and going into battle in helicopters. Roy got pretty good in getting out of helicopters fast and getting his wounded and dead marines on dust-off helicopters quickly as well. Finally, Roy received some shrapnel in his buttocks from a grenade blast, which required the marine commander to send him to the hospital for treatment. After Roy got back to base and was told to go to the hospital, his commander said that Roy was to take two weeks off on R&R and get "healed up."

Unknown to Roy, Lieutenant Commander Bucher had been in touch with Roy's commander and told him that she had some plans of her own to heal up Medic Roy Emerson. The, marine commander thought that some time away with a lovely nurse would do Roy some good. Why? When he returned, he was going to be sent up-country toward the ill-named Demilitarized Zone to be a medic at the marine forward base at Khe Sanh.

Roy walked over to the hospital, bleeding from his buttocks. His fatigue pants were soaked with his blood, and he could feel shards of shrapnel in his butt. When he got to the hospital, he sat in his usual chair until the other marines were treated. He fell asleep again, but this time his blood was seeping from his wounds onto the chair and dripping on the floor.

Finally, Nurse Margaret Mary came over to him, woke him up, and took him into surgery. There, the staff stripped him down and gave him an IV to knock him out. The surgeon removed shrapnel from his buttocks and lower back and stitched him up. When he woke up in the recovery room, he saw Margaret Mary standing over him. When she saw that he was the only patient in the room and no other staff was present, she bent down and passionately kissed him, whispering in his ear that when he was healed they were going on R&R to Thailand together.

"No arguments!"

Roy was too woozy from the anesthesia and said feebly, "Okay, when I feel a little better."

Roy passed out again, and when he awoke, he was in a hospital bed on his stomach, with his buttocks exposed to the air and with two or three pillows under his groin. There was an anti-infection light shining on his backside, and Margaret Mary frequently changed his bandages, letting his bare skin soak up the healing light, and then rebandaged him. He found that he had a Foley catheter in his penis to remove his urine, but he had little appetite and did not frequently have a bowel movement. If he needed a bowel movement, Margaret Mary would give him an enema and hold the feces pan under his anus as he expelled the water and fecal matter.

Roy could heal up pretty quickly, and in a couple of days he felt well enough to walk around with a walker and, in about a week, to seek his discharge from the hospital. He still hurt in the rear end, but Margaret Mary told him she was going to take him where he could really heal up—Thailand.

She got orders for R&R for both of them; they got down to Saigon Airport and took a commercial flight to Bangkok, Thailand, where they then took a taxicab to a hotel she had picked out. Roy was still sore as he got out of the cab and walked into the hotel. Nurse Margaret did the registration for them and led him up to a nice room for *both* of them, with a large *single* bed.

As soon as the doorman placed their little bags were placed in their room, and Margaret Mary had tipped him, she closed the door and began passionately to make out with Roy. He reciprocated with all his might, despite his hurt buttocks. Soon, they disrobed, went into the bed and had foreplay, sex, and intercourse for several hours, falling asleep exhaustedly in each other's arms. Roy had not felt such love in his whole life; he really loved this older nurse, and obviously, she loved him.

They would be together for two weeks; this thought made him smile as he looked over at his lovely naked companion in bed with him.

When they awoke in the other's arms the next morning, they looked at each other and kissed tenderly. Margaret said they should shower, but Roy pulled her over on top of him and kissed and fondled her passionately; they had another act of intercourse and lay side by side, napping for a short time. When they awoke, Roy asked Margaret's permission to pose a couple of personal questions to her.

She replied, "After what we did last night and this morning, you can ask me anything that you want. Go ahead."

"Margaret Mary Bucher, nurse and navy lieutenant commander, I have fallen in love with you. I would like to have you with me for a long, long time. I come from a poor background, have little money, an incomplete education, and a couple more tours of duty in Vietnam, starting when we return in-country up to Khe Sanh."

"Roy, get to the point; what are you asking me?"

Stuttering, Roy said, "I have never felt toward any woman—ever—the way I feel toward you. I would like to marry you and make you my wife. This trip isn't just for sex, I hope; my wish is that you'll find something in me worth holding on to. Oh, I've been invited to motels before by girls, but I haven't gone. What they wanted was sex; I wanted companionship and true love. I think I have found that with you. I'm not sure, though, that you have found true love with me."

At that point, tears came into Roy's eyes, and he couldn't finish his talk and questions with Margaret. She said nothing but was looking at him intensely. He wiped his eyes with the sheet and slowly continued. "After I finish my tours, I want to go to college on my GI Bill and my saved-up money and get my degree; then, believe it or not, I would like to go to law school. But all this is dependent upon whether I survive the combat in Vietnam. So, I'm worried and confused; how can I ask you to marry me when I might not be alive in a few years?"

Margaret took Roy's two hands in her hands, placed them on her breasts, and then brought them to her lips and kissed them. "Isn't it a better question to ask as to whether you could be happy with a woman like me who is ten years your senior?"

Roy immediately replied, "I don't care one bit about your age. I care about you—the 'you–ness' of you—not about your age. Your body is beautiful, your lovemaking is spectacular, but best of all, you are my angel—my healer—my love. I think we could be companions for life, irrespective of the age difference. Personally, if we were out of the service—and I would want you to complete your twenty years in the navy—and we were both civilians, I would like to have a child by you. If you couldn't conceive a child, then I would like you and me to adopt a child. I think you would make a wonderful mother, as you would make a wonderful wife. What do you say to all this?"

Margaret Mary began to cry. She laid her head on Roy's chest and massaged his chest hair. He tenderly caressed her hair and kissed her head. She looked up at him and asked, "Do you really—and I mean really—mean what you are saying and what you have asked me?"

"Yes, oh yes. While we're here in Bangkok, I could buy you a small ring. We would be engaged, and we could get married in a year or so when I'm getting ready to finish my tours in Vietnam. But you may have to wait on me because you'll probably be promoted and sent to a naval hospital back in the States. After we got married, we would be separated for a while, but when we are both out of the service, we could move to Indianapolis, where I could finish college and go to law school—if I get accepted—and you could continue with your nursing. I would hope, though, that when we are civilians, we can have a child. I would love to be a father to a child, whether a boy or a girl. These are my ideas."

"Roy," Margaret said, "I think I have been in love with you from the time you gave me that first kiss at the Da Nang base hospital. My answer is yes. I will marry you if you'll have me. We can do it like you have said—have an engagement for about a year, then marry, and allow both of us to finish our navy careers; then go to Indianapolis where I can do my nursing, and you can do your education on the GI Bill. I love you so very, very much, and I think you will be a loving, kind, and honest partner with me for life, not like the last guy I married and divorced. So, yes; let's get a ring here while we're on R&R. It doesn't have to be expensive, but I'd like to pick it out together. If you don't have quite enough money, I'll put up some of my money—I make more than you! So, again, yes. I would be honored to be your wife."

With those statements both Roy and Margaret were weeping and clutching tightly to each other. They returned to lovemaking and didn't stop until they showered together and got dressed to go to the hotel bar and restaurant for drinks and dinner. They bathed each other in the shower, and they kissed and hugged each other frequently.

They almost decided not to go out for dinner, but both of them were famished and thought it best to get some food into their stomachs before drinking liquor. They dressed in their naval outfits and went downstairs to the bar. There, Roy ordered a bottle of champagne, and he toasted his new fiancée and gave her a passionate kiss.

They had a wonderful Thai dinner that night, some more drinks in the bar, and a little dancing to Thai love songs on the little dance floor in the bar. They were both pretty tired and a bit jet-lagged, so they went up to their room and resumed their romancing, seemingly with more passion than the night before. The next day, they agreed, they would go shopping for Margaret Mary's engagement ring.

Just before falling asleep, though, Roy asked his beloved to give him some pictures of her that he could keep in his barracks and inside the web-gear of his helmet while he was in the field. With that request, Margaret gave him more hugs and kisses, and then both fell sound asleep.

The room Margaret had rented at the Thai hotel was an expensive one, with a tub large enough for two bathers simultaneously and fine soaps and shampoos provided by the hotel. Before going ring shopping, Roy took Margaret into the bath, and they proceeded to wash each other's hair and bodies. Margaret sat in front of Roy in the tub.

As Roy was washing her hair, she looked down at her hands and found age spots. She said to Roy, "Will you look at these age spots on my hands, Roy? Are you sure you still want to marry an old woman like me?"

Roy looked over her shoulder at a few age spots on her hands. He took her arms and kissed each of her hands. Speaking very solemnly, Roy responded, "It's not those little spots on your hands, which I have just kissed, that bother me; it's those huge red nodules in the middle of each of your breasts that have me worried." He reached around and massaged the engorged nipples on Margaret's breasts. She turned around in the tub and tried to push his head under the water, but he was a strong guy, and he got Margaret in a bear hug. Passionately, they kissed, and they had an act of intercourse in the bathtub.

After their act of intimacy, Margaret rested her head on Roy's chest, and he gently stroked her hair. Roy surprised Margaret, saying, "You know, darling, I've been thinking. I'm not much of a thinker or all that intelligent, but I've been thinking about this a lot lately. I don't really want to wait a year before we get married. I have known you for some time, and you have treated me at the hospital a number of times and taken me out to dinner. We have been passionate and intimate together. So why should we wait? What about this: when we go out to shop for your ring today, why don't we buy three rings—your engagement ring, your wedding ring, and my wedding ring, if we have enough money? Then let's cut short our vacation here in Bangkok by a couple of days, fly back to Saigon, go to Da Nang earlier than our reporting date, find a chaplain, and get married right away?"

Margaret raised her head from Roy's chest, passionately kissed him on the lips, and asked, "Are you really, really sure you want to marry an old biddy like me?"

"Yes, Margaret dearest, I do. I know you are the one for me, and with a little bit of your tender loving care, I think I can be the one for you."

Margaret could feel an engorgement in Roy's male member. She replied, "The answer is yes, but if we don't finish our bathing and get out of this tub soon, we're going to stay here all day having glorious sex and will never go shopping for those rings. I'm all for your ideas. Let's go."

Margaret and Roy finished bathing each other and got out of the tub before there was more sexual intimacy. Getting dressed, Margaret asked Roy, "Do you think we should buy some civilian clothes?"

"Why? I'm not going to be able to wear them where I'm going at Khe Sanh, and as my wife, I don't want you going out with a bunch of younger sailors, all dolled up in fancy clothes, showing your glorious cleavage."

Margaret tried to slap Roy, but he grabbed her, and they made out for several minutes. Finally, she pulled away from him and told him that they just had to go.

In their navy uniforms, Margaret and Roy strolled hand in hand as they window-shopped and stopped in several jewelry stores. Diamond rings were too expensive, but they finally found a jeweler who sold a beautiful ruby engagement ring with a gold band and a small gold band to match the engagement ring. There was a matching small gold band for Roy. Both of them put up their money and split the bill. Roy carried the rings out in two small felt boxes.

The days of their R&R passed by quickly; they strolled and strolled, wearing their navy uniforms. It pleased Roy when a couple of guys whistled at Margaret. Roy looked over at her, smiling, and said, "You see? You really are a catch."

She just clutched him tighter. They ate, drank, danced, and made glorious love together at the hotel. Finally, the time came to leave Bangkok if they were to be married before the end of their R&R. They flew back on a commercial flight to Saigon and then hopped on a military truck for the final leg of the trip to Da Nang.

After going to their separate billets to drop their small bags and get on some fresh clothes, Roy located an army chaplain who had a female secretary and a male chaplain's assistant. The chaplain agreed to marry the couple right away since Roy was leaving tomorrow for a new assignment with the marines in the field. The chaplain called to Margaret's billet and asked her to come over right away.

Roy was standing at the little chapel entrance, dressed in his cleanest navy whites, Margaret was in her best uniform, with her badges of rank and her ribbons. Roy did not wear any of his awards. When she got out of her sedan, he came to her, kissed her tenderly, and led her into the chapel, where the nuptials were performed by the chaplain and witnessed by the chaplain's assistant and the secretary. The chaplain gave the newly married couple the military marriage certificate, which Roy asked Margaret to keep.

The newlyweds drove in the sedan back to the little restaurant where they'd had that first dinner together. They enjoyed drinks, dinner, and Vietnamese desserts. They admired each other's rings. Roy told Margaret that she did not have to change her surname unless she wanted to do so; she could continue to be a Bucher or become an Emerson—the choice was hers. Roy said that he had just married Margaret, but he didn't own her—she would be her own person. Margaret said she would not change her name until they were both civilians.

They drove back to Roy's billet in Margaret's navy sedan. For nearly an hour they talked, petted, and necked very hard. Roy was proud of his ring and said he would wear it everywhere. Margaret cried when Roy kissed the rings on her left ring finger. Roy said he had to go; tomorrow, he was on orders for Khe Sanh. He would write to her every day, but there might be a delay in delivering those letters. He urged her to stay at the hospital in Da Nang—too dangerous to be at other facilities now in Vietnam. She said she would do so but would expect a promotion and orders to report somewhere else. They pledged their love each for the other and indicated their determination to stay in touch and to take more R&R's whenever they could get the time.

Roy went into his bunk and packed up his gear for his morning departure. Margaret cried all the way back to her barracks. When she entered, she found out that the word had gone around from the chaplain's office that she had married Roy. The girls got out of bed, hugged and kissed Margaret, and said they were planning a postwedding shower for her at the Officers' Club in the near future. Margaret cried and cried; about all she could say to the other girls was she loved Roy Emerson more than any other man in the world, except for her father. The girls in the barracks cried with her, crowded around her, and assured her that the good Lord would be looking out for her husband. Finally, she peeled off her clothes and went to sleep, crying into her pillow.

9

HILL 861-A AT KHE SANH

Roy was up early the next morning, proudly wearing his new wedding ring. He went to the adjutant's office and changed the beneficiary on all his military insurance and pay amounts to his new wife, Margaret Mary Bucher Emerson. He turned in any extraneous equipment, got his orders, and, wearing his battle gear (Margaret's two new medic kits crossed over his chest and a new Red Cross helmet), he boarded a plane for Khe Sanh.

Flying north toward the Demilitarized Zone (DMZ) over the Vietnamese countryside, all he could think about was his new bride, Margaret. War, death, and wounds seemed far out of his mind. All this changed as the plane neared the landing strip at Khe Sanh. The pilot announced that the landing would be a scoot-and-run affair, meaning to grab gear, get out quickly and run to the sandbagged headquarters. Roy was near the plane exit. When the aircraft touched down, he opened the door and took off running as fast as his fat legs would carry him, along with his gear, to the sandbagged headquarters. Mortar shells and rockets began to bracket the plane which was slowly taxiing down the runway. When the last passengers had exited, the plane took off with maximum thrust, running a gauntlet of antiaircraft fire as it banked out toward the sea. It had to have been hit several times by shrapnel and gunfire.

In the headquarters, the adjutant told Roy to wait awhile; the base was undergoing an attack, and the commander and operations officer were busy at the sand table (which was a scale model in sand

41

of the base and of the believed enemy positions, with appropriate labeling). Roy sat down on a chair and fell asleep. In a couple of hours he felt someone kicking him awake. Opening his eyes, he saw the base commander smoking a cigar and standing in front of him with the adjutant.

The commander said through his cigar smoke, "So you're our new navy medic—wounded three times and winner of the Bronze Star with 'V' device. Those medals entitle you to stay down here with us at our base hospital."

"I don't like to sit on the bench, Colonel," Roy said. "I want to be where the fighting is. I told my last commander that I didn't deserve the medals—they should go to *my* dead and wounded marines—but the commander wouldn't take them back. I don't wear or display my medals. I'm no hero, Colonel."

"Emerson, you played football, didn't you? So, you really want to get into the game."

"Yes, sir. *Semper fi.*"

"Okay, Adjutant, send him up as our medic on Hill 861-A. Watch your ass up there, Emerson. The last medic came back from the hill in a body bag!"

"Yes, sir," Roy replied.

The adjutant said to grab his gear and get out to the helicopter pad. Roy picked up his stuff and walked to the helipad, where one of the aircraft was taking off. He hopped aboard. The copilot leaned around and asked if Roy was going to 881-South or 861-A.

Roy said. "Hill 861-A."

The pilot leaned around and said, "Good luck. Scoot and run."

When the helicopter touched down on Hill 861-A (showing its height in meters and a twin to Hill 881-South nearby), a violent mortar and rocket attack started on the hill. Roy bailed out with his gear and medical bags. He really didn't have any place to run, but when he heard the cries of "medic, medic," he left his gear where he dropped it and ran down the hill to treat the wounded.

Bullets, rockets and mortar bombs were coming in thick and

fast, but Roy tended to his charges. He applied all his bandages, syrettes of morphine, compress packs, sulfur, and blood expanders until his medical packs were empty. Tourniquets were still needed. Having no more supplies, Roy stripped off his fatigue shirt and fatigue pants and began to cut them into strips with his scissors. He was going from injured man to man, stripped down to his undershirt and skivvies and wearing his socks and combat boots with his Red Cross helmet on his head.

A shot grazed his helmet, and a small dent left in the helmet caused a little blood flow down his forehead; he brushed the blood away. When he'd used up all his strips from his clothing, he took off his boots, removed his socks, and cut the socks into strips; he applied the last of his strips to the wounded. Unfortunately, the wounds on several of his charges were too severe, and they died before they could be evacuated. Due to bombing by marine aircraft and long-range artillery fire on the enemy lines by 155 mm Long Tom cannons at the Rock Pile several miles from Khe Sanh, as well as every marine firing fiercely into the enemy, their trench lines, and bunkers, the shelling of the base and of Hill 861-A stopped.

The lieutenant and top sergeant came down from the crest of the hill and stood over Roy. He was cradling the head of a dead marine and crying. Roy wore no outer clothes, socks, or boots; he wore no medic bags—they were empty and discarded at the end of the trench. Roy was rocking the dead marine in his arms as if he were his own son.

The lieutenant looked at the top sergeant, who said to Roy, "Welcome, Medic Emerson to Hill 861-A. You have done a good job. But we need to get you some clothes and some new medical supplies."

"Sergeant, please have them send up as many as they can spare," Roy said. "Look at me. I ran out of bandages, and we need a lot of tourniquets. Please get me as much as you can. Also, I need some bags for sand. I want to build a medical hooch on the top of the hill beside the landing area."

The lieutenant spoke up. "That's a dangerous place to be during an attack, Emerson. When a helicopter comes in, it's the target for all the mortars and rockets from the enemy."

"Sir, I don't care," Roy responded. "I have to have my hooch there so that I can get the dead off the hill quickly before their bodies are torn apart by shelling."

"Okay," the sergeant answered. "We'll put through your orders, General Emerson."

All of them laughed at that remark, including the wounded guys in the trench. Roy's names among the marines after that attack were Pantless Roy or Doc Roy or Doc Emerson. He was very pleased by these names; they showed he had finally been accepted by the marines on Hill 861-A.

As soon as Roy got some new clothes, medical supplies, and bags for putting dirt into and building his hooch, he sat down and wrote a letter to Margaret, telling her how much he loved and missed her. In time, Roy would keep up his daily letters to Margaret, writing in the evening in his hooch by candlelight; also, he would write to his parents, his sister, Emily, and to Becky and Mary, telling them of his marriage to Margaret and of his Purple Heart medals and Bronze Star medal. All letters had to go through the marine censor, so he wasn't sure how much of what he wrote got through.

After he had been on the hill for a couple of weeks, Roy had his hooch completely sandbagged and covered with a piece of metal provided by helicopter from the airstrip down near Khe Sanh headquarters. Roy put the body bags of the dead into his hooch so that they would not be scattered all over the hill during a barrage of mortars and rockets from the enemy. The marines humorously named his hooch Roy's Ranch, and the name stuck as long as he was up on Hill 861-A.

Roy got to know some of the marine helicopter pilots; he showed them the picture of his wife, Margaret, which he carried in the webbing of his helmet. Roy asked, if they ever got down to Da Nang's hospital, if they would please to tell her that he was well and loved her very much.

10

ROY'S DECORATIONS

Stories about this oddball marine medic began to go up and down the hill and even got down to base headquarters. The things that Roy was doing to and for the marines were for their benefit, although they seemed a little loony at the time. One marine came back from R&R, seriously scratching his groin. Roy knew this marine very well, and he had a medical history of sexually transmitted disease (STD).

The marine was not too tall or stocky, and he was really scratching when he got off the helicopter. Roy was working out on the crest of the hill by doing push-ups and lifting some of the sandbags from his hooch. Whenever a helicopter would land and there was not a barrage going on, Roy would go over to helicopter to see if it had brought him any medical supplies. This time, there were some medical supplies aboard, which Roy off-loaded.

As he was carrying off the last box of blood expanders, the short marine got off the helicopter, scratching his groin like mad. Roy asked him if he was bringing back anything to the hill but himself. The marine gave Roy a smart-mouthed reply. Roy picked him up bodily and pulled down his pants. The guys in the trench near the helipad saw what Roy was doing, and all heads turned toward the scene. Roy had the marine's pants completely down around his boots, so when the marine tried to run away, he tripped and fell down.

Roy went over to him, reached into his privates, and saw blood and discharge. He picked up the marine and carried him over his shoulder into Roy's Ranch. Some of the guys from a nearby trench went up to the entrance watched Roy throw the marine on his cot, look him over carefully, pronounce that he had an STD, and wash his crotch with antibiotics. He had a syrette of penicillin (which he kept for this type of situation inside cold packs) and plunged it into the marine's buttocks.

As the marine got up from Roy's bed and pulled his pants up, Roy told the guy to stay clean, and "Don't bring that sh—up here to the hill." The marine thanked Roy. The guys from the trench were amazed. Roy reached into his piled-up medical supplies and tossed a pack of condoms to each of the idlers standing outside of Roy's hooch.

Roy said, "For your own sakes, please use these so I don't have to pull down your pants and inject you with penicillin when you come back from R&R."

The guys took the packs he distributed and nodded their heads affirmatively. Within a week, the shorter marine was feeling better. He came up to Roy's hooch and thanked him again. Roy asked him to lie on the bed, and Roy got another syrette of penicillin and shot him up in the buttocks.

Other stories went around about Mother Roy. After a particularly heavy rainy season, he stocked up on extra pairs of fresh socks. He began to comb through the marines in the trenches and demanded that they remove their shoes and socks for a "Roy's toes examination."

The guys would raise hell with him, but they finally did as he commanded under his threat to put them on report. Roy had no authority to put anybody on report, but he spoke so forcefully that the guys believed he did, and they didn't want to face an irritated lieutenant or top sergeant about noncombat wounds that could be prevented.

Roy went down the trench line, giving out fresh pairs of socks and demanding that the marines look out for their feet and come to him for fresh socks and for foot treatment whenever they needed new socks and ointments for the feet. The story went around that one marine, a pretty strong guy, refused to take off his shoes so that Roy could examine his feet.

Roy had seen this marine limping around, but the marine uttered obscenities at Roy when Roy asked him to remove his shoes. Roy simply picked up the guy, threw him over his shoulder, and forcibly took off his shoes and socks, exposing terrible trench foot. The guy was pounding with all his might on Roy's helmet, shoulders, and back, so much so that he left black-and-blue marks on Roy's shoulders and back after the encounter.

He put the guy back in his trench, treated his diseased feet, gave him new socks, and had him promise that he would keep in touch with Roy to make sure that the his trench foot cleared up. The marine whispered to Roy that he acted as he did because he didn't want to be sent off the hill. He and Roy hugged and gave each other a high-five.

The base commander heard the funny rumors about the nutty navy medic on Hill 861-A. He decided to go up for an inspection and to say "good job" to Roy. However, unexpectedly, the assistant marine division commander came to Khe Sanh for an inspection tour. Surprisingly, when his plane landed on the base airstrip, there was no firing by the enemy.

The brigadier general went in to meet the base commander and go over the situation at Khe Sanh. They spent time at the sand table and looking around personally over the defense positions. The general said he wanted to go up on the hills; a helicopter took him and the colonel up to Hill 881-South, and there was no firing upon the helicopter's landing from the enemy lines.

The helicopter flew the general and colonel and the general's aide-de-camp to Roy's Hill 861-A. No sooner had the helicopter landed than a massive barrage of gunfire, rockets, and mortar bombs came onto the hill from top to bottom. Shrapnel hit the helicopter, and the general's aide told the copter pilot to take off. As the helicopter exited the hill, it was hit by gunfire from the enemy lines. The North

Vietnamese regulars must have smuggled antiaircraft equipment up into their front trenches, along with mortar tubes and rocket-launching racks.

Roy was out of his hooch in a minute and gestured to the general, colonel, and aide to come inside Roy's Ranch before they got killed. They stumbled into Roy's hooch; the strong smell of dead bodies in body bags reached their nostrils. Roy did not stand on ceremony with his upper-echelon visitors. He gave them greetings and salutes, but he took off running out of the hooch and down the hill to tend to his wounded marines, hearing urgent calls of "medic, medic."

Roy tended to the wounded as best he could, using up all his medical supplies. Even during the continued shelling, he ran back up to his hooch and refilled his medical kits, nodding to his visitors still located in his hooch. He packed as many blood expanders into his pockets as he could carry. Out of the hooch and down the hill he went running; more cries of "medic, medic" were heard as the heavy shelling and bullets flying around from both sides continued.

The heavy combat went on for over an hour, and Roy ran out of his medical supplies. He resorted to his old standby—stripping off his jacket, shirt, and fatigue pants and cutting them into strips to use as tourniquets. He bandaged as many marines as he could, particularly those for whom tourniquets would stop heavy bleeding. When he ran out of strips, he pulled off his shoes and cut up his socks.

He used the last bit of strips on the wounded. Finally, the enemy decided to use timed sky bursts of mortar shells, raining shrapnel down on the trenches. There were four very badly wounded marines in one trench, upon whom the shrapnel would have rained down but for the fact that Roy lay his half-naked body on top of them. Shrapnel from the air bursts pierced his helmet, back, shoulders, and buttocks. A massive piece of shrapnel stuck in the back of Roy's helmet, knocking him senseless.

Eventually, the guns of the marines, the cannon fire from the

Rock Pile, and marine aircraft's low-level bombing stopped the shelling of the marine lines. The enemy lines were left destroyed, burning, and smoking.

The general, his aide, and the base commander emerged from Roy's Ranch and walked around the hill, coming down to the trench where Roy was stretched out on top of the four wounded marines, unconscious and bleeding heavily from perforations of his body from top to bottom. The general and his aide lifted Roy off the wounded marines. They were still alive, but Roy was out cold.

The general and his aide just looked at the colonel and said, "This man is a real fool or is a true hero." The colonel said that Roy was the navy medic everyone was talking about around base headquarters.

"This is how he functions; putting his own life at risk to save what he calls *his* marines."

The general said to his aide, "Put this man in for a high award and get him to the hospital. I heard from the colonel that he's married to a navy nurse down at Da Nang. See to it that he's transferred there."

Roy was still unconscious and wearing the Red Cross helmet with a huge piece of shrapnel in it. The helicopter that came to pick up the general, aide, and colonel was directed to leave the officers on the hill for further inspections. "Take this man to the hospital in Da Nang," the general said, "and send another helicopter to pick us up."

"Will do, General," the helicopter pilot said and took off for Da Nang, with Roy wrapped in a blanket wearing only his underwear, his boots without socks, and his helmet with the shrapnel still sticking out of it.

The helicopter had to avoid antiaircraft fire from the Viet Cong, so it flew to Da Nang in a route over the sea.

The pilot had radioed ahead to the Da Nang hospital that it was delivering a patient with severe back injuries. Margaret was on duty; there had been extensive combat in Happy Valley the previous day, and there were numerous wounded marines crowding the hospital's wards. The helicopter pilots and the hospital staff members carried

Roy in and placed him, still unconscious, on his face on a gurney in the hallway. He was covered with a hospital blanket, and his smashed helmet was still on his head—the staff fearing that if it were removed, they might injury his skull or, more seriously, his brain.

Roy lay unconscious on the gurney in the hall for some time; he had a tag hanging around his neck with his name, rank, injuries, and location at Khe Sanh, but Margaret and her staff were working vigorously with other injured patients. Finally, one of Margaret's junior nurses stopped at Roy's gurney and thought she recognized him. He was still unconscious, but she looked at his tag.

She let out a cry when she realized it was Roy Emerson, Margaret Mary Bucher's husband, lying in the hallway. She hastened to Margaret, who was tending a patient, and whispered to her that Roy was seriously wounded and was lying on a gurney in the hallway. Margaret Mary let out a scream; the young nurse took over her duties with the patient she was tending, and Margaret went running to her husband's prone and unconscious body, embraced him, wept over him, and asked the surgeon to bring him into the operating room whenever he could fit him in.

During the next hour, Margaret stayed with Roy, who would come in and out of consciousness but could not recognize his wife. Eventually, he was taken into the surgery; the surgeon gave her permission to scrub in on the operation. The helmet was cut off Roy's head. The staff was amazed that the huge piece of shrapnel had been stopped by the webbing in the helmet, cutting up and bloodying Margaret's pictures in the webbing but only superficially injuring Roy's scalp.

However, Roy's back, buttocks, and legs had received numerous shrapnel penetrations that had to be removed one by one, and some of the larger wounds needed stitches. Roy was given anesthesia and painkillers; he did not stir, even in the recovery room.

When Margaret and the recovery room staff were satisfied that he was out of danger, although still unconscious, they sought a bed for him, but none was available. Instead, the nursing staff kept Roy in the recovery room until a bed opened up later that day. He was wheeled to his bed, still unconscious from the anesthesia, antibiotics, and pain medications.

As tired as Margaret was, she stayed constantly by his bedside, even sleeping in a chair until he woke up. Finally, he awakened in a clean hospital bed, laying on his front side with his back heavily bandaged and an IV running into his arm. Margaret was asleep in the chair beside his bed. She was within touching distance of Roy's bed, and he reached over and took her hand in his. She woke up, saw her husband looking lovingly at her, and passionately hugged and kissed him, weeping heavily.

He touched her face to dry her tears and then fell back to sleep.

Roy stayed in the hospital for at least a week while his wounds healed; eventually, he was able to walk around with a walker. Margaret practically moved into the hospital to be with Roy all the time and to help the rest of the staff with the other patients, leaving only to go to her barracks to shower and get a clean nurse's uniform. Her uniform was always covered with blood but, thankfully, not from Roy.

Margaret toiled with the patients, including Roy, around the clock, stopping for very little sleep. At one point she passed out and was put to sleep by her staff on one of the empty gurneys. Her staff was very worried about Margaret because she had the responsibility of tending to her husband as well as supervising all the nurses in treating the other patients in an overflowing hospital.

As soon as Roy could walk under his own power, he left the hospital and went to his barracks to rest and to recuperate. One day Roy went over to the marine adjutant's office and said he wanted to report for duty and receive his orders to go back to Khe Sanh. The adjutant said that Roy was not going anywhere until he was cleared by the doctors at the hospital.

One day, unexpectedly, Margaret showed up at his barracks. She was dressed in her best uniform. She got him up out of bed, helped him put on his clean navy whites, and pinned his medals on him.

She helped him to walk to the marine headquarters building. There, she was met by all her off-duty staff nurses.

As a group they went into the headquarters where a navy captain was awaiting the awardee, his wife, and their friends. The adjutant called everyone to attention. Roy stood up straight, but he swayed a little. There he was in his navy whites, wearing his Purple Heart medals and his Bronze Star with V device.

The adjutant called out, "Attention to orders." Then the adjutant read a commendation for First Class Navy Medic James Elroy 'Roy' Emerson, USN. By order of the commanding general of the Marine Division staffing the Khe Sanh base, Roy was awarded three additional Purple Heart medals for wounds received under heavy combat with a hostile enemy force, attacking his duty station on Hill 861-A at Khe Sanh base.

Roy now had Purple Heart medals strung across his chest. He was still a little ill, but he shook the hand of the adjutant and the navy captain as vigorously as he could.

Then the captain turned to Margaret—she now called herself Margaret Mary Emerson—and read two commendations for Roy of great valor on at least two occasions under serious enemy artillery, mortar, and automatic weapons fire during attacks on his duty station at Hill 861-A at Khe Sanh Forward Marine Base, saving many marine lives. For his valor, first he was awarded the Silver Star medal, which was pinned onto his chest by the marine adjutant.

Then the navy captain said that for great heroism under heavy enemy fire and having saved the lives of many wounded marines, Roy was awarded the Navy Cross medal, which Margaret pinned to the chest of her proud husband. Tears ran down Margaret's cheeks as she finished with the clip on Roy's Navy Cross.

The captain and adjutant stepped back and said, humorously, to Roy, "You may now kiss your bride."

Tears came into Roy's eyes, and he passionately hugged and kissed his wife; both of them kept holding on to each other and failed to pay full attention to the adjutant, who handed one of

Margaret's nursing charges orders for both Margaret and Roy to have two weeks of R&R together, beginning immediately.

By now, Roy had served two tours of duty in Vietnam, and Margaret was on her third tour. The navy captain and adjutant went back to the work in their offices. The young nurses crowded around Roy and Margaret, who were still locked in a tight embrace, finally got them separated, and escorted them out for a dinner at their favorite Vietnamese restaurant.

Roy was a little shaky in walking to Margaret's sedan, in the back of which two of her nursing charges would be riding to their celebration. One of Margaret's staffers was carrying boxes for all of Roy's medals. Slowly, Roy took off his medals—over Margaret's protests—handed them to the lovely nurse in the backseat of the sedan, and asked her to "box them up for later display, when Margaret and I have a child or two to whom I can show the medals."

The nurses in the backseat pulled Roy's head back, kissed it, and patted Margaret on the head, telling her how happy they were to hear Roy's remarks.

They kidded Margaret, saying, "We wish we had a hunk like Roy to help us to make a baby!"

Margaret just laughed and replied, "If he keeps getting shot up like that, I'll turn him over to you. If he keeps receiving such wounds it will probably kill me, so he'll be all yours."

At the Vietnamese restaurant, all the off-duty doctors, nurses, aides, and staff members were waiting and cheered Roy when he came in. They toasted him repeatedly, but Margaret told Roy and the others to go easy on feeding drinks to Roy. He was just out of the hospital. The group had great gaiety and mirth and a wonderful Vietnamese dinner. At the end of the dinner, the group told Margaret and Roy that as a wedding gift, a nice hotel room had been rented for them in the town. Air transportation had been arranged for the next day for them to go on a two-week R&R—first-class commercial, round-trip, from Saigon to Bangkok.

They were signed up to stay for nine days in Bangkok, all

expenses paid, including all meals in the hotel's restaurant, drinks in the hotel's bars, and entertainment at the hotel's nightclub, including all gratuities, and champagne in their room. Roy and Margaret both broke down crying and embraced everyone. The staff members said they would get rides back to the base; Margaret and Roy could have the sedan for the evening. Someone would pick them up in the morning to take them to Saigon Airport.

The young nurses whispered to Margaret that they didn't think she would need many things to wear on their two-week R&R because they doubted that she and Roy would be fully clothed all the time.

Roy was still in a joyous fog, but Margaret said, "You girls are bad, but you are absolutely right. I'm going to keep him naked as a jaybird most of the time and will try to make that baby!"

That night at the hotel in town, Margaret and Roy made the most passionate love and fell asleep in each other's arms. The next morning they were picked up by the sedan, driven to the Saigon airport. They departed on Thai Airways for Bangkok and nine days of glorious romance.

Arriving at Bangkok, they went by taxi to the hotel and found they were registered for the room they had when they were previously on R&R. They tipped the doorman who brought in their few belongings. Then they passionately made out and went into the two-person tub to bathe each other and remember the day that Roy convinced Margaret to get married upon their return to Da Nang.

They got dressed in their navy uniforms, went down to the restaurant, and had a wonderful meal, drinks in the bar, and intimate dancing to slow tunes in the hotel's nightclub. Up in their room, they were in a passionate embrace in the bed, but practically nothing happened sexually because they were so exhausted and soon fell asleep in each other's arms.

When they woke up the next morning, neither would let go of the other. They just kept hugging and kissing. They were very much in love. Margaret turned Roy over and examined his sutures and bandages. There was some leakage of blood through some of the bandages on his back, so Margaret told him that they would have to take a stroll to find a druggist where she could get bandages and some salves and disinfectants.

Roy looked intensely into Margaret's eyes and asked her fondly, "What happened to Margaret Margaret Bucher? Did she die before I saw her again at the Da Nang Navy Hospital?"

Margaret laughed and replied, "Yes, like a snake sloughing off its old skin, Margaret Mary sloughed off Bucher and is now Emerson. Do you have any problem with that new name?"

"Yeah, I'm really mad about that last name," Roy replied as he began intensive foreplay and then intercourse with his beloved wife.

When they woke up after intimacy, Roy stroked Margaret's head and said, "You have made me the happiest man in the whole world. I don't deserve you. You mean more to me than all the medals and commendations I have received. Margaret, don't ever leave me. Please, please, don't ever leave me."

Kissing Roy, Margaret said, "You don't need to worry about me leaving you. You need to worry about you leaving me by getting your stupid self killed up on that hill at Khe Sanh. You have to be more careful."

Roy reminded her, "I'm a health professional, like you. I have to do what I can for my marines. Darling, I've protected you. I changed all my military benefits to your name."

"Roy, please don't tell me that; it's bad luck,"

Roy exclaimed as she started crying, "Margaret, why don't you stop crying and try to make a baby with me right now. Okay?"

Margaret laughed a little, remarking, "I suppose I have to do that because we're both in the nude in the bed, and you're stronger than me."

Their intimacy continued as both craved the companionship of the other, just as if they were still newlyweds (which they really were, although separated by geography in Vietnam and a violent war).

After a while, they finally got out of the bed, went into the big tub in the bathroom, and shampooed and washed each other's bodies. Dressing in their navy uniforms, they went downstairs for dinner, drinks, and entertainment, forgetting about a pharmacy. Margaret never did get to that pharmacy, but she washed Roy's back and his wounds very carefully. This couple was as much in love as if they were teenage boyfriend and girlfriend.

Unfortunately, their nine days in Bangkok flew by quickly, and they had to catch the plane back to Saigon and then to Da Nang. There, both Margaret and Roy went to the adjutant's office. The adjutant welcomed back the young lovers but apologized for giving Roy orders to leave on the morrow for Khe Sanh.

The navy captain came out of his office; both saluted the captain, who gave both Roy and Margaret hugs. He presented Margaret a set of new badges of rank—she had been promoted in her absence to the rank of full commander. With that new rank, she could request reassignment out of Vietnam or stay in Da Nang and become superintendent of nurses at the hospital.

"The current nursing superintendent just got promoted to my rank, Captain, and has orders of reassignment to Bethesda Naval Hospital in Maryland. She has to leave immediately, but she said she would stay until we have her replacement."

"Captain, you now have the new nursing captain's replacement—me, Mrs. Margaret Mary Emerson, RN, USN, who wants to stay here in Vietnam very much and is now of a proper rank to be superintendent of nurses at the Da Nang Hospital."

Margaret reached over, grabbed Roy's hand, and said, "I stay in Vietnam as long as my husband, Medic First Class Roy Emerson, is still stationed here. We don't leave each other, even though we are separated by miles. Please give me those orders to this Da Nang Hospital, Captain."

The navy captain replied, "I thought you would say that, Commander Emerson; here are your orders, assigning you to the Da Nang Hospital as superintendent of nurses. Good luck to both of you."

Both Roy and Margaret saluted the two officers and exited the adjutant's office. Margaret dropped off Roy at the marine quartermaster's department, where he picked up all new equipment. Then she took him over to the hospital, where she got two new medic bags and hung them around Roy's neck. She kissed him passionately, wished him goodbye, and dropped him off to pack up for tomorrow's departure.

The next morning Roy reported to the marine airport, got aboard the first helicopter leaving, and told the crew he had orders for Khe Sanh. The pilot and copilot looked at Roy and said, "You'll be sorry. When we land there, you've got to scoot and run."

Roy replied, "I see that things have not changed since my departure about a month ago."

The helicopter came into a hot landing field, with mortars and rocket bombs landing all around. Roy jumped out of the helicopter as soon as it touched down and made a beeline for the sandbagged headquarters. Just as Roy was about to enter the headquarters, the helicopter took a direct hit and burst into flames. Immediately, Roy ran from the entry to the headquarters and back to the helicopter.

There was a roaring fire, and the pilot and copilot were knocked out and leaning forward on the controls. The helicopter was still operating, with the main and rear rotors rotating. Roy charged into the cockpit and dragged out the copilot, who was unconscious and burned. Then Roy ran around to the other side of the helicopter and pulled as hard as he could on the pilot's door, burning both of his hands. He used all the strength that he still had (realizing he was still convalescing from hospitalization at Da Nang and a two-week R&R, where he had little exercise) and freed the door. Roy reached into the burning helicopter and struggled to get his arms around the unconscious pilot. The pilot's legs were somewhat tangled around the controls, and Roy was in the process of dragging him when the fuel in the aircraft exploded, blowing off all the rotors and spewing flaming fuel all over the burning helicopter and onto Roy, the pilot in his arms, and the unconscious copilot on the ground on the other side of the furiously burning aircraft.

Roy was on fire himself. He put down the pilot and threw dirt over his body to extinguish the flames, which stopped blazing and left the pilot's clothing smoldering. Very seriously burned, Roy ran around the burning wreck, went to the copilot's prone figure, and dragged him away from the burning aircraft. He moved toward the entry to the sandbagged headquarters.

At that point there was another violent explosion from the helicopter, showering Roy with burning debris as he turned his back to shield the copilot's body from the airborne flaming debris. At the entry of the headquarters, he turned over the copilot to the command staff, which had emerged to give aid if they could. Roy's clothing and red-cross helmet were smoldering when he raced through the debris burning on the ground around the wreck, He grabbed the pilot's body and carried it toward the entry to the sandbagged headquarters.

Releasing the pilot's severely burned and injured body to the headquarters staff, even though rockets and mortar bombs were still falling all around the airstrip, Roy collapsed.

A navy doctor, by coincidence making an inspection visit to Khe Sanh, began treating the pilot, copilot, and Roy. The helicopter crew members had serious injuries as well as third-degree burns. Roy was diagnosed with a concussion, some internal injuries, and third-degree burns, particularly on his back and legs. All three needed immediate hospitalization, and the colonel arranged for a dust-off helicopter to fly in amid the bombardment and pick up the crew members and Roy for transport to the Da Nang Navy Hospital.

The crew chief on the dust-off transport helicopter could do very little for these seriously injured, burned, and unconscious men, other than to comfort them as best he could. He was cautious about administering syrettes of morphine, given their condition.

When the helicopter landed at the Da Nang helipad, an ambulance and crew met the plane and took the patients immediately to the hospital. Emergency aid was given to all three marines, but the copilot did *not* survive. The pilot remained unconscious with severe injuries, including serious burns and a fractured skull. Roy had a concussion, some internal injuries and serious third-degree burns on his neck, back, buttocks, and legs.

The medical staff had to carefully remove Roy's clothing and helmet because these items were nearly melted into his skin. Roy was burned on his face, but the more serious burns were around the back of his neck at the base of his helmet and completely down his back.

Margaret had worked twelve to fourteen hours daily for the past two weeks. She got a few hours of sleep after a long day of providing direct patient care. Margaret was not the type of supervisor who stayed in her office, playing with paperwork, when there was hands-on work that needed to be done with patients.

After the medical staff got the three new patients stabilized as best as could be done at that hospital, which did not have a fully staffed burn unit, one of the young nurses went to Margaret's barracks and, gently waking her, told her that Roy was once again a patient at the hospital. Margaret shook off her sleep, splashed water into her face, donned a clean uniform, and took off running with the other nurse to the hospital. When she arrived, Roy was on a gurney outside of the surgery, as the doctors were operating on the severely injured pilot.

Margaret lifted Roy's coverings on his body, was shocked, and began crying.

She looked at her young charge and said, "He was just here. He left yesterday. How in the world did he get so injured to come back here? I hope and pray that he can be saved."

The young nurse said that the adjutant had come over from the marine on-base headquarters to inform the hospital staff that the three severely injured men were en route by helicopter for the hospital and that Roy was aboard, having saved the two fellow patients but was seriously injured in the process. Two teams of doctors were operating on the pilot and copilot simultaneously in the cramped surgery.

Unfortunately, the copilot never regained consciousness and his heart's flatline on the monitor told the staff that he had expired. The pilot was expected to live.

After finishing the operations on both of the aircrew members, the medical staff turned its attention to Roy. Margaret was permitted to scrub in on Roy's operation. His body was thoroughly x-rayed, and he was found to have a ruptured spleen, which was removed surgically. He had a concussion but no skull fracture. His brain seemed to be intact and only showing bruising where he experienced the concussion. He had no broken arms or legs, but he was severely burned on both hands and arms and all down his back, to the beginning of where the top of his boots were on his legs.

Margaret bore up pretty well during Roy's surgical procedures, x-rays, and treatments. When he went into the recovery room, she stayed by his bedside. He would be unconscious for a while. Margaret was so exhausted by the events surrounding Roy's treatment and her general lack of rest during the preceding hectic two-week period that she fell asleep beside Roy, with her head resting on his bed.

After a careful examination by the medical staff and the surgeons' conference with Margaret, a decision was made to keep Roy at the Da Nang Hospital rather than transfer him to the hospital ship, USS *Repose*, cruising off the coast of South Vietnam. The helicopter pilot's injuries and burns were so severe that he *had* to be removed to the *Repose*, but the *Repose*'s wards were crowded, and the ship's medical staff was overwhelmed with very serious cases, many of which turned out to be fatal.

If patients could get care elsewhere, the *Repose*'s medical staff requested that any new patient be cared for elsewhere. Even the hospitals in Japan and stateside were getting full with evacuated Vietnam Conflict's casualties.

Roy would be at the Da Nang Hospital for about two months, but eventually he would walk out of there, holding Margaret's hand, and get a new set of orders from the nearby adjutant's office. About two weeks after Roy's admission to the hospital, there were unexpected visitors.

The brigadier general, who was the marine division's assistant commander, appeared, along with his aide-de-camp and the navy captain stationed at Da Nang. The trio came into the hospital with bags full of medals for all the patients, including Roy. Word went around—and especially to the nurses' billet—that there were award ceremonies going on at the hospital for all the patients.

All off-duty medical, nursing, and staff personnel got dressed and came quickly to the hospital to meet the general and the captain as they distributed the medals and greeted those patients who could speak. The ceremonies would take several hours because the general and captain wanted to spend time talking to all the patients and meet staff members who were introduced to them at the hospital. Either the general or the navy captain pinned a Purple Heart on every patient in the hospital who could speak to the trio.

For those patients who were sleeping or under anesthesia (such as Roy), the medal was pinned to the patient's pillow and the box containing it was left at his bedside table. The nursing staff helped to get the patients sufficiency awake and erect in their beds to greet these officers and the aide.

After a couple of hours, the general and captain had met just about all staff members of the hospital, and they had distributed Purple Heart medals to everyone except Roy. Roy's bed was the last stop on the tour, but for very good reasons. Margaret was asleep with her head resting on Roy's bed when she heard the commotion connected with the awards ceremonies. She got up, straightened out her uniform, and went into the staff bathroom to comb up her hair and put on a little lipstick and perfume so that she would be presentable to meet the trio at Roy's bedside.

The captain introduced Commander Margaret Mary Emerson to the general, noting that the commander was Medic Emerson's wife, was the superintendent of nurses at the hospital, and was just beginning her third tour of duty in Da Nang's hospital. Margaret saluted the general and the captain—and then a strange thing happened.

The hardened marine general, who had seen more death and carnage on the fields of battle than anyone currently serving in the Corps in South Vietnam, who had advanced from the enlisted ranks, who was known to troops as Grizzled Bill Elliott, USMC, and who was a recipient of the Congressional Medal of Honor in the Korean Conflict (another undeclared war), tenderly hugged and kissed Margaret. Margaret began to cry; the young nurses who were in her charge began to cry as well.

The captain and the general's aide were a little surprised but not when the general said to Margaret, "Margaret Emerson [making no reference to her rank], you are married to this unconscious man in this bed, Roy Emerson, who is a true hero. He has saved more men than I can count, including the pilot of that ill-fated helicopter, which had just dropped him off at base headquarters at Khe Sanh and was destroyed by rocket fire. Roy risked his life to save the pilot, who is now on the hospital ship, and tried to save the copilot, a brave man who unfortunately succumbed to his wounds. Therefore, I, the captain, and my aide have something for both you and Roy."

Roy was still unconscious because of the continuous morphine drip through the IV in his arm. Roy was resting on his stomach, and his head was turned sideways on his pillow. A number of the young nurses were clustered around Margaret and around Roy's bed.

The adjutant spoke up but not in such a tone as to disturb the other patients, "Attention to orders: for wounds received at the Khe Sanh Forward Marine Base in the Republic of Vietnam, while administering medical aid to two downed marine flyers, Medic Roy Emerson is awarded the Purple Heart medal."

The aide handed the navy captain the medal, and it was pinned in Roy's pillow next to his head. The aide handed the commendation paper to Margaret.

Then the adjutant continued, "For the highest bravery exhibited by Medic Roy Emerson, above and beyond the call of duty in saving one pilot of a downed marine helicopter and attempting to save one copilot on the same aircraft, all while being under enemy mortar and rocket attack and having suffered severe wounds in the rescue effort, an award is made of the Distinguished Service Cross (DSC), the second highest award for bravery granted to members of the American Armed Forces."

The remove handed the DSC medal to the general, and the general pinned the medal to Roy's pillow next to the Purple Heart. He kissed Roy's head, saying, "This is one of the most highly decorated men I have ever known in all my years of Marine Corps service."

The adjutant continued. "To Commander Margaret Mary Emerson, RN, USN, superintendent of nursing services at the United States hospital at Da Nang in the Republic of Vietnam, for tireless attention to her many hospital patients and complete devotion to her relationships with the medical, nursing, and clerical staffs for long years of duty, an award of the Bronze Star is made."

Margaret was shocked. The young nurses crowded around and hugged her as the captain pinned the medal on her bloodstained nursing uniform. Everyone expected Margaret to cry when she received the medal, but she composed herself and spoke up, saying, "General, Captain, and General's Aide, I am honored to accept this medal, not for myself but for all the staff, past, present, and future, of the Da Nang Hospital. With the officers' permission, I will have the medal and the commendation framed and placed on the wall inside the front entrance to this hospital as a reminder to everyone who comes here that the award is given to me as the representative of all staff who have served or will serve at this hospital."

The general and captain nodded approvingly. Margaret asked if she might speak further and plainly to both high-ranking officers:

"General and Captain, I know my husband, Roy Emerson, unconscious in the bed there with the new decorations pinned on his pillow, better (I think) than anyone else in this world. I believe because of his bravery and injuries, he would probably be entitled to orders when he leaves this hospital for stateside duty for the remainder of his four tours in the US Navy. But speaking for Roy, if he is ordered out of Vietnam before his four tours of duty are finished, he will *feel*—for the remainder of his life—as if he were a *coward* running away from the duty that he has pledged to fulfill for the men of the United States Marine Corps. Again, speaking for Roy, when he walks out of this hospital, he will go right to the adjutant's office and *demand* orders to return to Khe Sanh. I would rather see him die of combat wounds here in Vietnam than spend the remainder of our lives with my living with a broken and dispirited man who felt that he had run away from the troops when they needed him the most. So, when his wounds heal, and the doctors here at Da Nang Hospital pronounce him fit to return to duty, *please*—please reassign him to Khe Sanh. I will remain as the superintendent of nurses at this hospital as long as my husband is in Vietnam and my health permits such service. *Please*, Captain and General, hear my pleas on behalf of my beloved husband, Roy Emerson."

The staff of the hospital clustered around Margaret were shocked by her words. The general's aide just shook his head in disbelief.

The general looked at the captain, and the captain spoke up to the general. "You see, General Elliott, it's just as I predicted. Roy and his wife are no quitters. They know their duties and want to carry them out here in Vietnam. I would ask you to honor Commander Emerson's request wholeheartedly. I will put in a letter officially recommending the same to your office and the Division Commander's Office."

Old, grizzled General Bill Elliott nodded his head approvingly. Astoundingly, he again hugged and kissed Margaret and then kissed Roy on the head, saying, "I will recommend his reassignment to Khe Sanh when your medical staff discharges him from this hospital."

With those words, the adjutant announced that the award ceremonies for that day were concluded. The trio walked toward the front exit, but the general stopped at the doorway to Roy's ward, turned around, and snapped off a smart salute to Margaret and her unconscious husband. Margaret and all her staff members saluted back.

The general then departed the hospital, went with the captain and the adjutant to post headquarters, and instructed the adjutant to "cut orders reassigning Medic Emerson to Khe Sanh Forward Marine Base upon his release from the medical staff at the hospital. Leave the date of the orders blank; when Roy is discharged, I will sign them at that time."

The navy captain saluted the general and his aide, and the duo departed in the general's private Piper Cub Marine aircraft. The entire hospital was abuzz for days afterward over the ceremonies, the awards distributed, and particularly Margaret's words to the general, his aide, and the navy captain about her Bronze Star medal and her husband's future in Vietnam.

The nursing staff was clucking around Margaret just as if they were her chicks, and she was their mother hen. Margaret took off the Bronze Star medal, put it in its box, and handed the box and her commendation to one of the youngest and prettiest nurses who was standing around her.

Margaret startled the nurses, saying to the young woman, "Emily, immediately please take this medal and commendation over to Army Lieutenant Fuller in the Army Quartermaster Depot. Please have him frame these items and have them hung inside the front door of the hospital."

Then, with a smile on her face, as her other nursing charges stood around her and Emily, Margaret said, "And while you're over at the depot, Emily, please don't have intercourse with Lieutenant Fuller, with whom you are deeply in love."

Emily's face reddened, but she knew that Margaret was speaking the truth.

Then Margaret said, "Why don't you and that handsome lieutenant stop sneaking around, and do what Roy and I did: find the base chaplain and get married. I'll be one of the witnesses, and we can have one of the lieutenant's army friends be the male witness."

Emily was weeping silently, but she said, "Commander, he has proposed to me three times, but I keep saying no. However, I do want to have as much intercourse with him as I can and make him happy with children. So when I deliver these items for framing, I'm going to tell the lieutenant that I am under orders from my nursing superintendent to marry him and am now saying yes. I am so glad you have given me this assignment and spoken to my heart as to what I need to be doing with my life and with my love."

With those parting remarks, the young pretty nurse saluted Margaret, borrowed her car, and hurried over to the lieutenant's Army Quartermaster Depot where she delivered Margaret's message to him. While Roy was still in the hospital, Emily and the lieutenant were married by the base chaplain, with Margaret as one of the witnesses.

Roy was still too disabled to attend the premarriage shower for Emily, which Margaret and the girls threw for her at the officers' club, or the nuptials and the reception. He heard about all this later from Margaret.

Roy made slow progress, but his wounds did heal sufficiently for him to be returned to duty. As promised by the general, Roy and Margaret walked over to the adjutant's office, where Roy received his orders to return to Khe Sanh, but he had two last days to spend with Margaret.

Immediately, they drove in Margaret's sedan to a nice, clean hotel in Da Nang City, where they registered and had glorious sex for two days straight. When they were about to check out of the hotel, Margaret announced to Roy that they had been having intercourse during her most fertile time of the month. Both of them wept a little and hoped that a child had been conceived as a result of their activities.

As it turned out, their hopes came true. The pregnancy, though, would send Margaret on medical leave back to her parents' home in Milwaukee, Wisconsin, where she would deliver a beautiful baby girl, Mary Margaret Emerson, but would end her tours of duty in Vietnam. Until she completed her twentieth year on active duty with the navy, she would be based at Roy's old training facilities at Great Lakes, north of Chicago, where she could be near her parents and where her mother could reside off post with Margaret and care for the baby when Margaret had to be on duty.

While Margaret's pregnancy was developing, Roy was up at Khe Sanh on Hill 861-A once again, undergoing furious enemy attacks during what became called Tet I, Tet II, and Tet III, after the countrywide attacks of the Viet Cong and North Vietnamese regular forces, beginning on the Chinese New Year and continuing throughout the year.

Having completed their stay in the hotel, Margaret delivered Roy back to the enlisted marine barracks and passionately kissed him goodbye. He promised to write, as before, and wanted her to take care of herself and to inform him of any *changes* in her medical condition (if you get what I mean).

Having new uniforms, a new Red Cross helmet (with some new pictures of Margaret in the webbing of the helmet), and twin medical bags slung across his chest (provided by Margaret), Roy flew by helicopter back up to Khe Sanh and reported in at base headquarters. Things were surprisingly quiet when he arrived, but soon things would change for the worse.

After a brief discussion with the adjutant and base commander about his physical health and his most recent awards, making him the most decorated person on the base, Roy flew by helicopter (filled with medical supplies) up to Hill 861-A and found that the marines up there had repaired Roy's Ranch. He off-loaded his medical supplies and set up shop once again in his hooch, going up and down the hill to greet *his* marines and criticized them if they had not been taking care of their feet during his long absence.

The marines told him, "Go to h—, Pantless Emerson." Everyone laughed, including Roy, who told the marines it was good to be back on *his* hill with them. He reminded them that without him, they would all probably end up with jock-itch!

Upon the arrival of the Chinese New Year, or Tet, two full divisions of North Vietnamese regular troops began a sustained, all-around attack on the Marine Forward Base of Khe Sanh. The enemy used every type of bullet and weapon in their arsenal—rockets, mortar shells, and bullets rained down on the base. The enemy broke through the marine lines at various points and started advancing up twin hills, 881-South and Roy's 861-A.

The firing by both sides of the conflict was merciless and deadly. Destroyed enemy bodies piled up in the front trenches facing the marine forward line and up and down both of the hills. The stench from decomposing and burned flesh became a terrible annoyance and made some marines vomit. Wounds and deaths among the marine defenders of Hill 861-A were horrible, but the marines held the hill, mowing down the attackers who were bold enough to come through mine fields, claymore mines, and stretched barbed wire to get into the marine foxholes and fight hand to hand with Roy's marines.

The attackers were mowed down to a man but not before they did terrible damage to the marines on Hill 861-A, which kept Roy running around, treating wounded and bagging up the dead, for days on end, practically without any rest, chow, or sleep. Roy stayed at his post, though, and came through as a marine hero (although he was a navy medic) was expected to perform.

Roy suffered all kinds of minor injuries and even had a bullet pass through the red cross on his helmet without killing him, but he self-medicated so that he would not have to be pulled off *that* hill. Sustained bombing by air force jet aircraft dropping cluster bombs, marine jets releasing napalm canisters, and high-flying B-52 bombers discharging tons of bombs in an action called *arc light* stopped the enemy attacks, rocking the ground and practically causing an earthquake, sending the ground and the two hills shaking.

After the severe attacks of Tet I, things calmed down at Khe Sanh and on Hill 861-A. The dead and seriously wounded were evacuated; new replacements arrived; and Roy replenished his medical supplies. There seemed to be a lot of rain, which would be appropriate for a country subject to a monsoon season.

One day there was a light rain falling on Roy's Ranch, but Roy paid no attention to it. He was writing his daily letter to Margaret and some catch-up letters to his parents, his sister, Emily, and to Becky and Mary. A helicopter came in for a landing near his hooch, discharging some marine replacements and more medical supplies for Roy. Roy knew personally all the helicopter crew members on all the helos that flew up to and down from Hill 861-A. Roy sprinted out to the helicopter that had just touched down and whose crew chief was putting Roy's medical supply boxes on the helipad. The crew chief grinned at Roy. The pilot turned down the rotations of the helicopter rotors so that Roy could hear him speak.

With a very serious look on his face, the pilot said, "Hey, Roy, do you know any medic up here at Khe Sanh by the name of Emerson? The Shore Patrol guys are trying to track down this Emerson for rape! It turns out that someone by the name of Emerson raped a pretty older nurse at the Da Nang Hospital by the name of Margaret Mary Bucher. She claims the assailant was some type of navy medic named Emerson! It seems that she's two months' pregnant, so if you see anybody by the name of Emerson up here, tell him to watch out for the Shore Patrol, although I doubt if those guys will come personally up to Khe Sanh because they're afraid of getting shot at!"

These words hit Roy like peals of joy from a huge bell. His wishes for him and Margaret had been fulfilled—she was going to have their baby! How he loved her! Looking up at the helicopter pilot and crew chief, who were smiling down at him, and the copilot, who was waving at him, Roy yelled out, "Get your asses out of that aircraft and come to where I am before I tell the North Vietnamese to rocket your craft!"

The pilot turned over the controls to the copilot, who was still waving at Roy, and the pilot and crew chief came over and embraced

Roy. Roy was bawling like a baby! Tears were running down his cheeks and onto his fatigue top. He hugged and kissed the pilot and crew chief and got his tears on their outfits. The pilot and crew chief were equally affectionate toward Roy.

The crew chief spoke up. "Roy, that pilot you saved is doing well on the hospital ship. He'll survive, although he'll be a little nicked up, and be headed for home soon to his wife and two children. He owes his life to you."

Roy was still bawling but wiped his tears and his nose with the sleeve of his fatigue shirt. "I can't thank you guys for what you have just told me. I am so very, very happy. If you see Margaret, please give her my love. I'll write to her right away. Does she seem okay?"

The pilot said, "Yes, she's okay, but no one wants to date her now that she's pregnant by some navy guy."

Roy gave the pilot a slight punch in the shoulder and hugged and kissed him again. Roy looked at the pilot and crew chief as they remounted their helicopter. Before the noise became too great, he said so that all three could hear, "I would give all my medals if I could have saved that copilot's life. I feel I let him and his family down. I should have dragged him farther away from the burning aircraft before it exploded. Then maybe he would have lived."

The pilot yelled out of the plane at Roy, "You did your best. We're all glad you were decorated for heroism and have recovered from your wounds. *Semper fi.*"

11

MARGARET'S CAPTAIN'S MAST

The end finally came for Margaret in Vietnam at a captain's mast. It had been months since she had seen Roy, but the baby was growing healthily within her womb. Roy had been through another series of attacks by Ho Chi Minh's favorite military commander, General Giap, on Khe Sanh. Although the dead and wounded piled up throughout the base and on both hills, including Roy's Hill 861-A, the marine lines held. Extensive artillery fire from Camp Carroll and bombing by air force planes and bombers and marine low-level support aircraft had wreaked havoc among the North Vietnamese regulars. The masses charging up both hills were caught up in minefields and on marine barbed wire and shot down mercilessly. It was kill or be killed throughout the Khe Sanh base.

The Tet II offensives throughout the South Vietnamese countryside and the reaction of the allied forces, particularly the marines, brought a huge number of casualties into Margaret's hospital. Hour after hour, seven days per week, practically around the clock (pregnant and all), she helped hergirls and the surgeons with the wounded and dying men brought into *her* hospital.

Several times she collapsed and had to be laid on a gurney to sleep for a few hours; then, even against the doctors' advice, she would get up once again, without changing her bloody uniform or taking a shower in her billet, and go back to nursing *her* patients.

Finally, the Tet II offensives disappeared as quickly as they had come, and both sides of the Vietnam Conflict seemed to calm down for a while to lick their wounds. Roy finally got a little shut-eye on Hill 861-A. Miraculously, through all the fighting and carnage, he was not seriously hurt—a few nicks here and there, which he self-treated. Margaret was practically carried out bodily by her girls over to her billet, where she fell asleep in her bloody uniform and slept for twenty-four hours straight.

The nurses, surgeons, and staff at the hospital held a conclave and went to the navy captain, demanding, "Something must be done about that crazy pregnant nurse of ours."

When Margaret was finally sufficiently rested to shower and put on a clean uniform, she returned to the hospital. The staff, behind her back, gave the signal to the marine adjutant, a grizzled warrior by the name of Captain Jim Brady, USMC (who had come up through the ranks to this, his last tour in Vietnam) to do something about their beloved Margaret.

Jim Brady came across from headquarters himself, found Margaret tending a patient, and told her she was wanted immediately in the captain's office.

Suddenly, Margaret was frightened as she walked behind Jim Brady because she anticipated that bad news about Roy had come through. She walked slowly because her pregnancy was really beginning to show. Margaret thought something was up because as she was leaving the hospital and trailing behind Jim Brady, the staff was silent, but everyone seemed to be looking at her.

Arriving at headquarters to appear before her captain, Margaret asked Jim to excuse her for a few minutes while she freshened up in the bathroom. There, she combed her hair and put on a little lipstick and a little perfume. Coming out, Jim said that the captain was waiting for her. As she was entering the captain's office, she noticed that the furniture in Jim's office was unusually scattered around and the papers were all messed up on his desk and in his in-and-out bin.

Margaret stood at attention and tried to stand up straight, but she was beginning to feel a little heavy in the tummy. The captain looked up from his papers and said, "Margaret, you are going home tomorrow!"

Margaret knew something was up and responded, "I refuse to go, Captain. I will not leave Vietnam and that hospital of *mine* until that stupid, foolhardy husband of mine, Navy Medic Roy Emerson, is off that damned Hill 861-A at Khe Sanh and is back here in my arms and is patting my tummy to feel our baby coming. I won't go. I disobey your order. If you court-martial me, I'll resign from the navy, deliver my baby here in Vietnam, and will come back to work as a *civilian* nurse at *my* hospital, even if I have to bring my baby there to nurse him or her when I have a few minutes' rest. Captain, I am disobeying your order and will take the consequences!"

With a slight smile on his face, the captain said, "What you have just said to me is *mutinous* to your captain. If we were in the old British navy, I could hold a 'captain's mast' right here and now, find you guilty of mutiny, and have you hung from the yardarms of the sails. So I'm giving you one last chance: Commander Margaret Mary Emerson, I order you to leave Vietnam and go to your home."

Margaret held her ground, folded her arms over her now-growing belly and said forcefully, "I refuse."

The captain replied, "Okay, Margaret, I'm going to have to take action against you right now. Please sit down in that chair while I call the Shore Patrolmen."

Margaret was glad to sit down because she was really dead on her feet, but she began to cry because of her disobedience to her navy captain, who had been like a second father to her throughout her tours of duty at the hospital.

The captain picked up his phone to call Jim Brady, saying, "Captain Brady, we have a mutinous woman in here. Hold up in calling the Shore Patrolmen, but bring in those orders for her court-martial and the setting that we put out for visiting brass. Thank you."

Pretty soon, Jim Brady entered the captain's office with papers under his arm and carrying a very beautiful tray holding three glasses of ice, a bottle of fine scotch whiskey, and some Vietnamese delicacies.

The captain told Jim to pull up a chair and prepare to take custody of this "lovely prisoner, who is mutinous toward her captain!" Jim smiled, sat down, poured everyone a good scotch, and put some delicacies on the captain's desk in front of Margaret. The captain apologized about offering good scotch whiskey to a pregnant woman, but he said, "This mutinous occasion demands it."

Margaret stopped crying, took a good draft of the scotch, ate a couple of the Vietnamese delicacies, and finally knew that something unusual had happened. She asked the captain, "It's Roy, isn't it? He's hurt or he's dead, isn't he?"

The captain replied, "The way my colleague, the base commander at Khe Sanh, says Roy performs on that hill, he ought to be wounded severely or dead. But as far as we know, he's fine. It's *you* we're worried about. Now, do you want to hear why?"

Margaret took another drink of her scotch, which was beginning to relax her (particularly with the news about Roy at Khe Sanh), and said, "Yes, sir, I do!"

"Commander Margaret Mary Emerson, RN, USN, you have caused a near mutiny at *your* hospital. Did you see the messed-up chairs and papers in Jim's office?"

"Yes, sir, I did notice something unusual."

"Well, this morning we had a mob of your colleagues in here, making demands of me. We had the chief surgeon of your hospital, your assistant director of nurses, and particularly the off-duty nurses and staff assistants at your hospital in this office this very morning, making serious demands of me and giving me personal threats if I did not do what they demanded. I was even given a written ultimatum by a pretty young married nurse who called herself Mrs. Fuller, who says, *you* made her marry a young army officer by the name of Fuller. This Fuller, now a captain in the Army Quartermaster Depot, was in here with his wife, holding her hand as she read a manifesto signed by everyone at the hospital. Do you know what it said?"

Margaret put down her scotch glass and said, "Yes. Oh my. They must have cooked up something behind my back. And you say the chief surgeon was here and my assistant superintendent of nurses, and that Mrs.—I mean, Lieutenant—Fuller was the spokeswoman, holding the hand of her new husband, Captain Fuller—I stood up as a witness recently at their wedding by the base chaplain)—was here too?"

"Commander, I don't lie. Yes, they were all here. They messed up the furniture in Jim's anteroom and threw around the papers on his desk and his in-out basket until their demands were met. Now, I'm going to tell you what they demanded, which to me, as a naval officer of forty years' service, was mutinous! They demanded that *you* be reassigned back to the States and given maternity leave and another Bronze Star medal for yourself."

"Why in the world would they do that to me?"

"Let me go on. They threatened—all of them, even the chief surgeon—to immediately resign their commissions unless Jim and I immediately cut orders returning you to the States for maternity leave. They also threatened to call the United Nations on me and claim that *I* was personally guilty of human rights abuses by working a beautiful, pregnant nurse between ten and twelve hours a day, seven days a week." Margaret put down her glass and put her hand to her mouth. "However, Margaret, do you want to know the real reason they were here?"

"Yes, please, Captain."

"It was because they were concerned about you *and* the health of your baby."

Margaret replied, "Well, they have a point there. I am getting a little heavy. Previously, they knew that I had a miscarriage. I certainly don't want to lose this baby—he or she is Roy's and my baby!" With that, Margaret broke down crying.

The captain came around from his desk and hugged and kissed her and stroked her hair. "Margaret, you are like a daughter to me. To lose you here is like losing one of my own children. But for your sake and, most important, for the baby's, you have to leave Vietnam and go back to your parents' home in Milwaukee. Look out for yourself and for the baby over these next few months, and deliver a beautiful baby boy or girl for your hero husband, Roy Emerson, who will survive this conflict and come home to you and to his firstborn child! I know you'll go now because of what we've just said. I am going to spare you the reading of another commendation for you. But here it is."

Jim Brady handed Margaret a commendation, a set of orders immediately granting her emergency medical leave and transportation to her home in Milwaukee, and a beautiful box. Margaret opened the box. Inside was a Bronze Star medal, A paper covered front and back with the signatures of all the staff members of the hospital and the navy captain and Jim Brady.

Jim reached over, hugged and kissed Margaret, and said, "We'll really miss you. You have been one of the best personnel with whom the captain and I have ever served in our long careers in the military services."

Jim helped Margaret up. Jim and the captain walked her to the door and patted her hair. She said goodbye to both of them. A tearful Margaret, carrying her commendation, orders and box with the medal, came across to the hospital to say goodbye to her staff. When she walked in the main entrance, Margaret was mobbed by the staff, including the doctors, and cheered by some of the patients who had heard rumors and were healed enough to pay attention to the goings-on with Margaret and the staff.

Margaret made a special effort to hug and kiss not only Mrs. Fuller but her husband, now Captain Fuller, who was standing beside his wife with a big grin on his face.

Margaret made a mock fist to hit Mr. and Mrs. Fuller, but the chief surgeon grabbed her, folded her into his arms, and gave her a tender hug and kiss, telling her, "This is from a heroic navy medic, Roy Emerson."

Margaret cried and cried in his arms. Her assistant director hugged and kissed Margaret and said, "You are leaving immediately for the States on a US Navy plane. We will pack everything up for you and send it to your parents' place in Milwaukee. When the baby is born, we want the news and plenty of pictures. You're going to get transferred to Great Lakes, north of Chicago, to finish out your career. When we see you again, it'll be back in the States."

Margaret went around to every patient in the hospital, saying goodbye and hugging and kissing the ones who were awake. She said to the staff, "Look out for that crazy husband of mine, Roy Emerson, if he ends up here as a patient once again." Everyone assured her that Roy would be fine, would survive, and would come to her and the baby as soon as he could get R&R.

With those parting remarks, a very tired Mary Margaret Emerson went over to her barracks, packed up a few things—including her commendation and Bronze Star medal with the signed paper from her hospital colleagues, Jim Brady, and the navy captain—walked over to the airport on base, and departed on the next plane for Saigon. From there, she would go back to the States, via Guam, and to her parents' place in Milwaukee. This was one captain's mast where the mutinous accused was not hung from the yardarms.

12

TET III

The silence at Khe Sanh did not hold for long. When the offensive launched by General Giap and his Viet Cong allies, called Tet III, commenced, the North Vietnamese forces were able to cut off and surround Khe Sanh. A lucky North Vietnamese rocket hit the ammunition dump at Khe Sanh base, and the explosions and scattered ammunition and shrapnel rained down for a long time. Luckily, none of Roy's people on Hill 861-A was hit.

Also, a large cargo plane landing on the Khe Sanh airstrip was rocketed, caught on fire, and burned out. Foam had to be used to douse the flames, and a bulldozer pushed the blackened wreck off to the side of the runway. Larger aircraft coming to Khe Sanh thereafter would touch down briefly and keep rolling forward as their crew chief ejected supplies and equipment from the back doors while the plane was preparing for departure. Antiaircraft fire usually hit such planes as they banked to go out to the sea.

Back in Saigon, General Westmoreland, overall American commander in Vietnam, decided that Khe Sanh would *not* be overrun by the North Vietnamese regulars. The base would be—and was—relieved by a massive armed column of US Army troops that broke through the surrounding North Vietnamese lines and entered Khe Sanh base. However, the time for usefulness of Khe Sanh base had expired, and the American military now conducted search-and-destroy missions. A base such as Khe Sanh was a sitting duck for massed enemy attacks and could be surrounded, as Khe Sanh had just been surrounded, and cut off from other American forces.

So, the commander in chief in Saigon made a determination to abandon the base at Khe Sanh. Amid intensive shelling and bombing of the North Vietnamese lines, the marines began a slow pull-out of troops from Khe Sanh. Roy was one of the last men off of Hill 861-A, combing the hill to make certain that all marines had been evacuated, and all marine body parts had been picked up for later identification and return home.

While Roy was finishing his work, the North Vietnamese were crawling up the other side of Roy's Hill 861-A. Low-flying marine jets, dropping canisters of napalm on the massed attackers, drove them away, and saved Roy from imprisonment and/or death. The marines came through again for a navy medic!

Roy returned to Da Nang with the last contingent of marines and checked in with his commander there, his old friend Captain Brady, USMC, the navy captain's adjutant.

He offered himself for reassignment there and for working in the field with his marines. They told him his help was needed, but he didn't have a lot of time on his fourth tour. He told them that when his time was up, he wanted to return to the States, be with Margaret and their child, and go back to finish his college education. Also, he said he might like to study law.

By now, Margaret had been home with her parents for a while and had delivered a beautiful baby girl—they named her Mary Margaret Emerson—and Roy learned that he was going to have one last R&R before his discharge from the navy so that he could see Margaret and his new daughter.

Roy indicated he would like to have R&R for two weeks in Hawaii before he went back into the field, and the adjutant told him he would see to it that he got the appropriate orders.

It didn't take Roy much time to get his orders for R&R. He had contacted Margaret, and she, her mother, and the baby were going to meet him for R&R in Honolulu, Hawaii, where they could stay in two rooms in a navy billet. Roy organized his things, even packing his boxes of medals, and departed for Hawaii.

Margaret, the baby, and her mother (Mrs. Bucher, who had not yet met Roy) flew from Milwaukee via Los Angeles to Hawaii. The group had agreed to meet on the navy's base at the visitors' billeting building.

When Roy arrived at the navy billet, he found Margaret, with the baby in her arms, and her mother waiting for him at the front entrance. He ran to Margaret and passionately hugged and kissed her; both cried. He admired his new baby and cradled her in his arms, crying without any shame.

Mary Margaret was a beautiful baby, favoring her mother and Margaret's mother, with a little bit of Roy mixed in.

Fortunately, Roy said, "Mary Margaret looks like her mother and grandmother rather than her ugly father!"

Margaret's mother embraced all three of her now children; they hugged, cried together, and said how happy they were to be together and for Roy to meet his mother-in-law, about whom she had heard much from his wife.

Margaret's mother liked Roy immediately.

The party checked into the visitors' billet and went to their rooms, side by side with an connecting door from one room to the next. Roy and Margaret would be in one room, and Margaret's mother with the baby would be in the other.

Margaret's mother surprised Roy by speaking up. "Tonight, Roy, you are going to get dressed up in your navy whites and are going to wear all your medals. You and my lovely daughter, your wife, Margaret, are going for a nice dinner at the officers' club."

Roy was about to say something when his mother-in-law continued. "Don't say no because you are going and wearing all your medals. I am going to stay with the baby, and we are going to have a talk about her mother and father behind your backs." At that remark, both Margaret and Roy burst out laughing.

Roy said, "Okay. Let's change."

However, when Roy and Margaret got behind their closed door, you can easily imagine what went on between them for an hour. Finally, they stopped what they were doing, bathed, dressed in their outfits, and went over to kiss Mrs. Bucher and the baby goodbye.

The baby was sleeping, and Mrs. Bucher had the first opportunity see her son-in-law in his navy whites with all his medals. She was very, very impressed. She felt, as her daughter had told her, that Roy was a true hero.

When they reached the officers' club, the club secretary seated them at a very nice table. Looking around the room, Margaret spied the base commander, a rear admiral, and the base chief surgeon, with whom she had served at the hospital in Da Nang. The surgeon (a navy captain), noticed Margaret, spoke to the admiral, and together they walked over to Margaret and Roy's table.

Both of the diners stood up and greeted their high-ranking guests. The navy surgeon gave Margaret tender hugs and kisses, told her how happy he was to hear that she had had a baby girl, and introduced himself and the admiral to Roy. Roy was a little embarrassed, as an enlisted navy medic, to meet such high-ranking navy personnel in the officers' club, but the admiral asked to join them and offered to buy them a drink. He summoned the wine steward, who brought over a fine bottle of chilled champagne, which he poured in four glasses for all at the table. The admiral knew all about Margaret Mary, Roy and the baby from the chief surgeon, and he made a toast to Emersons and their baby. All of them drained their champagne glasses.

The admiral addressed Roy, "Chief Medic Emerson, you have more medals earned under combat situations on your chest than I have or the chief surgeon has. The navy is proud of you. I want to wish you and your lovely wife and baby happiness well into the future."

With that remark, the admiral shook hands with Roy and hugged and kissed Margaret; the chief surgeon did the same, and the duo returned to their dinner at their table. Roy was puffed up with pride at the fine greeting and toast, but his eyes were firmly fixed on his wife, whom he dearly loved. They held hands throughout dinner and as they strolled back to their billet.

Stopping in Margaret's mother's room, they found Mrs. Bucher was asleep in her bed, with baby Mary Margaret in her arms. Both Roy and Margaret kissed Mrs. Bucher and the baby good night. Roy and Margaret went to their room and had the most passionate and glorious foreplay and intercourse that they had had since the two-day stay at the hotel in Da Nang City, where Margaret had become pregnant.

The next morning, Margaret announced to Roy that what they had done last night had been during her most fertile period of the month.

Roy said, "Maybe something good will come of it, besides my enduring love for you and for my baby girl."

The two weeks' R&R seemed to fly by, with Roy carrying baby Mary as much as he could and learning to bottle feed her and change her diapers. When he burped her, she always would vomit on his shirt. We would just hug and kiss her harder when she did that. These were very special days for Roy, Margaret, the baby, and Margaret's mother, but the end of the vacation had to come. Tearfully, Roy departed for Vietnam, promising to write to Margaret every day. Margaret was now finishing her career as the emergency room charge nurse at Great Lakes. She resided with her mother off-base, and her mother looked out for baby Mary when Margaret was on duty.

Margaret said she was counting the days—a few more months— until Roy's fourth tour in Vietnam was over, and he could come home for good.

When Roy arrived back at Da Nang, he reported in, drew his equipment, and began to go on helicopter missions with his marines. There was much fighting; Roy tended the wounded and dying marines without regard for his personal safety. He was commended in reports by his commander frequently.

Finally, as he was nearing the next-to-last month of his fourth tour, he brought some papers to the adjutant, carrying them in his right hand. The adjutant knew that Roy's dominant hand was his left and asked why he couldn't carry the papers in his left hand or under his left arm at the shoulder.

Roy remained silent as the adjutant came around from behind his desk and grabbed Roy's left arm. It hung loosely at his side, obviously dislocated from the shoulder. Yet Roy was going to go back out on a combat mission the next day. It so happened that the captain was in the headquarters, and the adjutant called out to him, and he came out to greet Roy.

The adjutant said that Roy had a dislocated shoulder, about which he intended to do nothing but request a combat assignment for the next day. The navy captain said, "No way," and he ordered Roy immediately to report to the hospital for surgery on that arm and shoulder.

Roy did as he was told, going to his old favorite chair in the hospital. He waited until his other marines had been taken care of. Finally, Nurse Fuller saw him sitting there, alone and asleep. She hugged and kissed him, asking about Margaret and the baby. He said that they were fine and that he would be seeing them soon; he had about one month to go in his fourth and final tour.

"Why are you at the hospital?" she asked.

"The Captain sent me here," he answered.

"Why?"

He responded, "I don't know!"

The lovely nurse looked at him skeptically and told him to stand up. Roy had a hard time standing, and as he faced her, his left arm hung down uselessly. She tenderly reached for and tried to raise his left arm. She could see the pain on his face and said that he was going in for x-rays. In radiology, it was learned that Roy had a seriously dislocated shoulder and rotator cuff injury, both needing immediate surgery.

He was admitted to the hospital, prepped for surgery, and had a long surgical procedure, during which a surgical pin had was inserted to make certain that the bone would stay in the socket. Roy would need weeks of rehabilitation to get his arm to move around and go above his head. The doctor ordered him to stay in the hospital until he had regained appropriate use of his arm.

The new director of nursing services assigned Nurse Fuller to be his full-time nurse. When Roy came to in the recovery room following surgery, he looked up and saw the angelic face of Nurse Fuller smiling down at him.

He mistook her for his wife, saying, "Margaret, dear, you are the most beautiful woman in the world. You are my love—my healer—my protector. I can't wait to get up from this bed, hold you in my arms, and love you and baby Mary together." Roy then lapsed back into unconsciousness.

Nurse Fuller bent down and gently kissed and hugged Roy, saying "That's from your wife, Margaret, and your baby, Mary."

It took Roy about a month to recover from the shoulder surgery and to regain strength in and usefulness of his left arm and shoulder. During that time. he worked daily in the hospital's physical therapy department and tried to help the staff as much as he could with some of the needs of the other patients.

Finally, Roy's time in Vietnam was up. The adjutant and captain came over to the hospital from headquarters and confronted Roy and some of the nursing staff members. They presented him a final Purple Heart and a second award of the Bronze Star with V device for his work in the field with the marines outside Da Nang, where he seriously dislocated his left shoulder and injured his left arm putting dead and wounded marines on and off dust-off helicopters. The navy captain saluted Roy, and the adjutant gave Roy his orders home, where he would be discharged from the US Navy at the navy training facilities at Great Lakes.

Roy turned in all his extraneous equipment and flew out from Saigon to San Francisco and from there to Midway Airport in Chicago, where he met a navy van and was driven to the enlisted barracks at Great Lakes Training Center. There, he bedded down for the night, and the next day he was honorably discharged from the US Navy, effective in three days, and given a paper with a long list of the military training sessions he had attended, his long years of service in the US Navy, his awards, and the amount of his discharge pay, which was considerable. The adjutant shook his hand and said, "You're the most decorated navy medic I've had the honor to know."

Roy was still jet-lagged, so he stayed in his billet another night; he had two days left in the service. He arose early the next morning, ate chow in the mess hall, showered, and then dressed in his navy whites with all his medals. He walked over to the base hospital and went to the emergency room. The ward secretary recognized his name immediately when filling out paperwork, and she asked if he was Margaret's husband. When he said he was, they decided to cook up a little ruse to frighten Margaret.

Roy got on a gurney with a sheet fully covering his body. The ward clerk went running to Margaret and told her that the ambulance had just brought in what looked like a fatality from the indoor swim training area.

Margaret was looking very pregnant again, almost as if she were about to deliver her baby, but she waddled over as fast as she could to the gurney on which Roy lay covered by the sheet. Margaret looked over the hump under the sheet and asked the name of the patient. The ward secretary said quickly "Roy Emerson" and completely pulled the cover off of the "body." There lay Roy, smiling at his wife. Margaret was shocked beyond belief, punched the ward secretary lightly on the shoulder, and then embraced, kissed, and nearly become intimate (recognizing, of course, that Margaret was very pregnant) with her husband.

He hopped off the gurney and gathered his pregnant wife into his arms, and they embraced for a long time. Slowly, she took him from station to station in the hospital and introduced him to the staff and her coworkers who had heard so much about Roy. In the hospital adjutant's office, Margaret was handed orders, notifying her of immediate medical leave and her forthcoming discharge under honorable conditions from the US Navy.

She was instructed to go off duty that very moment to see what she could do about the "deceased patient" standing beside her. The staff gave her a fond farewell kiss, and she waddled out of the hospital to her automobile. Roy hadn't driven in years; so, Margaret had to drive to her off-base apartment, where Roy was reunited with his mother-in-law and his baby daughter, Mary Margaret, who was becoming a toddler.

In the apartment, Margaret's mother fixed dinner for everyone; the baby sat in a highchair. Roy couldn't keep his eyes off his very pregnant wife or his child. That night Roy slept with Margaret but could tell that she was in discomfort from the baby in her womb.

The next day Roy took a cab to the base, walked to his billet, gathered up his things, and left the Great Lakes facilities as a navy medic for the last time. He stayed in bed with Margaret for about three nights after she was rushed to the base hospital, where she delivered a healthy baby daughter; they named her Emily Louise Emerson, after Roy's sister and Margaret's mother.

Mother and daughter were doing fine, although Margaret was sore, as could be expected. Roy helped her to get out of bed, toilet herself, and walk a little around the ward. The hospital adjutant came to Margaret's bedside and gave her the discharge papers that showed her military classes, years of service, awards, and out-processing pay, including travel pay to Milwaukee (her home, from which she'd entered the US Navy over twenty years earlier).

Roy made arrangements to pay off the landlord of Margaret's apartment and have her things transported to storage for later shipment to Indianapolis, Indiana, where they had talked about living while Roy went back to school.

When Margaret was discharged from the hospital, Roy rented a large car for the drive from Lake Forest to Milwaukee, sufficient to accommodate Margaret, her mother, the babies, and him (although he was a little shaky with driving for the first time in several years). They made it to Milwaukee and got Margaret, her mother, and the little ones into Margaret's home, and Roy met her father for the first time. After putting down the two ladies and the babies for sleep, Roy and Margaret's father got to talking about old times over beers and became fast friends. Margaret's father was very glad to have Roy as a son-in-law. Roy told Margaret's father that he would like all the Buchers to meet his parents and his beautiful sister, Emily, down in Tippecanoe County, Indiana.

The time passed rather quickly for the Emersons (all four of them) while staying with Margaret's parents. Roy got his transcripts together from high school and Boyne, and he was accepted into Service University in Indianapolis, Indiana, with finances to be provided by the GI Bill. He and Margaret's father drove down to Indianapolis from Milwaukee and rented a very nice and large apartment with four bedrooms and two full bathrooms not too far from the Service campus for the new Emerson family.

Between some furniture items from Margaret's family house and the few things she had in storage (the transportation of which she had arranged from Great Lakes to the apartment in Indianapolis) and a few new purchases of bedding from local furniture stores, the apartment and its rooms got set up pretty well in about a month. Roy asked Mr. and Mrs. Bucher to move in with them in Indianapolis. Mr. Bucher said he should stay behind in Milwaukee to look after the Bucher household, but Margaret, the babies and Margaret's mother would move to Indianapolis with Roy.

Moving day came around, and a fond farewell with hugs and tears was given to Margaret's father. Roy drove a new Chevrolet he had purchased with his out-processing money and took his wife, babies, and mother-in-law to their new apartment. Margaret and Mrs. Bucher said the boys had done a nice job laying things out, and they were pleased with the accommodations. Margaret was feeling better and having her periods once again; for the first time in quite a while, she and Roy were able to be intimate in their new apartment.

They slept while tightly holding on to each other in their new large bed.

13

BACK TO SCHOOL

Roy began his studies at Service University, and with Margaret's permission, he got a part-time job on Saturdays and during school holiday periods with Indianapolis Township as a trash collector. The money supplemented his GI Bill payments and lessened the need to tap into Margaret's retirement and out-processing funds. The job helped Roy to keep in shape. Roy was not the very best student, so it took him a while to reacquaint himself with college studies, but Margaret and her mother helped him. Throughout his few years at Service, he kept up a straight B average, which, given Roy's previous performance in grade school, high school, and at Boyne, was a marked improvement in Roy's educational achievements.

Roy was really enjoying his schooling at Service. One of the reasons was that a lot of students there were from Indiana, some even from Tippecanoe County. Many students lived in the Indianapolis area. Roy enjoyed talking to his fellow students, whether men or women. Frequently, they would ask him where he hailed from and what he had been doing with his life between high school and Service. Roy never mentioned Boyne College, the marines, Vietnam, or his medals. He was not a proud man, and he still felt deep down inside that he had failed at Boyne and had failed miserably to save all his marines in Vietnam. (Remember he had told the commander to take back his first award of medals and send them to the families of the marines he could not save.)

By the time Roy was a junior at Service, he had to declare

major and minor subjects before he could qualify for his degree. He particularly liked history, so he chose that as his major. Because he was such a poor speller and a poor reader, Roy decided to challenge himself and chose English literature as his minor. He would struggle through these courses for the remainder of his years at Service but did much better in history courses.

Margaret and Mrs. Bucher really helped him to get through his English literature courses, where he scored B and C grades. He was an A or B student in history; he knew the content of each course, but he had difficulty writing down the answers to quiz and examination questions, even though the answers were floating around in his mind.

Another reason that he liked Service was his friendship with an older classmate named William Jay "Bill" Rice. Bill was pushing sixty years of age. He and Roy had a lot of history classes together. They would meet for coffee in the Student Union to review class materials and notes, and each got to know the other's background pretty well.

One day, when Bill invited Roy to go to a bar after class with him, Roy broke his rule and revealed to Bill his full background, including his upbringing, football, college suspension, and days in the navy and the heavy fighting during four tours of duty in Vietnam. It turned out that Bill had been drafted into the army as a young lad at the end of the Korean War. He came from a very humble background in the Valparaiso area; after Bill was discharged from the army, he used his GI Bill monies to begin buying low-cost furniture stores. Now, he was the owner of the largest chain of high-end furniture stores in Indiana and Kentucky.

However, Bill said he felt empty because he lacked adequate education, so he came back to school, finished at a junior college, and enrolled in Service. He was majoring in history with a minor in political science.

Bill had been married and had a son, William Jay Rice Junior. Young Bill was the apple of his father's eye; he had given young Bill the best education that money could afford, and young Bill lapped it up, earning several degrees from prestigious eastern universities, but young Bill was a bit of a Bohemian. He could speak several languages. After young Bill returned from a trip to Europe, he said he didn't feel well.

He was diagnosed with an early form of HIV. His mother, Bill's late wife, had been a nurse. She looked after young Bill and got him medications, which had prolonged his life. However, Bill Senior was awaiting the news any day that young Bill had developed full-blown AIDS. Bill's wife had died many years ago of breast cancer, and he had not remarried. He craved female companionship, but he felt that younger women who went out with him were only interested in his money. So he dated very infrequently.

Bill asked Roy a question about young Bill: "What should I do about him?"

Roy gave an immediate answer that surprised Bill Senior: "Love him as he is, support him, and tell him that you accept him as he is."

With that reply, Bill Senior hugged Roy and cried on his shoulder. Roy said he knew lots of gay guys and gay girls; that was their choice, and he accepted them as they were. It was, Roy indicated, no big deal.

The two Service history majors finished their beers and were thereafter the best of friends. In time, Bill Senior would become for Roy like an older uncle. Also, Roy would introduce him to one of his and Margaret's neighbors in their apartment building, Laura Angel Evans.

14

MARGARET, LAURA, GEORGIE, AND BILL

There was a gorgeous woman neighbor, Laura Angel Evans, who lived in the two-bedroom, one-and-a-half-bath apartment beneath the Emersons. Whenever Roy or Margaret would pass Laura, they would always say hello to her. She would just look at them and mumble a hello. It was obvious that the Emersons were going to be Laura's neighbors for quite a time because of Roy's schooling and Margaret's position as a charge nurse at Methodist Hospital in Indianapolis. Laura knew that Margaret and Roy had two children, Mary Margaret and Emily, and that Mary Margaret was just a little younger than her son, George.

One Sunday, when Roy was not working, he took his two daughters out for a walk. Outside the apartment on the spacious back lawn was Laura, sunning herself in a sexy bikini with the top unfastened. Her son, George, was playing with blocks and sitting next to her on his own blanket in short pants and athletic shoes. Roy stopped to say hello, and Mary Margaret (who by now could speak) went over to George and bent down to say hello to him.

George reacted favorably to Mary Margaret's greeting and asked her if she would like to play with his blocks. Mary Margaret said no, that she was taking a walk with her father, but she asked if George like to come with them. Laura, who was reading a fashion magazine, rose up from her blanket but had to hold onto the top of her bikini, which was untied on her back. Roy said hello to Laura and told her that he would be pleased to take her son on a walk with them if she would permit it.

George looked at his mom and asked, "Can I go?"

Laura looked at Roy and his two girls and at George and said, "Okay."

Roy took the children for a nice long walk. He pushed baby Emily in a stroller, and Mary Margaret held George's hand as they walked along. From time to time the foursome would stop, and Mary Margaret would pick some wildflowers to give to Roy, Emily, and George, who put them in his other hand. All through the walk George held hands with Mary Margaret. The foursome was gone for about an hour, and when they arrived back at the apartment, Mary Margaret asked George if he would like to come up and play.

Roy knocked on Laura's apartment door. She answered wearing the shortest shorts and tightest halter top he had ever seen. Mary Margaret did the talking and asked Laura if George could come up to her apartment to play blocks with her and her sister, Emily. She told Laura that she had a large set of blocks and that her grandmother, Granny Bucher, who lived with the Emersons, would probably join in the play.

George looked up at his mother and asked, "Mother, may I?" Laura looked at Mary Margaret and at Roy holding baby Emily and said, "Okay."

Roy told Laura they would be right upstairs, and whenever she wanted George to come home, all she had to do was to come upstairs and ask for him. Also, Roy told Laura that Granny Bucher was preparing a nice dinner, and she and George were invited to join his wife, Margaret, and the family for dinner.

Laura looked a little skeptical but said, "I will think about it!"

By this time in his academic life, Roy was forced to wear spectacles for reading; he was sitting in his rocking chair, reading a history text. Margaret and her mother were in the kitchen together, preparing dinner; and the children, with George, were in the kids' playroom, having a good time with the blocks.

After a couple of hours, a knock came on the door, and Margaret went to answer it. It was Laura. Margaret invited her in and offered her some refreshment. Margaret introduced herself and her mother and came in to the living room where Roy was napping in his rocking chair, with his spectacles down on his nose and his history book on his lap.

Roy roused himself when Laura came in with Margaret, stood up, and shook Laura's hand. Mrs. Bucher came out of the kitchen, from which emanated delicious smells of a meal cooking, and invited Laura and George to stay with them for dinner. Looking a little skeptical, Laura said, "Okay." Laura had wanted to meet some young friends for her son, George, in the apartment complex.

Roy asked Margaret and her mother if it was okay to break out the "good service" for a neighbor who was a first-time guest. Both said okay. Roy went into the kitchen and got out a fine serving tray, on which he placed four of their best glasses, a container for ice, and a very fine, expensive bottle of scotch blend whiskey.

Roy carried the tray into the living room and put it on the coffee table. Mrs. Bucher, who was wearing an apron, and Margaret, who was wearing shorts with her hair in a bun, sat down with Laura on the couch. Roy poured drinks for all the adults; Laura accepted the drink and crossed her lovely legs.

She was quite a sight. Margaret told Roy later, when they were in bed together, and Roy was definitely not concentrating on Laura's visit, that she thought Roy got red in the face when Laura crossed her beautiful legs. "Laura is good-looking enough to be a *Playboy* model," she said.

"You are my *Playboy* model," Roy told her, "and I will love you forever."

The four adults pretty well polished off a fifth of good scotch. Roy explained that they drank good scotch when there was company for dinner. George was having a high old time with the girls in the playroom.

Eventually, he came out and asked his mother if he could stay a little longer. Margaret looked at Laura and again asked her to stay, saying, "Mom has made a wonderful turkey dinner with all the trimmings, and there is plenty for everyone."

Laura, who was feeling her scotch a little bit, said yes, and they all had a wonderful dinner. After dinner, Roy offered some cognac which he had been saving for guests, and all the adults had a nice bit of cognac.

Margaret was very friendly to Laura and asked her mother, "Mom, if George wants to come up here and play with the girls when Roy and I are gone, will you look after him as you look after our two girls?"

Mrs. Bucher replied to her daughter, "Sure; it will be good for the girls and good for George to have some friends."

Margaret noticed tears come into Laura's beautiful eyes. Laura said, "You are really fine people. I am so glad that I have had a chance to meet you. And George can come up here as much as you will have him."

After a while, it was time for Laura and George to leave. Margaret escorted them to the door and spontaneously hugged and kissed Laura and George, calling them "our friends." Laura was dabbing tears from her eyes as she descended the steps, holding George's hand.

Thus began a long-lasting and dear friendship between Roy and his family and Laura and George. Bill Senior would enter the picture later.

Whenever the Emersons saw Laura or George (whom the girls began to call Georgie), they invited them to the Emersons' apartment for the kids to play or for dinner. Sometimes, Laura would come up with Georgie, and sometimes Georgie would come up alone.

After the first date for Laura with the Emerson family, Laura and Margaret became good friends. Late one Saturday afternoon, Roy got back from his part-time job as a trash collector for the nearby township. As he entered the apartment, Laura was sitting on the couch and was crying. Georgie was playing with Mrs. Bucher and the girls. Immediately, the smell of garbage from Roy's work clothes filled the living room.

Margaret said, "Roy Emerson, go right into that bathroom, take off those clothes, wash yourself up good, put on some clean clothes with some nice cologne and aftershave lotion, tie up those work clothes in a plastic bag for later washing, and come out here and visit with us two good-looking women."

Roy responded, "Aye, aye, Commander Bucher—I mean, Commander Margaret Mary Emerson, RN, USN, now retired."

Roy did as Margaret asked, got a good shower, bundled up his clothes, and put on some sexy cologne and aftershave. He wore his navy white pants and a white T-shirt, which showed off his muscles. He went to the kitchen; seeing that there was company and no drinks had been served, he got out the good service for guests and brought in glasses with ice and a full bottle of expensive scotch blend whiskey. As he laid the tray on the coffee table, he noticed that Laura, who had been crying heavily, turned away from him. He poured drinks for Laura, Margaret, and himself (Mrs. Bucher was too busy playing with the kids in the playroom) and offered a toast: "To Georgie—the girls' new best friend!"

Margaret and Roy raised their glasses and took a good draft. Laura slowly raised her glass. Margaret and Roy noticed that her hand was shaking, but she did take a good draft, trying to look away from Roy.

Roy spoke up. "Laura is everything all right with you?"

Laura was still crying. She looked at Roy and said no.

Roy observed that Laura had what the marines would call a shiner on her left eye and bruises on her lovely left arm.

Roy spoke up, "Laura, may I ask what happened to you? Maybe there's some guy that I need to have a serious talk with about mistreating you."

Laura cried some more, got up from her seat on the couch, and went into Margaret's arms like a hurt daughter. She cried and cried. Roy sat still, saying nothing and looking at the two women hugging tightly. Margaret finally let Laura go. Laura sat back down at the end of the couch, sipped her scotch, and said she would like to talk plainly to Roy and Margaret, if they would listen to her.

Margaret already knew what she was going to say; both said, "Of course. Fire away." Roy poured more scotch for them.

Laura explained that she was a high-priced escort. George was a result of one of her liaisons. She didn't even know who his father was. She put her last name on his birth certificate, so he was George Washington Evans. Her escort service charged $1,500 per night for companionship services and $3,000 per night of overnight services. Her last trick wanted rough sex and busted her up good.

"Look at me. Who would want to go out with me now?"

She said she gave her escort service manager one-third of her take for the night; if she earned three thousand dollars per night, she could take home two thousand dollars, which she really needed to take care of herself and Georgie. She had no health insurance, and she was always going to the doctor's office to make certain she had no sexually transmitted diseases. "Now, what do you think of me?"

Margaret and Roy looked at each other and then back at Laura.

Roy spoke up. "Laura, you are our friend and the mother of a beautiful boy, Georgie. Your work is *your* business. However, I think Margaret and I could help you get into another business that would support you and Georgie. We have come to love you as a dear friend. You tell me the identification of the guy who beat you up, and I'll give him some of the same. I mean it."

Laura responded, "No, Roy. I'm not even sure who the guy was. We were in an expensive hotel room. He claimed I didn't give him enough for the three thousand dollars. He wanted kinky sex with handcuffs and all. When I said no, he punched me out. That's why I look like I do."

Margaret reached over and took Laura by the hand. "Roy and I and my mother are glad to help you and Georgie. Just let us know what we can do for you."

Sobbing, Laura said, "Please, please, get me out of this profession."

Roy said, "I think I know just the person for you to meet who can help you do that. His name is Bill Rice; he's an older businessman. He needs someone to do his books, and that someone can work from home. He is a very attractive and decent man. He is a widower. He has a grown son. He is the owner of a chain of high-end furniture stores in Indiana and Kentucky. Would you like to meet him, Laura?"

Through tears, Laura said, "Yes, I would like to meet a decent unmarried man for a change!"

Roy responded, "It shall be done as you have asked."

Drying her eyes, Laura asked about Margaret's and Roy's backgrounds. Margaret gave her a brief summary, but Roy said nothing. Margaret spoke up for him; she told Laura about his background, their meeting and marriage, and the birth of their children.

Laura noticed that over the couch was a large plaque with many medals in it. "What are these?" she asked.

Roy and Margaret hesitated to answer Laura. However, Margaret surprised Roy by saying, "Roy, go into the bedroom, put on your Speedo bathing suit, and come back out here, and we'll show Laura what it takes to win all these medals."

Roy responded, "Margaret, do you really want me to do that? I'm thinking that with you two beautiful women sitting on that couch, I am going to have a bulge in my Speedo."

Margaret said, "Get in there, Roy Emerson, and do what I have told you to do."

Roy went into his bedroom, took off his clothes, and walked back into the living room in his Speedo bathing suit. As he stood facing both ladies, he posed as if he were a body-builder, first flexing one bicep and then the other. "Just admit it, ladies," he said. "I look like a model for a women's magazine, don't I?" A bulge was beginning to develop in Roy's Speedo.

Margaret said, "Now turn around and show her what a military hero is made of."

Roy turned around, and Laura let out a screech. Roy had burns from where his Red Cross helmet ended down his entire back to where his boot tops began. Additionally, Margaret pointed out the shrapnel scars on Roy's back and buttocks and an exit wound that she sewed up on his upper arm.

Margaret said, "It's lucky that bullet didn't sever an artery, or we might have lost him, and I would have no children by him. Now, Roy, turn around."

By that time, Roy really did have a bulge in his Speedo, but neither lady was looking at it. Instead, Margaret pointed out to Laura the burn scars on Roy's hands and scars from shrapnel fragments in his legs.

"Okay, Roy," Margaret said, "the beauty contest is over. Now, go back and get dressed and come out and have some drinks with us horny ladies!"

Laura started to laugh. Roy went into the bedroom, got dressed back in his clothes, came back into the living room, and filled up the trio's glasses.

Roy gave a toast. "To Margaret Mary Emerson, my angel, who saved my life several times, and to the nursing and medical staffs at the hospital in Da Nang, Vietnam." Everyone took a long draft of the scotch, and Laura seemed to calm down.

Roy looked seriously at Laura and said, "What you have seen on my body, I never want you to have to see on Georgie's body. I don't want Georgie to be sent where he can get these injuries to his fine body." Roy started to cry, and Laura and Margaret comforted him. Roy looked up and said, "Go ahead, you two, and sit down on the couch. Laura, if you only knew—if you only knew—how many *good,* really *good* men I lost when I was a navy medic, trying to save them in Happy Valley and up on Hill 861-A at Khe Sanh...

As General Sherman of the Union Army said during the Civil War, 'War is all hell,' and General Sherman was right. War is worse that you can ever imagine. Just ask Margaret what injuries and deaths she saw in her hospital, where she was one of the angels who saved my life on numerous occasions. Those men I put into body bags would have been proud to date someone with your beauty, would have been kind to you, and would have been honored to be your husband and to give you good children like Georgie. But they are gone."

At that point Roy broke down; he had to leave the living room and go into the bedroom, where he held his head in his hands, bawling like a baby. Fortunately, the door to the playroom was closed, but the happy talk of the children could be heard. Roy rocked back and forth on his bed. Both Laura and Margaret came into the bedroom, sat on the bed on each side of Roy, put their arms around him, and kissed him tenderly, touching his head and hair.

Finally, Roy composed himself and apologized to the ladies. He asked them to go back with him into the living room and have a little more to drink. "Sometimes," Roy said, "the visions come back to me, and they haunt me. Margaret has been a great help to me to get me to pull through."

They all got up and walked back into the living room. Laura paused in front of the couch and looked up at the framed plaque with the medals hanging on the wall. She said, "I'd never noticed them before, but now I know what you did, Roy, to win these medals." When everyone was seated again, Roy told Laura, "Margaret is too modest to tell you, but she was presented two Bronze Start medals for outstanding performance of her nursing duties in Vietnam at Da Nang Hospital, almost at the risk of her personal health and our first baby's."

Laura looked over at Margaret. "Is this true?"

When Margaret nodded, Laura gave Margaret a fond hug and kiss.

Roy asked, "Ladies, can I help you get a meal going?"

The answer was yes, and the three of them descended upon the kitchen; Roy set the table for all of them while the ladies got the meal started. In about half an hour, they called the kids and Mrs. Bucher, and everyone had dinner. There was ice cream for dessert, and Margaret put some chocolate sauce with whipped cream and a cherry on the sundaes for each of the kids, including baby Emily, who proceeded to get the sundae all over herself.

After dinner, Roy did the dishes while Margaret and Laura talked on the couch, and the kids went back to block-building in the playroom with Mrs. Bucher.

After doing dishes, Roy brought out some cognac and asked the ladies if they would join him. They said yes, and Roy poured cognac for everyone. Roy made a toast to Laura who, Roy said, caused him to get a bulge in his Speedo suit.

Margaret told Roy, "Shut up! You should *only* have eyes for me."

Roy said that was true. Laura, Margaret, and Roy laughed and took a drink of the cognac. Roy looked at Laura and asked, "Would you go out with Margaret and me on a double-date with my friend, Bill Rice Senior? We could have dinner someplace nice and, then go to a nightclub for some drinks and dancing."

Laura surprised Margaret and Roy by saying, "Yes, I think I would like to meet him. If he's anything like you, Roy, he is a nice man!"

They ended the evening, hugged and kissed Laura and Georgie, and Margaret walked them down to their apartment while Roy cleaned up the cognac glasses, washed them, and put them away.

The following week, when Roy and Bill Senior met to go over class notes, Roy asked Bill if he would like to have a double-date for dinner with him and Margaret—and Laura, a very attractive, nice, but younger woman. Bill said that he would be willing to do that this coming Saturday evening if—and only if—Roy and Margaret would allow him to make all the arrangements.

Roy said, "Why not? I'll ask Laura Evans if she is available, but I think she will be."

The week rolled by. Laura said she was available; Margaret was not working that weekend; and Roy went into work for the township early so that he could get off at four o'clock, in time to meet Bill and the others for dinner. Roy got showered and dressed in his best clothes.

Margaret dressed up and looked beautiful to Roy. Mrs. Bucher was back from a short airplane trip to Milwaukee, and she was looking after Georgie and the girls, who were playing nicely in the playroom. Laura came up to their apartment. When she knocked on the door, Margaret answered it, gasped and said, "I'm afraid for Roy to see you!"

Laura entered the living room, where Roy was rocking in his chair, with his reading spectacles on and looking over his history notes for a forthcoming quiz. Margaret's perfume brought Roy to attention, and when he looked over at Laura, he was pleased—she was gorgeous beyond belief.

"You'll be a wonderful date for Bill tonight," he said. They talked for a while, and soon a knock came on the apartment door. Roy answered it, shook Bill's hand, and brought him into the living room to meet Laura and Margaret.

Bill looked fabulous; he was an older man with silver hair, and he was a true gentleman. When introduced to Laura, he shook her hand. He gave Margaret a chaste kiss and a hug. He asked to meet Margaret's mother and see the children. Everyone walked with Bill into the playroom, where he was introduced to Mrs. Bucher and the children. Bill shook hands with the children, even little Emily, and with Mrs. Bucher.

Going back into the living room, he said they had a reservation at a nice restaurant, and a car was waiting for them. Roy had expected to drive, but when they went to the parking lot, there was a limousine. Bill opened the door and helped everyone into the limousine.

As the vehicle was proceeding to the restaurant, Roy and the ladies said they were very impressed to be riding in such a fine vehicle.

Bill said casually, "I have several of these, but as Roy knows, I don't have a lot of friends I think appropriate to take out in one of my limousines. You people are the type of people I need to have as friends, and I am proud to drive you to where we are going in my vehicle."

It was a half-hour's drive to the finest restaurant in Indianapolis, on the top of the tallest building in town. The chauffeur came around and opened the door for the passengers, and Bill helped the ladies to exit the vehicle. The limousine would wait for them until it was needed.

In the elevator, riding to the top of the building, Bill stared straight ahead. Laura kept looking at his profile but said nothing. Roy was holding hands with Margaret, and he reached over and gave her a kiss on the ear.

She punched Roy in the chest and told him to mind his manners. "We're out with friends tonight, and I want you to make a good impression!" Margaret straightened Roy's tie.

Bill and Laura chuckled at Roy and Margaret. Arriving at the top floor, Carl, the maitre d', met the foursome, said, "Good evening, Mr. Rice," and showed the foursome to Bill's favorite table at the window, overlooking the lights of downtown Indianapolis.

Roy, being Roy, told Bill, "I have never been in a place as nice as this, but I wonder if the food is as good as the chow in the Da Nang Hospital, where I first met and wooed my wonderful wife here, Margaret Mary Emerson."

Margaret started blushing but held Roy's hand tightly under the table.

Bill said with a smile, "I think all of us will find the food and drinks to our liking."

Bill had preordered everything, from the wines, champagne, and scotch, to appetizers, salads, and entrees, to desserts and after-dinner drinks. All the party thoroughly enjoyed Bill's hospitality and told him so. Laura said that this was the nicest place she had ever been.

Roy spoke up, "You should have been with Margaret and me at the officers' club on my R&R in Honolulu."

Margaret nudged Roy and exclaimed, "Roy Emerson, you know on that visit we didn't spend much time eating out!"

All of them burst out laughing and took another drink of their after-dinner liqueurs.

They were pretty full, but Bill said the evening was not over yet. They descended from the restaurant, met the limousine, and were driven to one of the finest nightclubs in Indianapolis at a top-rated hotel. A band was playing slow tunes in the nightclub, and there was a small dance floor. Roy couldn't wait to get Margaret in his arms to dance.

Bill asked Laura to dance, and all of them had a wonderful evening, dancing, drinking, and chatting. Roy also danced with Laura, and Bill with Margaret. Toward midnight, they decided to go back to the apartment building to check on the children. Bill's limousine drove them there and was asked to wait until Bill decided to depart. They checked on the children and found all of them asleep in the same bed with Margaret's mother. Laura teared up because the kids looked very happy and beautiful sleeping beside Margaret's wonderful mother.

Laura invited the adults down to her apartment for some champagne. They went downstairs, had champagne, and talked for two hours. During the conversation (prompted by Roy), Bill offered Laura a job keeping the books and doing the bill-paying and accounting for the Rice furniture chain. She could work by computer at home. He would supply all the equipment. He would provide her with benefits, a fine salary, and even a company car. She would have her free time for herself. If she liked what she was doing, she could become a permanent employee of his company.

Laura looked at Margaret and Roy, and they nodded. Roy remarked, "This will be a good opportunity to learn some new skills." Roy looked at Bill and said, "Laura would do a good job for you if she takes the position."

Laura asked Margaret what to do, and Margaret urged Laura to take the job.

Laura hesitated but said, "All right. When do I start?"

Bill (who knew about Laura from talking to Roy) replied, "You have already started. Tonight was your hiring interview. Here is your first paycheck. Just do a good job for me and pay attention to the teachers, one of my accountants, and another representatives from my information technology staff, who will come over on Monday, begin your instruction, and set up the equipment. It will take you a couple of months to learn the routine. Take your time, and don't be afraid of making mistakes. None of us is perfect. God knows, I'm not perfect, but Roy and Margaret *are* perfect."

People were beginning to get tired, and Margaret and Roy said it was time to retire upstairs.

Laura invited Bill to stay for a while.

Politely, he declined. "I have to study for some tests at Service next week, so I've got to be going." As he got up, he reached into his pocket and took out an envelope. He handed it to Laura and said, "Get ready to work hard. If you make it, there's more where that came from. I pay my people well!" Bill bid the group good night and left in his limousine.

Laura asked Margaret and Roy to stay for a moment while she opened the envelope. Margaret and Laura sat on the couch and Roy in the easy chair. With somewhat shaking hands, Laura opened the envelope, which contained a certified check payable to Laura Angel Evans for three thousand dollars on Bill's business account at Regions Bank in Indianapolis.

Laura put her hand up to her mouth and stifled an outcry. Margaret looked over at Roy, and Roy nodded. Margaret said, "If you work out, Laura, three thousand dollars per week before taxes, even *without* costing out the additional benefits, such as health insurance, sick leave, vacation time, and retirement, amounts to $156,000 per year."

Laura gasped.

Margaret and Roy bade her good night, told her to let Georgie sleep with them tonight, and, if Bill called again and wanted to take her out with them, she might think of saying yes.

"Bill," Roy told Laura, "is a very successful businessman, but he is a stickler for good work. So, you have a lot to learn!"

The accountant and information technician arrived at Laura's apartment promptly at nine o'clock on Monday morning, began the installation of equipment, as well as starting Laura's schooling in the accounting functions of the Rice furniture chain.

During their visit, Laura's escort manager called for her. She said "I've retired," and promptly hung up the phone.

Laura was a lot smarter than she let on, having completed a college degree in business with honors. She picked up the system and the use of the equipment and was functioning to Bill's satisfaction within three months. Margaret, Roy, and Bill were pleased with her progress.

15

THE GROWING EMERSON FAMILY, LAURA, AND BILL

As the months passed, Laura, the Emersons, and Mrs. Bucher became very close, and with Georgie, they were almost one family. One day, Laura, who had been working in her downstairs apartment on the Rice Company accounting pages, came up to the Emerson apartment, where Mrs. Bucher was sitting with the three kids.

"Would you come down to my apartment," she asked Mrs. Bucher, "and teach me some domestic skills? I'm pretty deficient!"

Laura and Mrs. Bucher told the children that the adults would be downstairs; Georgie said he would watch out for the girls.

The two adults laughed and walked downstairs. Laura was not the best housekeeper, and for the next couple of weeks, she and Mrs. Bucher straightened up the apartment. During that time, however, Laura did not slack off her work for the Rice Company. Sometimes, Georgie would stay overnight with the Emersons while Laura worked until late at night or into the early morning on the Rice books.

With a little embarrassment, Laura took Mrs. Bucher into her bedroom and asked, "Would you help me go through my wardrobe and get rid of some things?" All sex toys, inappropriate underwear, short-short skirts, overly tight tops, and numerous other overly sexy articles went into the Dumpster behind the apartment building.

Mrs. Bucher taught Laura how to cook wholesome meals for her and Georgie from scratch, rather than eating out of boxes of preprepared food. After a cooking lesson one afternoon, while both women were sweating from the kitchen's heat, Laura led Mrs. Bucher to the couch in the living room, saying she wanted to talk to her *confidentially.*

While sipping on a cup of tea, Laura broke down, crying, "I am nothing but a dirty old whore. I feel that I have no business even being with you beautiful people. I'm condemned to the life of a filthy escort."

Mrs. Bucher surprised Laura with her reply: "Laura, you are a beautiful woman with a wonderful and intelligent son, Georgie. You are *not* a filthy whore. Personally, I can understand the life of an escort because when I was younger and before I married Mr. Bucher, I was a waitress at a strip club and sometimes had to fill in for the girls on the pole. Margaret doesn't know these things about me, so please don't tell her or Roy—although, knowing them both very well, they wouldn't change their opinion of me one bit. They love me for who I am. I am so proud to have Margaret as a daughter and Roy as a son-in-law. To tell you the truth, Laura, you are my grown daughter, and Georgie is another of my grandchildren. I will love you forever, Laura, despite your past. People can change. I do not condemn women who work in strip clubs or for escort services. A girl has to do what a girl has to do! Fortunately for you, you got off the downward slide before you got hurt again. Margaret and Roy told me about what that one trick did to you. That situation will never happen again, as long as you are part of the Emerson family."

Laura cried and cried and hugged and kissed Mrs. Bucher and asked her, "When you and I are together, just by ourselves, may I call you Mom or Mother? But I don't want to hurt Margaret's feelings."

Mrs. Bucher reached out, took Laura into her arms, stroked her hair, and said, "All the Emersons, particularly me, love you dearly and consider you and Georgie as members of our family for as long as you want to be a part of our family. Laura, you can call me anything you want, whether we are alone or with others. You can even introduce me as your mother. Margaret Mary, Roy, and my grandchildren would be proud to have you call me Mother or Mom. Don't worry about it! If either Roy or Margaret would say anything, I would punch each of them in the nose. I am one tough broad. After all, I used to work in a strip club, so I know how to handle groping hands!"

Laura held on to her, stroked her hair, and called her "my lovely mother."

Mrs. Bucher said, "I think there's something nice in store for you with Bill Rice."

Laura answered, "I really hope so. He is as fine a man as Roy."

The calendar pages turned; Bill did not come around until one Sunday before the final examination in history. The semester grade in an important course hung in the balance on the final examination. Bill came over to study with Roy. Bill had agreed to stay for dinner, and Mrs. Bucher and Margaret (who had one of her few weekends off from the hospital) were in the kitchen preparing a nice pot roast, with potatoes, onions, and carrots. Georgie was in the playroom with the girls. Mrs. Bucher was setting the dining room table.

Bill and Roy were really going at it on the coffee table. Roy had a medieval map of Western Europe, and the two men were discussing the Hundred Years' War and its goals and accomplishments for the nation-states of Western Europe, and for the war's contributions, if any, to a revised map of Western Europe. These types of questions were certain to be on the examination. Bill and Roy were deep in conversation when a knock came on the Emerson apartment door.

Mrs. Bucher went to the door and ushered Laura in. Laura said hello to Margaret in the kitchen.

Margaret whispered to Laura, "You really look beautiful. The boys are in the living room, deep into their discussion about history. Why don't you ask them if you can bring out the special serving tray for guests?"

Laura agreed and walked into the living room, saying in a low voice, "Hello, Roy and Mr. Rice."

Roy looked up and saw Laura—she was absolutely gorgeous but dressed in less explicit clothing and with the look of a proper lady.

Roy said hello, but Bill was still rubbing his chin and looking carefully at the map on the coffee table.

Roy gave Bill a poke and said, "We have a guest we would like you to meet."

Bill was wearing his reading spectacles but took off the glasses and looked up. There was Laura, a gorgeous woman but somehow changed for the better. Bill's mouth just hung open, and he couldn't speak.

Laura said again, "Hello, Mr. Rice." Bill stood up, and, surprisingly, he went over and shook Laura's hand and asked, "May I hug and kiss you hello?"

"I've been hoping you would do that for some time," Laura answered.

Bill hugged and kissed Laura, and they held that pose for some time.

Finally, Bill came out of his reverie with Laura when Margaret announced, "Dinner is served." The kids were rounded up, everyone sat down, and Margaret and Mrs. Bucher served up the dinner. Laura was seated next to Bill, with Roy at the head of the table and Margaret at the other end. Roy asked Bill to recite a prayer of thanksgiving for a fine meal and for the fellowship of all the people around the table. Bill was a little embarrassed, but he recited a prayer that he had not uttered for a long, long time.

The hungry group dove into the food, and everyone had an enjoyable dinner. Margaret poured some good white wine for the adults. The adults never had a chance to have their scotch before dinner, but they enjoyed their meal and wine. Sundaes were served for all the kids, but the adults, rubbing their full bellies, declined.

When everyone was finished with his or her meal and wine, Margaret said she had an announcement to make.

Laura put her hand to her mouth and said, "Oh my God. You and Roy aren't getting a divorce, I hope."

The adults laughed except Laura.

Margaret said, "Oh, no. First of all, Laura, you've seen all the scars on Roy's body. Nobody else would want him. But since I took care of his fecal matter"—everyone laughed—"at the hospital in Da Nang, I guess I'll have to keep him around for a number of years."

Roy piped up, saying, "I couldn't find anyone better anywhere than my lovely and wonderful wife, Margaret Mary Bucher—oh, and I forgot, Emerson."

Margaret went on, "No, the announcement isn't all that complicated. I'm two months' pregnant. But this is the last child. Roy and I have discussed this, and in a couple of days, Roy has an appointment with a urologist."

Roy and Mrs. Bucher knew Margaret's secret, but Laura, Bill, and the kids were thrilled to learn the fact for the first time. Bill and Laura hugged and kissed Margaret and then congratulated Roy and Margaret for the great news.

Three of the adults went into the living room; Mrs. Bucher brought in the fine service for only three because she was going to the playroom with the children. There were fine scotch blend whiskey and cognac with glasses, ice, and smaller glasses for the cognac.

Bill and Laura sat next to each other on the couch. Bill reached over and took Laura's hand. Glasses of scotch and cognac were served all around. Each of the adults took a good drink and toasted Georgie and Mary, who were about to start school—Georgie into kindergarten and Mary into preschool. Everybody took a good draft of both drinks.

As Bill held Laura's hand on the couch, he said he had an announcement himself and would like to ask Laura a question. The three adults were all ears. Bill said he had kept tabs on Laura every week since she became employed with Rice Company. He had a spy within the Emerson camp.

Roy pointed to himself and said, "It wasn't me. I've been at school and was working."

Margaret replied, "It wasn't me; I've been getting pregnant and working in the emergency room at Methodist Hospital." Then she said, "Hmm." She got up and went into the playroom and brought out her mother to face the adult jury. "Mother, have you been talking to Bill about Laura?"

Mrs. Bucher said, "That's for me to know and for you to find out!" She turned on her heel and went back into the playroom, totally ignoring the adults to concentrate on the kids.

Roy said, "We've had a fifth columnist in our midst!"

Bill gazed at Laura and said with a loving look in his eyes, "I think the time has come for the Rice Company to fire you, Laura. You're dismissed!" Laura almost began to tear up, but Bill continued. "Instead of being my employee, I would like for Laura to become my companion, be on my arm at various functions, and travel with me to furniture shows. Also, I would like you to be my wife."

Everyone's mouth fell open. Bill reached into his pocket and pulled out a small felt box. He handed it to Laura and asked her to open it. Slowly, Laura lifted the top of the box to find a three-carat perfect diamond ring with a platinum band.

Bill looked at Laura and asked, "Laura Evans, will you marry me? I'm an old fart, but I am very much in love with you. I've just concealed my feeling for you. I fell for you when we went out for dinner at the restaurant in downtown Indianapolis."

After kissing Bill tenderly, Laura said, "Bill, you don't know my background. I used to work for an escort service and sometimes spent nights with strange men sexually. I stopped when the Emersons took me in after I had been beaten up by my last trick."

Bill responded, "I don't care about your past. I care about your present, your son, Georgie, and *our* future together. I'll ask again: Laura, will you marry an old fart like me? I'm sixty years old, but I think I'm still fertile." Everybody, including Bill, laughed.

Laura took the ring out of the box, put it on her finger, and said, "Yes, Bill Rice, I will marry you. But I don't think you're getting such a good deal."

Mrs. Bucher poked her head around the corner of the living

room wall and saw Bill and Laura embracing. Margaret Mary gave her mother a thumbs-up sign. The two newly engaged ones were embracing passionately on the Emerson couch.

Laura asked Bill, "Will you spend the night with me at my apartment if the Emersons will keep Georgie?"

Bill surprised her. "The answer is no. Let's wait awhile. I don't need to go into the sack with you, Laura, to love and marry you!"

Laura reared back, looking at Bill and said, "I never—and I mean, never—thought I would ever hear a man say those words to me. I'll wait too, although it will be hard."

Bill said, "I have two more things to ask."

Mrs. Bucher had joined the group.

"First, I'd like to have Margaret or her mother go with you to get some clothes so you can go with me to a big Republican function next week at the hotel where we danced in downtown Indianapolis."

Laura said, "I would like to do that and wear my new ring too."

"Then I would like us all to fly down to my villa outside Puerto Vallarta on the Gulf of California and the Pacific Ocean. I'll provide all the transportation and expenses. Our classes will be out. Margaret, can you get a little leave from the hospital? Roy, you'll have to miss a weekend of work for the township."

Mrs. Bucher spoke up, "Flying to Milwaukee is all that I can take in the air. I'll stay here with all the children. You adults go with Bill to Mexico."

Margaret, Laura, and Bill looked at Roy, who responded, "Okay, let's go!"

The evening ended on a happy note, with Laura passionately embracing Bill when he had to leave. Laura, Margaret, and Roy cleaned up.

Roy and Bill got an A on the final history examination. Margaret and Roy got fill-ins for their week away with Bill and Laura. The accountant and technician from the Rice Company came over to Laura's apartment, removed all the records and equipment, and congratulated Laura on her engagement to Bill. The woman accountant from the Rice Company told Laura that in Bill Rice she was getting a very good man as a husband.

The Republican function Bill had asked Laura to attend was a very expensive political fund-raiser for the Indiana Republican Party.

Roy was always kidding Bill about Bill's allegiance to the Republican Party, claiming that Bill had become an aristocrat and really believed in monarchism.

Bill would fire back at Roy that, given Roy's declaration as a Democrat, in the Middle Ages, with feudalism, Roy would have been classified as a peasant and would have only been able to carry a pike in the Lord's army. Roy would correct Bill and say that in the Middle Ages, as a peasant, all Roy may have been able to carry was a pitchfork; pikes were too expensive for peasants to own!

Both guys would laugh, touch coffee mugs together in the Student Union, and say neither one of them would have been good fighters in the Middle Ages. Both were afraid of being cut with knives or swords.

Bill confided in Roy a great deal about his future plans and his son. One of the reasons they were such good friends was that neither one was trying to con the other or trying to get work or money from the other.

Roy turned Bill's job offers with the Rice Company many times. Roy said that lifting trash and garbage cans for the township, plus school and a family, was about all he could handle. It was fair to say that Bill and Roy became as attached as if they were brothers.

Just before the event for the Republican Party, Bill gave Mrs. Bucher a credit card on his personal account and asked her to take Laura out and, as he put it, "get her really dolled up" for the forthcoming event.

Bill sent his limousine to pick up both ladies for two days straight. Roy did the baby-sitting for the kids, letting Margaret, who was getting bigger in the belly every day, sleep as much as she could. Margaret was working the afternoon shift at the hospital (which was a busy shift), and she was on her feet practically for eight hours.

The night of the big event came. Mrs. Bucher and Roy took over the baby-sitting duties. Georgie had been at the Emersons' apartment all day, playing with the girls. The girls felt that Georgie was their older brother; even baby Emily, as she began to speak, said Georgie was her older brother. As mentioned, the Emersons and Mrs. Bucher treated Georgie as one of their family.

The Republican function started early. Bill and Laura were to be at the hotel by five in the evening for a predinner reception. The details of the evening were to be related later to Roy in a late-night meeting with Bill and Laura. Mrs. Bucher and Roy set up an early dinner for the kids and themselves. By four thirty, everyone was properly fed, and the kids were back romping with Mrs. Bucher in the playroom.

Roy was sitting in his rocking chair, reading a history text for next semester's classes, when a knock came on the apartment door. Mrs. Bucher, who knew the persons knocking, said that she would answer the door as Roy was about to get up from his chair and walk toward the apartment door. Mrs. Bucher gave out a sigh at the door, and she led the most beautiful couple into the living room to see Roy.

When Roy saw Bill and Laura, he was speechless. Bill was dressed in a beautifully fitted black tuxedo with black tie, cuffs with Republican cufflinks, and highly polished dress shoes. He was wearing very expensive cologne and aftershave (lotions that Roy could never afford to buy but which he would *not* accept as gifts from Bill). Bill looked liked an elder statesman; he was shaved very closely, and his silver hair was newly trimmed.

On his arm was the most gorgeous woman Roy had ever seen. Bill was about six foot one, and Laura was about five foot eleven. She wore a stunning green satin dress, with one arm open at the shoulder. Mrs. Bucher had the beautician give Laura the works— pedicure, manicure, facial, and an absolutely fabulous hairdo, with hair hanging down over the open sleeve portion of her dress.

The dress had slits up the sides to expose beautiful legs, ending in lovely feet wearing open-toed high-heel shoes that showed her highly polished toenails. She wore a short string of pearls and pearl earrings. She had on her three-carat diamond engagement ring. Laura had perfect skin and very white teeth. (Her years as an escort certainly hadn't done her any harm.)

Roy got out of his rocking chair to hug and kiss both of them, saying to Bill, "As a former navy medic, having worked with the marines for four years, my marines would say that you ought to forget about the Republican function and go downstairs and make love to this beautiful creature at once. To heck with politics and tonight's political function with a beauty on your arm like that!"

Both Bill and Laura laughed and hugged Roy. Mrs. Bucher came out, stood behind and then in front of the couple, and pronounced them "fit to be seen in public!"

Bill and Laura embraced Mrs. Bucher, and Laura had tears in her eyes as she said, "Thank you, Mother." The couple left for the function in Bill's limousine, but Bill asked Roy to wait up for them; they wanted to talk to him. Roy said he would be up late, reading next term's history books so that he could get a better grade in each history class than Bill. Bill laughed at this remark.

Roy spent the evening reading; Mrs. Bucher put the children down in her bed early, reading them a bedtime story. She herself was asleep with the kids by ten o'clock.

Roy avoided getting into the scotch because he had not any company while he was reading. Long ago, for weight control, Margaret had gotten him to swear off scoffing of a big bag of Indiana corn nuts and a half pint of peppermint schnapps.

He found the reading interesting, as the book was getting to the point of the Napoleonic Wars, which he was very curious to learn about. There was a light knocking on the apartment door; he knew it was a little too early for Margaret to be home because she didn't get off until eleven, and it was just that time now.

Roy answered the door and greeted the handsome couple, Bill and Laura, and invited them in for a nightcap. Roy got a chuckle out of the look of both of them—Bill's bowtie was undone, he smelled of Laura's perfume, and he had Laura's lipstick on his tuxedo shirt collar. Laura's dress was a little disheveled, and her lipstick needed to be refreshed. Roy went into the kitchen to get the fine service for guests,

Bill sat on the couch while Laura went into the bathroom to freshen up and check on the kids—she came back with tears in her eyes, having seen all the kids in bed with Mrs. Bucher, clustered around her as if she was a mother hen. Laura sat close to Bill, while Roy poured good scotch blend whiskey for everyone. Roy made a toast to the two lovers, and everyone had a good draft.

Bill said, "There are some things to tell you and some things to ask you, Margaret, and Mrs. Bucher."

"Margaret probably will be home in about forty-five minutes. She has to do a nursing report from her shift before she leaves the emergency room." As Bill was about to speak, Roy just came out with it: "While we're on our way to Puerto Vallarta, why don't we stop first in Las Vegas and get you two married. You look married already; let's make it official."

Bill and Laura gazed at each other and started laughing, and Bill said, "Your suggestion was our first request to you and Margaret. Would you both go with us to Las Vegas before reaching Mexico and be the witnesses at our wedding?"

Roy responded, "If you don't get married on the trip, Margaret and I will be very disappointed."

At that point, Bill and Laura passionately necked on the couch. Roy spoke up. "I certainly hope, Mr. Rice, that you are not going back to *your* home tonight. I think there is a lady who would very much like to have you spend the night with *her* in *her* apartment downstairs."

Laura said, "We were going to ask you if Georgie could spend the night up here."

Roy responded, "He already is, and we'll get him cleaned up, clothed, and fed in the morning."

Bill knew that Roy had his urologist's appointment the next

afternoon. He said he wanted his limousine to take Roy to the appointment and wait for him to come home.

Roy said, "That's fine. I really appreciate it. I don't want Margaret to have to sit around and wait for me in the urologist's office or in the hospital, wherever the urologist takes me."

Bill replied, "The next couple of things are much more complicated. Tonight's dinner at the hotel was ten thousand dollars per plate. The reception was an extra ten thousand dollars per person. I kicked in fifty thousand to the Indiana Republican Party, and Laura and I had a chance to meet the dignitaries, led by the vice president of the United States, in a small cocktail reception. Laura just glowed, and the men could not get their eyes off of her. I noticed some of the women whispering among themselves. I think they were jealous of Laura."

Roy responded, "They should be. Look at her; she is gorgeous. What's more important, she is a fine woman too."

With that statement, Laura got up from the couch and gave Roy a tender hug and kiss.

Roy laughed and said, "I'm glad my wife's not home to see this scene. Remember the Speedo incident? Do you know why I got a bulge in my Speedo?"

Laura said, "You hush up, Roy Emerson. You have the most wonderful wife in the world in that Margaret Mary Bucher Emerson."

Roy said, "I know, and that's why I had a bulge in my Speedo—*not* because of you, Laura Angel Evans."

Laura laughed and said, "Liar!"

Roy raised his scotch glass and gave a toast to the bulge in his Speedo.

"I'll drink to that!" everyone said.

Bill said, "On a more serious note, some of the high-ranking state Republicans reminded me that our senior United States senator would announce his retirement following the completion of his current term at the end of this year's session. They want me to run for United States senator next year. What do you think of that?"

Roy chuckled. "I think it's a good idea. But you need to get your grades up in your political science courses at Service before the campaign, or you'll be criticized for not knowing enough about politics."

"Seriously though, Roy," Bill said, "I am willing to run for US senator, and Laura says she supports my decision. But I know how lowdown political campaigning can get. My opponents will throw the 'negative-find gang' on my case and Laura's. My slate is clean, but, as you know, my son is HIV positive, and we have just learned from his doctors that he now has full-blown AIDS. They will attack me through my son."

Roy answered quickly. "So what? We'll look after your son. I don't know where he stays now, but a newly refurnished one-bedroom apartment with a large bathroom has just opened up on our floor near our apartment. Bill, why don't you rent the apartment, move him in there, and let me, Mrs. Bucher, and Margaret look out for him while you and Laura are out campaigning?"

Bill asked, "Aren't you and your family afraid of contracting AIDS by taking care of my son, Bill Junior?"

Roy answered, "Of course not. Margaret and I have talked about your son. We're not afraid of HIV or of AIDS where the patient has his own place, and there are sufficient toilet and washup facilities. I think the apartment would not have to be fixed up too much to accommodate him. And we would be honored to take care of your son. If anyone criticizes your son, that person or group will have to contend with me, my wife, and Mrs. Bucher. Let 'em criticize; it will backfire on them."

"But there's another matter," Bill noted. "And that is Laura. Her escort service manager is mad about her retirement. He's said she was one of his best girls. He will contact my opponents and say that Laura was an escort and had sex with many men. Also, they'll criticize her about Georgie, who has no father listed on his birth certificate. How do we deal with this situation?"

Roy answered, "I seem to remember something I leaned about

former President Harry Truman in one of my modern history classes. He was supposed to have said, 'If you can't stand the heat, get out of the kitchen.'" Looking Bill and Laura right in the eyes, Roy said, "Laura backs your decision. She is willing to take the heat in the kitchen. I know how to handle this situation. With Laura's permission, when you and Laura are married, why don't you adopt Georgie and give him the Rice name. I think Georgie will like that. Georgie will stay with us while you and Laura campaign around the state. As a matter of fact, if Laura is gone with you for extensive periods of time, as I think she will be, Mrs. Bucher could live with Georgie downstairs in Laura's apartment and use your company car to drive Georgie to and from school and Mary Margaret to and from her day care center. Woe be to anyone who attacks a child who was born out of so-called 'wedlock' but who has been adopted by a wonderful man. Every social worker dealing with adoptions in this state, if not the nation, will attack that individual or group. As far as Laura is concerned, she is a changed woman. Let them show pictures of her when she was an escort, criticize her and condemn her. I remember that a powerful Jewish prophet once said, 'Let he who is without sin cast the first stone!' Margaret and I will personally appear at a press conference and, although we may not be able to wear our navy uniforms and our medals, we will stand up for our beloved friend Laura, whom Margaret and I would never have urged you to marry if we thought she was a trashy person. So how about it, Senator William Jay 'Bill' Rice Senior? Are you and your lovely bride-to-be ready for some heat in the kitchen?"

Bill looked at Laura; Laura said nothing but kissed Bill passionately.

Roy responded, "Well, that's the answer—no sweat! So you better get going on your campaign as soon as the senior US senator announces his retirement. The Emerson family and Mrs. Bucher are right behind you, even though you are a lousy Republican. But there is one condition, Senator, that I will impose on you—in future years, when I run as a Democrat for county prosecutor in

Tippecanoe County, I want you to say a kind word about me from your Washington, DC, office."

Bill got up from the couch to hug and kiss Roy. Just then, a pregnant Margaret walked in the front door of the apartment.

Roy said, "Look who's our company tonight! Please stand up, you two, and face Commander Margaret Mary Bucher Emerson, RN, USN, for close-order inspection."

Margaret's mouth just hung open; finally, she uttered some words. "God, what I wouldn't give to look like Laura. She is truly fabulous!"

Margaret went into the bedroom to change into some comfortable clothes. She came back out, sat down, and said, "Boy, am I pooped."

Roy offered her a scotch, but she said, "Absolutely not. With this baby I'm carrying, I am not drinking alcohol or being around smokers for the duration of my pregnancy. Roy, can you make me some tea?"

Roy responded, "Sure, darling." As he walked to the kitchen, Roy sang out, "Oh, by the way, Margaret... I think you look especially beautiful pregnant, and I want more children. So I have canceled my appointment with the urologist for tomorrow."

Margaret said, "Roy Emerson, stop your joking around. Get me some tea and a piece of that leftover pound cake that Mary, Emily, you, Georgie, and my mother nearly demolished!"

Roy replied, "Aye, aye, Commander Bucher—I mean, Emerson." Everybody laughed. Roy gave Margaret tea and cake and freshened up his, Bill's, and Laura's scotch glasses. Roy gave Margaret all the news.

She was so happy that she got up and hugged and kissed Bill and caressed Laura's hair, saying, "You are a gorgeous, lucky woman and are getting a very fine man. I hope he is not going home tonight but is staying here with you."

Roy said, "That's the plan. We have Georgie for a while."

Margaret responded, "We love Georgie and will care for him and for Bill's son as much as we can. We'll all pitch in: Roy, me, and my mother. We'll stand up for you at the wedding, and we'll really stand up against anyone who criticizes you, Bill, over Georgie, or your son, Bill Junior, or Laura. I mean that!"

Roy decided to end the evening with a recitation of how he and Margaret got together.

Margaret gave him a dirty look and said, "Don't you say anything."

"I learned in my history classes that America is a democracy," Roy said, "and that I can speak freely, so I am going to give out the true facts."

Margaret got red in the face and looked at him sternly.

Roy went on, "Just imagine: here you are, a wounded navy medic just back from a fierce fire fight with the enemy. An angel treats your wounds at the hospital and then takes you out for dinner and passionately kisses you at the end of the evening. Then, instead of letting you go out with the troops for two weeks and save marines, she kidnaps you and takes you for a two-week R&R to Bangkok, Thailand, where she rents a room, seduces you, and makes you promise to marry her. Then, when you two are bathing each other in the tub, she puts your hands on her beautiful breasts, passionately kisses you, and makes you have sex with her in the warm water. Then, in order to get out of the tub, you have to promise that you'll marry her as soon as you get back to Da Nang base. There she forces you into a permanent marital relationship, stopping you from running after beautiful women such as Laura Angel Evans. That's a true story, folks, about my life with Commander Margaret Mary Bucher, now Emerson, RN, USN."

Margaret burst out laughing, as did Bill and Laura.

Laura spoke up. "Nice try, Roy. We have some true facts about your courtship, but I think you have your facts reversed a slight bit, wouldn't you say?"

Roy did not respond but offered a toast to the two-person tub in that wonderful hotel in Bangkok.

"I'll drink to that," everyone said again.

The evening ended on a happy note. Laura went in and kissed Georgie and Mrs. Bucher lightly without waking them up. She led Bill by the hand down to her apartment.

The next day, Mrs. Bucher and Roy made pancakes for everyone, including the late-arising Margaret, Bill, and Laura. Before leaving on the plane, Roy had his urologist's appointment, and he was little bit sore when he was walking around. The foursome packed a few things to travel, first to Las Vegas and then to Puerto Vallarta. Bill forbade them from bringing a whole lot of things because he said a good bit would be provided en route or in Mexico.

Bill rented the apartment Roy had mentioned for Bill Junior and paid for a full year's rent in advance.

Bill's limousine took the foursome out to the general aviation portion of the Indianapolis International Airport, where Roy, Margaret, and Laura learned for the first time that Bill owned his own executive jet (not titled in the Rice Company's name and not paid for during personal outings with Rice Company's funds).

As the couples emerged from the limousine and espied the plane, Roy, Margaret, and Laura gasped.

Laura went up to the fuselage at the front of the plane and touched the newly painted name—"Ms. Laura"—on both sides of the plane's nose section. On the plane were comfortable seat-beds for all the passengers, and the stewardess served alcoholic drinks to all but Margaret Mary (who got iced tea, unsweetened, with lemon) and some finger-foods as the plane flew out to Las Vegas.

Landing at the McCarran Airport's private plane section, a rented limousine took the two couples to the Clark County Courthouse, where Bill and Laura got their marriage license. Then the foursome went to a wedding chapel, where Bill and Laura were married, with Roy and Margaret Mary as their witnesses. Then it was back to the clerk's office to report the wedding, off to the plane, and a take-off for Puerto Vallarta, Mexico.

Roy was still walking around gingerly. Everyone slept on the route to Mexico. The plane landed at the small Puerto Vallarta airport, where the foursome was met by another of Bill's limousines and driven to Bill's magnificent hacienda overlooking the Bay of California and the Pacific Ocean. Bill introduced his guests to the Gomez family, who lived on the premises and took care of the place for Bill.

Bill felt that they were his own family members, and Mr. and Mrs. Gomez and their grown daughter hugged and embraced all four of the newly arrived persons. Mrs. Gomez and her daughter prepared a glorious Mexican dinner for everyone, served at poolside—Bill had a large in-ground pool with a diving board—around which everyone sat in bathing or lounge gear.

Laura had on that skimpy bikini covered with a white robe that Mrs. Bucher had allowed her to keep for the honeymoon.

Bill and Roy were in their Speedos, covered with short white robes. Margaret had a one-piece bathing suit with a short robe and a little bulge in her stomach. All but Margaret enjoyed Mexican *mojitos* (Mrs. Gomez made a nice fruit-punch drink for Margaret), delicious appetizers, and a fine Mexican dinner. Everyone had a wonderful evening but retired early. Roy and Margaret hugged and kissed the newlyweds good night. Roy was still sore, so there was little lovemaking in bed with Margaret that night.

The next morning the couples slept until nearly noon. Mrs. Gomez and her daughter made a wonderful Mexican brunch for the guests, and they enjoyed their meals outside. It was quite a treat for Margaret and Roy to get out into the sun; they tended to be cooped up in their apartment too much. Laura got out more frequently than the Emersons.

Bill was always busy with his work or school. All agreed that it was too bad the children were not with them; the kids could use some sun and would really enjoy the pool, although they would have to be watched carefully and probably have parents with them all the time because of their ages.

Roy and Margaret observed to Bill and Laura that they looked wonderful: relaxed, happy, and fulfilled. They had made a good marriage.

Bill indicated that as soon as they returned to Indianapolis, he would have his lawyer draw up papers to adopt Georgie. "I only need Laura's consent," he said, "and she is willing to have me adopt Georgie and give him my surname."

Roy and Margaret asked Laura what surname she wanted to use. Immediately, she said, "Rice."

Jokingly, Margaret and Roy threatened Bill that they were going to tell the adoption judge that they objected to the adoption because the Emerson family and Mrs. Bucher loved Georgie like a son, and he had already been adopted by them.

Bill and Laura laughed and said, "Believe us; we will never take Georgie away from you. All of us are one big—and, I think, happy—family already."

Margaret spoke up with some tears coming into her eyes. "Thank you, Laura and Bill, for being so wonderful to us. It means a lot to Roy and me to be with you at your wedding and on this splendid vacation. We just wish it wouldn't end, although we dearly miss seeing all the kids."

"Speaking of the kids," Roy said, "where are you and Laura going to live as a married couple?"

Bill responded, holding Laura's hand, "That's a good question. I travel a great deal in my executive jet, upon which you have just flown. I do not want to leave my beautiful wife behind for one moment while I am on the road, so to speak, so I think she'll be away a lot, if she will consent to go with me everywhere."

Laura spoke up. "Of course, darling. I want to go with you everywhere."

Then Margaret said, "When the adoption for Georgie is completed, and the judge has signed the final papers, why don't you and Laura give a handwritten note to me, as primary, and my mother, as alternate, that if you are absent when Georgie needs attention at school, at a doctor's office, or a hospital or clinic setting, or he has to see the dentist or the eye doctor, I or my mother would have your permission to act on your behalf?"

Bill responded, "Say, that is a good idea, if it's okay with Laura."

Laura said, "For sure, yes!"

Margaret went on. "Why doesn't Laura keep the apartment below ours? My mother can stay with Georgie, or he can stay with us whenever Laura is gone, and either Roy, my mother, or I—if we can use Laura's company car—can get the children around to school and for other activities."

Bill looked at Laura, and she nodded approvingly.

Bill spoke up. "I'd like to pay you to take care of Georgie if Laura is away with me."

Almost angrily, both Margaret Mary and Roy spoke out. "No way. No way. No way. Georgie's not going to cost you anything. We love him and think of him as our own. We will not—and I mean, not—accept any money for his care, activities, or schooling. Just keep health insurance up on Georgie so that if he does become sick, we can have an insurance card to show the health care provider."

Bill looked at Laura, and she nodded approvingly. With tears in her eyes, Laura came over to Roy and chastely hugged and kissed him. Then Laura went to Margaret Mary, cried with her, and hugged and kissed her fondly.

While Laura had her arms around Margaret Mary, she said, "Do you know your mother and I had a talk, and Mrs. Bucher permits me to call her Mom or Mother. How do you feel about that?"

Margaret responded, "That's fine with me but on one condition."

"What's that?" Laura asked.

"Only if I can call you sister, and Roy can call you and Bill sister-in-law and brother-in-law. Is that okay?"

Laura looked at Roy, and he nodded. Laura cried; Margaret Mary cried; the two women held onto each other a seemingly long time.

"I love you, sister Margaret Mary and brother Roy Emerson."

Roy responded, "We love you, Laura, and your husband. Now,

I think he has a big home in Indianapolis. And you should feel free to spend time with him there and not feel that you are abandoning your son. Is that okay with you both?"

Laura and Bill looked at each other. Laura answered, "That seems like a good arrangement as long as Georgie doesn't feel hurt by my being gone too long."

Roy said, "When we get back home, why don't you and Margaret's mom talk to Georgie about such an arrangement and see if he has any problems with it."

Laura and Bill, who were now seated and holding hands, looked at each other and responded, "That sounds like a good idea."

"Now," Roy mentioned, "Bill—about your future. You're a wealthy guy. I'm not sure you're going to have to do a lot of fund-raising. It looks like the Rice Company is pretty well organized, so it should be able to function well while you are out campaigning."

Bill responded, "Sure it will, if you're president of the company, Roy Emerson."

Roy answered, "Mr.—or rather, Senator—Rice, you and I are students of history. I believe it was General William Tecumseh Sherman, who didn't like journalists or politicians much (although his brother, I think, was a US senator from Ohio), who once said, 'If nominated, I will not run; if elected, I will not serve.' So my answer to your generous offer of company presidency, probably with a pretty good paycheck and benefits, is a flat-out no. With Margaret's support—and she and I have talked about this—after I finish at Service, I am going to try to go to law school at Indiana University's campus in Indianapolis. If I graduate and pass the bar examination, the Emerson family (and Georgie, if we have him with us) is packing up and moving to Tippecanoe County, Indiana, where I am going to practice law and, hopefully, one day be elected the county prosecuting attorney on the Democratic ticket. If I *lose* and you are, as I believe you will be, a US senator, you can have me appointed as postmaster of some small Indiana town, where I can be a big fish in a small pond. That's my final answer. Right, Margaret, my darling, pregnant wife?"

Margaret said, "That's what we've agreed, and we'll stick with our agreement."

Bill went on, "The job pays $500,000 per year, Roy, with full benefits and bonuses if the company makes money. Are you still sure your answer is no?"

Roy answered, "Absolutely. Even if the job paid a million dollars a year plus benefits, the answer is still no. All I would do with that much money is give it to Margaret, and she would throw me over and marry a more handsome man!"

Margaret tried to give Roy a kick in the leg, but he was too far away. So she got out of her chair and came over to him. Now, Roy was a strong guy, so he just swept Margaret off her feet, pressed her to his body, and gave her the most passionate kisses and embrace.

As he was kissing Margaret, he spoke to Bill and Laura and asked, "Would you please excuse us for a few minutes? I think we're back in that bathtub in Bangkok, and I would like to make another baby with my beautiful Margaret, right here and now."

Everybody laughed as Margaret said, "Roy Emerson, you let me go immediately."

Roy tenderly kissed Margaret's belly and listened carefully for fetal sounds. He put his hand on Margaret's abdomen and announced that he could feel life in there. Margaret, who was still in Roy's arms, just kept kissing him. Laura then started kissing Bill just as passionately. Finally, Roy and Bill let go of their ladies;

Roy spoke up. "If we keep doing this around the pool, people will think that Bill's hacienda is a brothel! Stop attacking us men, you women!"

Laura had a drink that contained a maraschino cherry; she threw the cherry at Roy and said, "Liar." There was laughter all around.

Bill said, "Let's stay here tonight and go shopping tomorrow. Then we can eat out and go to a nightclub."

Margaret said, "I'm all for going out tomorrow but no smoky

places. We should eat outside, and I won't join you at the nightclubs, where there's sure to be smoking."

Roy responded, "I'm all for tomorrow's events, but I'll come home here to the hacienda with Margaret while you two newlyweds take in the town. After all, without Margaret around, some beautiful Latina may take a shine to me because of my good looks and wonderful masculine physique."

Margaret spoke up. "Roy, you are a real dreamer! I've seen your gonads since you've met the urologist; and you're not doing much of anything, anywhere."

Everybody laughed at that remark. Roy pointed to Margaret and said, "You've got me there."

Margaret said sexually, "No, I don't. When I tried to get you there last night, all you did was yowl." Everybody cracked up.

Roy told Bill, "Aren't you glad you never married a nurse?"

The ladies went in to change out of bathing wear, but Roy and Bill stayed at the pool and began discussing late medieval and modern history topics. Bill was particularly well versed on the so-called Korean War, which was really a conflict, just as Vietnam had been a conflict for Roy and the marines. When the ladies returned, the two husbands were drawing battlefield maps on the back of napkins and ignored the ladies.

Margaret spoke up. "Well, the hell with you two guys. Laura and I are going to take the limousine downtown to some smoky nightclubs and find some younger and fitter men to spend the evening with."

Bill and Roy got red in the face and begged to be forgiven. Each woman came over and passionately embraced her husband.

A nice meal was had by all. The talk centered around home, children, and their futures. Margaret said someday she would like to teach nursing.

Bill said, "That should be possible, given that Terre Haute in Monroe County is right next to Tippecanoe County and isn't a far drive away from where you'll be living."

Margaret answered, "I hope you're right. However, I don't have a master's or a PhD degree, and given my current condition and family responsibilities, I'm not planning on going back to school anytime soon."

After dinner, the group retired to Bill's library, which was rich with books. Roy looked around and was amazed at Bill's extensive collection of history and political science books. While the ladies talked about female fashions, Bill and Roy pulled a couple of history books from his library and got to talking about historical topics.

It was getting late, and the couples decided to retire. Margaret and Roy hugged and kissed Bill and Laura and told them how happy they were to have Laura, Bill, Georgie, and Bill Junior (whom they hoped to meet soon) as their friends.

That night, both couples had glorious sexual relations in their separate bedrooms, even with Roy's hurt gonads and Margaret's pregnancy.

After a good night's sleep and another wonderful Mexican brunch prepared by Mrs. Gomez and her daughter, the two couples got in Roy's limousine and went into Puerto Vallarta. They drove around and saw the sights and particularly enjoyed the views along the beachfront. They stopped to walk along the beach walk and the sand for a while, until Margaret said she felt tired. After getting back into the vehicle, Bill had his driver take the ladies to a clothing store and beautician, where he bought them some nice Mexican-made clothing and got them the works at the beauty parlor.

Bill offered to buy Roy some clothes, but all Roy wanted was one set of warm-weather wear for the time he would be spending in Puerto Vallarta and a single pair of sandals. Then both Bill and Roy went to a barber shop, where each got a shampoo, haircut, and a shave. The barber applied some nice cologne and aftershave lotion, and Bill tipped generously.

Bill and Roy met up with the ladies and drove to a fancy jewelry store. After all, the wedding had occurred so swiftly for Bill and Laura that Laura really didn't have a wedding ring; neither did Bill.

In the jewelry store, Bill had Laura select a very expensive wedding ring; he bought himself a similar gold band. Bill offered to buy jewelry for Roy, but Roy held up his wedding ring.

"I'm totally satisfied with my ring, which my darling Margaret Mary and I got in Bangkok. However, if you want to get something for Margaret Mary, that would be your choice." Roy and Margaret wanted to stroll a bit until Margaret got tired. The Emersons did some window-shopping and really enjoyed the sights, aroma of Mexican cooking, and the sunlight. When Bill and Laura tracked Roy and Margaret down with their limousine, the driver took all four to a nice restaurant with an outdoor patio where the couples could eat and drink out of a smoky atmosphere, for Margaret's sake.

Three had mojitos, and Margaret ordered a fruit drink. The diners enjoyed the house specialties of appetizers, salads, and entrees. The meal was so delicious that the foursome still had a little room left for Mexican desserts. The town was beginning to rock, with music seeming to fill the air.

However, the bars and nightclubs would be smoky. Margaret asked if she could be taken back to the hacienda up on the hill. Bill had his driver take the couples back to his home, where Margaret told them that she was just going to rest but that Roy could accompany them to the bars and nightclubs. Joking around, Roy said that was a good idea; with his new haircut, close shave, and cologne, the ladies couldn't resist him and would be asking him to dance to sexy music until the wee small hours of the morning.

Margaret said, "Go ahead, but just remember you're a married man and keep on that wedding ring."

Everybody laughed, and Roy scored a few romantic points with Margaret by saying, "Downtown I couldn't find anyone as fine or as beautiful as you." Then Roy said to Bill and Laura, "Would you excuse us for the evening? You two enjoy yourselves downtown as much as you want."

Laura hugged and kissed Roy and Margaret and slipped a nice felt box into Margaret's hands, saying it was a present from Bill.

Margaret opened the box and inside was a beautiful pearl necklace and matching earrings.

Margaret started to tear up. She hugged and kissed Bill and Laura, saying, "You are my wonderful sister and brother." Roy thanked Bill profusely and hugged and kissed Laura.

Bill gave Roy some presents: newspapers and international news magazines in the English language.

Roy chuckled and said to Bill, "By reading these, Senator, I'm going to get better grades than you at Service next school year—probably your last two semesters at Service before you leave for a new job in Washington, DC."

Bill laughed as he and Laura boarded the limousine and took off for a fun-filled evening. Roy insisted that Margaret go into the bedroom and take a long nap while he lounged around the pool and read his new literature from Bill. Margaret was bushed and took a long slumber until nighttime. Roy put on his Speedo and swam off some of the pounds from the fine brunch and Mexican dinner. Then he put on a white robe, as it was getting a little breezy, and he stayed at poolside until after dark, reading his newspapers and magazines by candlelight.

Mrs. Gomez fixed him a nice Mexican fruit drink and offered him finger foods, but Roy rubbed his belly and turned down the food offer. Mrs. Gomez's daughter brought Roy drinks throughout the late afternoon and evening and asked if she could speak English to him. He was pleased to speak English to this beautiful Latina and tried to pick up a few of her Mexican words.

They talked about their lives in the United States and Mexico. The Gomez daughter asked Roy if the people in the United States had heard rumors of the healer who lived in a northern Mexican drug province.

Roy said, "No, I have not, but please tell me about the healer."

The young daughter with wide eyes related a lengthy story about a woman named Rebecca, who lived in a Mexican province infested with criminals. She had fought off the criminals and operated a healing clinic for free, where wonder cures were being performed by this healer. The Mexican people were talking about her, and she had been written up with photographs in all the Mexican newspapers. Excitedly, she told Roy there were even stories that this healer had miraculous powers to raise the dead.

"In Indianapolis, Indiana, where I live," said Roy, "no one has heard about this healer, but I promise to watch the American newspapers and news magazines to see if stories turn up about her." Roy thought this pretty young woman spoke fair English.

She thanked him for the conversation, which had lasted for probably two hours. Roy took a little snooze until his beautiful pregnant wife came out to the pool wearing her attractive bathing gear. She modeled her new jewelry for Roy, and he told her that she looked better than anyone in town.

Roy, being strong, grabbed Margaret and gently pulled her down on top of him and showered her with hugs and kisses and caressed her lovely hair. She smelled of wonderful shampoo and perfume. They nearly had an act of intercourse in Roy's chair, but neither Margaret nor Roy wanted to embarrass the Gomezes or show that the Emersons were not respectful guests in Bill's home.

Mrs. Gomez made fruit drinks for both Roy and Margaret (no alcohol) and sent out finger foods as well. Before eating, Margaret put the pearl necklace and earrings back into the felt box she had carried in her robe. She jumped into the pool and swam a number of laps. Even pregnant, Margaret surprised Roy with her swimming form.

When she got out from the pool, he complimented her on her swimming strokes, and she reminded him that she had been in the United States navy. Both of them laughed and held hands as they enjoyed the drinks and finger foods. They were not going to stay up to wait for Bill and Laura's return. When they felt tired, they went into their bedroom and made glorious love.

Roy felt he must be the happiest man in the world, with a wonderful family that was about to add a third child. Margaret predicted the baby was a girl, and Roy told her how pleased he would be to have another daughter; he loved Mary and Emily so much.

The next morning, Roy and Margaret were up before the newlyweds. Roy persuaded Margaret to shower together, and she agreed. They washed and caressed each other's bodies in the shower, and Roy repeatedly rubbed Margaret's abdomen and kissed it tenderly, saying, "There's a third Emerson in there." Margaret kissed Roy passionately.

Getting in bathing gear, the Emersons returned to poolside, with Roy finishing off Bill's newspapers and news magazines and Margaret snoozing for a short time in the sunshine until she decided to sit under an umbrella at a table.

Eventually, Bill and Laura joined them in bathing gear. Bill looked a little hungover, but Laura just glowed. Roy kidded Bill about all the fun he must be having down here in Puerto Vallarta. Bill replied, "A little too much fun last night, for which I am paying the bill this morning."

Margaret was moved by the sight of Laura. She looked happy and contented for the first time since the two women had become good friends. Margaret took Laura in her arms and tenderly hugged and kissed her, saying, "You're a wonderful woman, Laura. I'm very happy that you and Bill have become part of the Emerson family."

Margaret and Laura cried a little as they were in each other's arms, and Laura said, "I am eternally grateful to you, Roy, and especially to Mother Bucher for introducing me to Bill and giving me the opportunity to make a transition for the better in my life. Bill keeps telling me how much he loves me and wants continuously to be buying me things. I tell him, 'Our love does not need to be based on wealth and presents,' and I think I have finally gotten him to believe me."

Margaret let go of Laura and went over to hug and kiss Bill and congratulate him on having married one of the finest women on the planet. Bill embraced Laura and said to Roy, "I can't thank you enough, Roy Emerson, for introducing me to Laura. She is the love of my life. I have not been so happy in a long, long time."

Mrs. Gomez and her daughter brought out some fruit drinks and a delicious brunch. As the foursome ate at poolside, Roy made a few political comments to Bill and said that these few thoughts were about all he would tell Bill during his campaign.

"You know, Bill, poor people, little people, and the people who benefit from social welfare programs think that the Republican Party and its adherents don't really care for them. They say the Republicans are only interested in wealthy individuals and protecting America's corporations. Personally, I don't believe that broadband denunciation of the Republican Party. I would like to suggest to you that you reach out to a broad base of voters in your political campaign. When you are ready to announce your candidacy, why don't you hire a campaign bus and make your first stop the courthouse in Decatur, up in Tippecanoe County. Visit the courthouses, the county clerks, and chambers of commerce in all the smaller counties and town. Show the 'little people' that you are interested in them. I know that when you are in Washington, you'll have to take special care of the corporations—after all, they make jobs that hire people and support families and whole communities."

Bill replied, "You are talking a little bit like a Republican, Roy Emerson, but I totally believe what you are saying. I am taking your suggestions and going to do what you have said. I have budgeted twelve million dollars of my own money just for the primary election, and I can come up with the same amount for the general election. However, if I win the primary, the Republican Party will provide some financial support. Then I can devote some of my saved money for buying clothes for my beautiful wife. Look at her now; she doesn't have much to wear."

They looked over at Laura's beautiful figure in her skimpy bikini, and everyone laughed at Bill's remark. Laura was not one to forget to get in the last word.

She responded, "If he has that kind of money, then he can stop being a penny-pincher and buy me some maternity clothes."

Laura's statement hit Margaret and Roy like a rocket, and they went over together and hugged and kissed her, telling her that she and Bill would make wonderful parents. "Bill already has a son," Roy reminded Laura, "and so do you. Georgie now has a big brother, and we know both boys would love to have a youngster by your marriage."

Margaret said, "We are so glad you two are thinking along these lines."

Roy was so moved by these remarks that he hugged Bill tightly.

Bill said, "Who would not want to have children by this gorgeous wife?"

The time for the two couples went along quickly while they were in Puerto Vallarta, and the same routine was pretty well followed, although Margaret and Roy told Bill and Laura that they didn't need any other gifts. Margaret thanked Bill for the set of pearls and said, "I'll wear them to your election night reception in Indianapolis!"

Finally, it was time to fly back home to see the children and Mrs. Bucher. Roy and Margaret packed up their few things, and off they flew in Bill's executive jet with the new Mr. and Mrs. Rice to Indianapolis. There, they were met by Bill's limousine and driven back to the apartment building. By now, Bill's son, Bill Junior, had taken up residence in the one-bedroom apartment near the Emersons, and Mrs. Bucher had "adopted" Bill Junior as her own and looked out for him every day.

Bill Junior was very ill, and Mrs. Bucher gave him all the medications prescribed for him and fixed him healthy meals from scratch. The younger children were permitted to come to young Bill's apartment and play with their toys and blocks. Bill Junior was very pleased to get to know them. Every night, Mrs. Bucher tucked Bill Junior into bed, kissed him good night, urged him to get a good sleep, and said she would be there for him in the morning. When

Bill Senior later learned how tenderly Mrs. Bucher had been looking after his son, he wept and embraced Mrs. Bucher. So did Laura.

Mrs. Bucher said, "It's all in a day's work."

Bill Junior met his father, new stepmother, Laura, and Roy and Margaret. Without hesitation, Roy and Margaret embraced Bill Junior and told them he was welcomed into the Emerson family. From that point on, Bill Junior would be invited to come to the Emerson household whenever he felt up to it and to eat his meals together with the family. Bill Senior was overcome with gratitude for knowing these fine Emersons.

Margaret said she would communicate with Bill Junior's doctor (with Bill Junior's written permission, of course) and see how, as a health care professional, she could help Bill with his illness. Bill Junior was so moved by this offer that he cried. From that day forward until he died, Bill Junior was truly treated as a member of the Emerson family.

When he passed away, the Emersons and Mrs. Bucher were devastated, having lost the life of one of their family. Bill and Laura never forgot the generosity and caring from Margaret, Roy, their children, and Mrs. Bucher, who would not accept one cent from Bill for his son's care.

16

CAMPAIGNING

Bill Rice had plenty of his own private money (not the company's) to sink into his primary campaign, so he was not beholden to political action committees for funds as he announced his candidacy—the senior US senator having advised the media during Bill and Laura's absence that he was stepping down at the end of his term—on the steps of the Tippecanoe County Courthouse, in accordance with Roy's suggestion.

Immediately, the naysayers of both parties began to attack Bill personally and his candidacy, not because they could get anything on Bill but because of the medical condition of his son and his wife's background.

Although Roy, Margaret, and Mrs. Bucher were not active in Bill's campaign, they were ready to jump into the political affray to defend their dear friend, Bill Rice, his wonderful son, Bill Junior, and Bill's beautiful wife, Laura Evans Rice. And pretty quickly, they did just that.

Late one morning, while Bill and Roy were at Service, Mary and Georgie were at their schools, and Mrs. Bucher was with baby Emily at Bill Junior's apartment, preparing his lunch and his medications, there was a great commotion at the front of the apartment building. Looking out, Mrs. Bucher spied a couple of television satellite vans and a group of newspaper people and photographers.

Telling Emily to stay with Bill Junior (both were looking out of the window at the happenings through light window curtains), Mrs.

Bucher went downstairs and out the front door of the apartment building, where she demanded to know why the horde was about to invade her private apartment building.

Some bold reporters announced they wanted to see and photograph Bill Junior, whom they said they believed had AIDS.

"Anyone's medical condition, like Bill Junior's, is a matter between the patient and his doctor," Mrs. Bucher said. "Bill Junior is like a second son to me, and I am *not* going to have a mad group of wild media representatives invading my and Bill Junior's private space. I'll call the police if any of you try to enter Bill Junior's apartment."

One bold woman reporter said, "I'm coming in."

Mrs. Bucher replied, "Okay, I'm calling the police." Mrs. Bucher turned on her heel as the horde followed her into the building. She entered Bill Junior's apartment, locked and bolted the door, and put a chair up next to it for good measure.

While the media was pounding on the door and the television people were taking pictures of the building, Mrs. Bucher called the police and said she and her son were being attacked in their apartment. Soon, police sirens were heard, and when the police arrived they ordered the media out of the building. The public areas were fair game, the police sergeant said, but not private property.

So the media camped outside of the Emersons' apartment building for several hours but finally drifted away. Mrs. Bucher's confrontation of the media was the talk of the evening and late television news shows, and her picture was on the front page of the next day's newspapers with her arms folded in front of her as she confronted the media.

There were calls into radio talk shows and letters to the editor in newspapers, asking, "What is Bill Rice hiding in his campaign in respect to Mrs. Bucher and his son?" Mrs. Bucher would listen to the radio talk shows, call in, and give them a piece of her mind. Also, she wrote hot reply letters to the newspapers, responded to criticism of Bill Senior and his son. There was actually a political cartoon showing Mrs. Bucher in a Katie-bar-the-door pose in front of the apartment build, sheltering a cowering Bill Junior.

Mrs. Bucher had Roy get the cartoon framed, and she hung it on the wall of her bedroom. There was a strange political happening; after that confrontation with Mrs. Bucher, the matter of Bill Junior's medical condition vanished from the campaign format of Bill Senior's opponents and enemies. It appeared that the media did not want to face an angry Mrs. Bucher once again.

Turning away from Bill Junior, the naysayers jumped on Laura, showing skimpily clad pictures of her when she was an escort and claiming she had an illegitimate child. Roy and Margaret took to the podium in defense of their dear friend. As a retired navy officer and as a decorated navy medic, both Margaret and Roy received the permission of the secretary of the navy to wear their uniforms and medals to a press conference for Bill. (The secretary of the navy was a former marine and knew about Roy's and Margaret's exploits in Vietnam from grizzled General Elliott, now retired USMC, and he was a *Republican* to boot.)

At a hastily called press conference on the steps of the Indiana state capitol lawn, Margaret, Roy, and Mrs. Bucher, surrounded by television reporters and numerous newspaper people and photographers, appeared in their uniforms and blasted the media for denouncing their sister, Laura Evans Rice, and criticizing their "grandchild," Georgie Evans Rice, whom they dearly loved and respected. Roy reminded the media that Georgie was now Bill Senior's child, and the boy was only five years old.

The broadside by Margaret and Roy got a wide play on the television stations, the radio and television talk shows, and the national media. Their pictures in their uniforms were everywhere. An endorsement by these well-decorated navy people seemed to quiet down the furor about Laura, and thereafter, the campaign rhetoric focused on Bill Senior's lack of political experience and his political philosophy, or lack thereof, and not upon attacks of his family members.

As a matter of political fact, there was a backlash against the media for leading the charge in trying to attack Bill Senior's family members, rather than focusing on Bill's political beliefs. Bill tapped his assistant chief operating officer of the Rice Company (on an unpaid leave-of-absence from the company), a lovely woman, as his campaign chairperson, and the very nice woman accountant who'd helped Laura with the Rice Company's accounting books as his campaign treasurer.

All appropriate federal Campaign Finance Reports were turned in and on time; the audit of the reports showed everything to be in order.

On primary election night, Bill and Laura were down in campaign headquarters, watching the primary returns; the Emersons with the kids and Bill Junior were in their apartment, watching the same television station. After two o'clock, when everyone in the Emersons' apartment was asleep except Roy, Bill's Republican primary opponents conceded the primary election to him.

Roy had a broad smile on his face and said to himself, "Too bad Bill's a Republican!" Then Roy retired but was up at the usual time the next morning and back at his books, By primary election time, both he and Bill had graduated from Service. Roy was put on the waiting list for law school at Indiana University in Indianapolis (he still had some of his GI Bill benefits remaining) and would be slotted in to a vacant spot in the law school in January of the same year that Bill was sworn in as a United States senator.

Oddly enough, Roy and the children, except Georgie, did not attend the swearing-in at Washington.

Margaret had delivered the third Emerson girl, whom Roy and Margaret named Laura Rice Emerson, in honor of you-know-who. Roy was getting ready for law school, and Mrs. Bucher was busy, living in Laura's apartment and taking care of Mary Margaret and Emily Emerson and getting them to and from school.

Bill's general election had been no big a deal. The Republican Party brought in money and heavy political hitters to pitch his candidacy. When the votes were counted, Bill had won over a Democratic congressman and some minor party candidates with 62 percent of the popular vote.

In the general election campaign, the Democratic Party and other minor party candidates stayed away from references to Bill Junior and Laura. However, one Washington political columnist remarked in a social column in the Washington newspapers that Mrs. Rice was, in her opinion, the most gorgeous political wife on the new social scene in Washington.

When Laura went with Bill to the White House for a presidential reception for newly elected members of Congress, Laura glowed like a brightly burning bulb! Laura had certainly come a long way from the scared escort with a black eye on the Emersons' couch and learning domestic skills from Roy's mother-in-law, who treated Laura as a daughter.

Bill's election enervated Roy in law school, and Roy ended his first semester in some tough law courses with a C+ average. He was not going to be material for the Law Review or the Moot Court team, but he was not going to finish as the goat of his law school class.

The years for Roy at Indiana Law School in Indianapolis flew by. Roy scored a gentleman's C in most of his course, but he received an A in criminal law and another A in criminal procedure, a B+ in civil rights law, and a B in his two-semester constitutional law class. He graduated with a C+ average.

The graduation speaker, arranged by Roy, was junior United States senator William Rice from Indiana. Margaret, Laura, and all the children attended the graduation and the party hosted by the Law School dean afterward. The students were much honored to meet Senator Rice and his lovely wife, Laura Evans Rice, who practically stole the attention of all male members of the graduating class, except Roy Emerson. Margaret was wearing the pearl necklace and matching earrings from Bill and Laura at the graduation ceremony. (She had not been able to be present at campaign headquarters of

Rice for Senator on general election night to wear them, as she had promised.)

The Rices drove with Roy, Margaret, and the kids back to the Emersons' apartment, where they all kicked off their shoes and had a good Mrs. Bucher-prepared dinner, admired baby Laura Rice Emerson, and remembered everyone's lost son, Bill Junior, who, despite Margaret's and Mrs. Bucher's ministrations, had passed away during the summer.

Roy had gotten Laura's and Bill's permission to bury Bill Junior in the Emersons' family plot up in Tippecanoe County, where Emersons had buried their loved ones for a generation (Roy's parents had now passed away) and where burial plots had been purchased for Roy and Margaret. The Rices were pleased with the choice of burial place for Bill Junior and had attended all the funeral proceedings and burial.

Margaret and Roy would see to it that appropriate flowers were regularly placed on Bill Junior's grave when they moved back to Tippecanoe County.

The time had come for Roy to plunge into law practice. Although he got a low grade in the bar examination, he just passed by a whisker. Roy was sworn into the bar by the circuit court judge in Tippecanoe County.

Roy decided to live in Decatur so that Margaret would be able to drive over to Terre Haute, where she hoped to teach, but Roy established a small solo-practice law office in Dansville village, where many of his clients were minorities and people with very little money.

Roy had finally been evaluated by the US Department of Veterans Affairs and was rated as 50 percent disabled from his military service-connected wounds. So, Bill received a monthly VA check (and had access to *fine* VA medical care facilities in Indianapolis) and a small check as a wounded Vietnam veteran from the state of Indiana; he used these monthly VA and Indiana monies to support his modest law practice, so he could keep his fees low for his clients.

Roy became the talk of the village and its environs as being a very fine lawyer who was for the little people. This reputation would stay with Roy throughout his entire legal career and would really help him when he ran, eventually, for Tippecanoe County prosecuting attorney.

17

DECATUR, DANSVILLE, AND GEORGIE

The Emersons were now a pretty good-sized family. There were Roy, Margaret Mary, their three girls (Mary Margaret, Emily, and Laura) and Margaret's mother, Mrs. Bucher. They had asked Mr. Bucher to move from Milwaukee to join them in Indiana, but he said that he would miss his old pals too much if he left Milwaukee and, after all, Mrs. Bucher traveled back to Milwaukee from time to time.

Periodically, when Bill and Laura were traveling extensively, they would drop Georgie off at the Emersons, and he was treated, as always, as another member of the family. Unexpectedly, one day Bill and Laura showed up at the Emersons' household with Georgie and explained that they were sorry to drop in without contacting Margaret and Roy first, but something very important had come up. All the Emersons were glad to see Georgie, none more so that Mary Margaret and Mrs. Bucher.

The kids went to play in the playroom and started to run around the big house that Roy and Margaret Mary had bought in Decatur from their combined savings and Margaret Mary's navy out-processing monies, which they had not touched and which had been invested at interest in the Navy Credit Union up at Great Lakes (far away from where the family was located so that before the selection of their first house, Roy and Margaret would not break down and get into the funds earmarked for the residential purchase).

The house the Emersons bought had been vacant for a couple of years due to a downturn in the real estate market in Decatur. They were able to get it for cash, so there was no mortgage due. The house had many rooms, many bathrooms, and a huge living room, dining room, and kitchen. There was even a finished basement with a bathroom.

All of the Emersons and Mrs. Bucher loved this new old house. There was still plenty of room for guests. Laura and Bill had arrived on a weekend when Margaret was off from her job in the emergency room at the Terre Haute Hospital, and Roy had already been down to his Dansville office in South Tip that morning.

Bill and Laura asked if they might talk to Roy and Margaret Mary *privately*. Roy asked Mrs. Bucher if she could feed all the children, including Georgie, and let them romp around in the yard. Mrs. Bucher asked if she could walk downtown with the kids to buy ice cream cones. Roy said that would be a nice treat for Georgie, the girls, and Mrs. Bucher.

Roy, Margaret Mary, and the Rices went into the living room, and Roy broke out his best scotch for them. They sat down to talk, and Margaret Mary said that both of them looked wonderful and that it was a treat to have Georgie with them once again.

Bill lowered his voice and told the others that what he was about to say was very confidential. He explained that he and the president had become close personal friends; besides being members of the same political party, the president frequently called him to come over to the family quarters at the White House to seek his no-holds-barred advice on pressing political matters waiting for the president's decision.

Bill always gave him straight answers and would even argue with the president over policy as they shared drinks, but they always parted friends, even after a heated meeting. Bill said, even as he lowered his voice further, that the secretary of defense, a mutual friend of Bill's and the president's, had been offered a lucrative job in private industry that he could not afford to turn down.

So there was going to be a vacancy in the cabinet, and the president had asked Bill to fill the job of secretary of defense. Bill was squeaky clean, and his nomination and appointment should sail through the United States Senate; after all, Bill was one of the Senate's own. Laura was an absolute smash hit in Washington, and her parties at the Rice household were *the places* to be on social nights, outside of White House receptions.

Roy interrupted Bill's presentation because he knew where the conversation was leading.

Looking at Margaret Mary, Roy said to Bill and Laura, "Let Georgie live with us; we love him. You know he's like a son to us. The girls and Mrs. Bucher are very fond of him. We'll send him to Mary Margaret and Emily's school."

Laura said that Georgie had not been happy in Washington. He really missed the Emersons and asked about them all the time. Laura said she and Bill seemed to be busy all the time, and they felt they were neglecting their son. They wanted Georgie to be happy, but an opportunity like that offered by the president came along only once in a lifetime, and Bill and Laura, talking about everything, thought Bill should accept the president's appointment.

However, Georgie's placement was critical.

Both Roy and Margaret Mary congratulated Bill and Laura on the nomination, told Bill he would make a wonderful cabinet member, and wanted Georgie to come to live with them and Mrs. Bucher. Their girls would be overjoyed to have Georgie staying with them; they thought of him as a brother.

The Emersons thought Georgie would enjoy attending the girls' school.

About that time Mrs. Bucher was returning with the kids from the ice cream store; Margaret Mary asked Mrs. Bucher to join them in the living room with the children.

Laura put the question bluntly to Georgie: "Would you like to stay here with the Emersons and Mrs. Bucher while Mother and Dad had to travel around a lot?"

Georgie looked at the Emersons, the girls, and Mrs. Bucher and answered, "Yes, Mom and Dad. I would like to stay here, but I hope I'll see you from time to time. Will I go to Mary Margaret's school?"

Laura said, "Yes; is that okay with you?"

Georgie responded, "That's okay. I hope Mary can help me make some friends there. I don't have many friends where I have been in school now."

Roy asked, "Why doesn't Georgie stay with us now while you fly back to Washington? You're going to have to spend a lot of time at the White House getting prepared for the nomination hearings up on Capitol Hill. We'll get Georgie enrolled in school on the first school day after this meeting. Will you, Bill and Laura, give Margaret Mary, as principal, and Mrs. Bucher, as alternate, a handwritten note allowing either of them to take care of Georgie's needs at school, at a doctor's, hospital, clinic, dentist's or eye doctor's office in your absence?"

Roy gave Bill and Laura a piece of paper, and they wrote out the authorization for Margaret Mary and/or Mrs. Bucher. The Rices walked upstairs with Georgie and the Emersons to select Georgie's bedroom and bathroom. Georgie liked his room and attached bathroom. His room was right next to the girls' rooms. There was a tearful farewell between Laura, Bill, and Georgie as the Rices left Georgie with the Emersons and headed for Bill's executive jet.

Margaret Mary and Roy teared up a little as they bid a fond farewell to Bill and Laura. The girls and Mrs. Bucher put their arms around Georgie, took him back to his room, and helped him unpack the clothing, toys, and books that the Rices had left for him.

By evening around the Emersons' dinner table, Georgie had calmed down. Over prayers before dinner, the Emersons welcomed Georgie back into their family. The next school day, Roy enrolled Georgie in the kids' school, and the following school day Georgie attended his first classes in Mary Margaret and Emily's building. Georgie would turn out to be a very fine student and a popular boy, as Mary Margaret introduced him to all of her and Emily's friends as their older brother.

Also, Georgie was gifted in athletics as well as schoolwork.

Bill's nomination hearings turned out to be very contentious. The minority Democrats in the Senate Committee dealing with military and veterans' affairs raked him over the coals, claiming that he lacked experience in military affairs (even though Bill had served in the army). They said he was not capable of running a huge organization such as the armed forces and the bureaucracy at the Pentagon, even though Bill had been the chairman and chief executive of a multimillion-dollar corporation in Indiana and Kentucky.

There was a divided vote in the Senate Committee to recommend Bill's appointment, with the voting strictly along partisan lines. There was more debate in the Senate, and the Democrats threatened a filibuster. However, the Democrats could not get enough votes to prevent a cloture of debate, so they consented to an up-or-down vote on Bill's nomination.

The voting was along partisan lines in the full Senate, and Bill was approved by just a few votes.

There was a White House swearing-in ceremony for Bill as the new secretary of defense, followed by a reception for all the military brass, particularly for the Joint Chiefs of Staff. Slowly, Bill settled into the huge job of running the Pentagon and being the president's front man with his military forces.

In taking Georgie into their home, Roy and Margaret Mary emphasized to the Rices that they would accept no funds for carrying for Georgie, but they did ask the Rices to keep Georgie on their health insurance and to provide to Margaret Mary or Mrs. Bucher an insurance card for Georgie.

In order to protect Georgie's security while he was living with the Emersons (given his father's new important position in the president's cabinet), the Secret Service provided for Georgie an American passport listing his surname as Emerson and a revised birth certificate listing his mother as Margaret Mary Bucher Emerson and Georgie's father as James Elroy Emerson. Not being associated with the Rices, Georgie's experiences at school and in the community were undisturbed as he grew up, and a Secret Service agent did not always need to be hovering around him. Also, the health insurance cards were provided for Georgie with the surname Emerson.

18

LAURA MOVES IN; ROY STARTS UP

Amid the glitter, glamour, and power in Washington, DC, Laura was never completely happy being there. She was forced to be polite to and to socialize with many unpleasant and phony people. Laura did not like the fact that Bill was away from home for so long, particularly when he became the secretary of defense. Laura and Bill were deeply in love, and Bill treated Laura with the greatest tenderness and passion.

Laura became pregnant twice but miscarried each time. She became pregnant for the third time, and the doctor examining her advised that she needed extensive bed rest, given her prior miscarriages. Laura was determined not to stay in Washington for extensive bed rest. She advised Bill that she wanted to be with her dear friends, the Emersons, during this third pregnancy.

"If I stay with the Emersons during the pregnancy," she told him, "I feel I will deliver a healthy baby." Bill protested, but in the end he agreed; however, his Secret Service detail did not agree and nixed Laura's whole idea. So Laura decided to pull rank on the Secret Service. She and the First Lady were very good friends; they shopped together, traveled together, and spent as much time together as they could.

During an afternoon tea with the First Lady and her aide, Laura asked her help to get free of Washington to have her baby in the company of the Emersons. She told the First Lady that Bill's Secret Service detail had convinced Bill of the security problems involved in Laura's moving away from Washington. The First Lady and her aide told Laura that they would take care of Laura's problem.

A short time after this meeting, the chief of the Secret Service told Bill's Secret Service detail commander to remove his objection to Laura's moving in with the Emersons to have her baby. The Security Service chief told the detail commander that the word had come down from *the top*.

Therefore, Bill's Secret Service detail chief retracted his objections to Laura's moving temporarily to Indiana under an assumed name.

Laura called the Emerson household; everyone was gone but Mrs. Bucher, who *commanded* the wife of the secretary of defense to get out of Washington right away and come to Mother Bucher's home to stay.

In order to protect Laura's anonymity from prying eyes, photographers, and gossip magazine editors and reporters, the Secret Service detail provided her with a revised birth certificate and passport, indicating her surname as Emerson. Her baby, when born, would bear the surname of Emerson.

Pretty soon, Laura arrived with her baggage (scaled down by Laura) on a commercial flight into Terre Haute's airport. Roy hired a limousine to meet her there. In the rented limousine awaiting Laura were Mrs. Bucher, Margaret Mary, Roy, and Georgie.

They embraced Laura dearly at the airport after she had passed into the passenger-greeting area. Roy picked up Laura's bags, and he and the limousine driver carried the bags to the trunk of the vehicle.

In the limousine Georgie hugged and kissed his mother; all the passengers hugged and kissed her. Mrs. Bucher was blunter: "You are now *my* patient, and *we* are going to help you deliver a healthy and happy baby!"

When Laura entered the Emersons' home, she found that the Rice Furniture Company had replaced all the furniture in the house and had paid completely for a special bathroom with a large tub with a seat for Laura and all the Emersons. The children were thrilled with their new furnishings.

Mrs. Bucher immediately ushered Laura, who looked bushed, into Laura's room. Laura used the bathroom; Mrs. Bucher undressed her, put her into night clothes, tucked her into bed, and fondly hugged and kissed her. Frequently, when Laura was tired, Mrs. Bucher, Margaret Mary, Roy, or the kids would bring Laura's food up to her room on a tray and sit with her while she ate.

Margaret Mary arranged for a doctor friend of hers, who had once been a nurse but who had attended medical school and become board-certified in obstetrics-gynecology, to come out to the Emersons' house from Terre Haute Hospital's Professional Center (where her professional offices were located) to examine Laura and make her a patient.

The doctor confirmed the previous diagnosis—this was going to be a difficult pregnancy, and Laura would need extended bed rest to deliver a healthy baby. The Emersons—all of them, even the children—pledged to make a healthy birth possible for Laura.

Roy found that what pleased Laura the most was the bedside reading before bedtime each night for the children. Margaret Mary allowed the new baby, Laura, to sleep with her namesake. Laura loved her namesake, but Georgie was getting too big to sleep with his mother.

All of the children would gather around Laura at bedtime, and Roy, Mrs. Bucher, or Margaret Mary would read a book to Laura and the children. Everyone enjoyed the experience, particularly Laura and the reader. Then everyone would hug and kiss Laura good night.

A couple of times Roy and Margaret Mary rented a limousine to drive Laura over to Terre Haute to see the doctor and then return to the Emersons' home for more bed rest. Being off of her feet was really helping Laura with her difficult pregnancy, and Mrs. Bucher hovered around her like a mother hen.

Eventually, the doctor convinced Laura that her labor should be induced because the fetus had a somewhat irregular heartbeat. Terre Haute Hospital had a neonatal unit, so the child could be cared for after birth there without having to be transferred to Indianapolis.

Laura delivered prematurely a baby girl, whom she named Louise Rice Emerson, but the baby was small and needed to be in the Neonatal Intensive Care Unit (NICU) for some period of time. Every day Laura and either Mrs. Bucher or Mary Margaret would visit Louise in the neonatal unit.

Louise was a little fighter, and with good care she clung to life and got bigger. After six weeks in the unit, the doctors pronounced Louise fit to be taken home, and the rented limousine drove the baby, Laura, Margaret Mary, and Mrs. Bucher back to the Emersons, where Laura commenced to nurse her baby.

The sight of Laura nursing her baby girl brought tears to the eyes of Laura, Margaret Mary, and Mrs. Bucher. Bill had been informed of the birth, and he told his wife how much he loved her and was proud of what she had been through with the help of Mrs. Bucher and the Emersons.

Several times he stopped at the hospital and, eventually, at the Emersons' home to admire the baby, but he could not stay long because of all the problems going on in the world.

On one occasion, Bill told Roy that the president, who was running for a second term, had asked Bill to run as his vice presidential candidate, and Bill had accepted the invitation. Bill did *not* want Laura involved in the campaign; her time with the Emersons and with new baby Louise were too important both to Laura and Bill.

Just to jump ahead in the story a little bit, Bill was successful at enhancing the presidential ticket, and the president and his new vice president were swept into office by a solid majority of popular and electoral college votes.

Laura decided *not* to attend the inauguration and festivities surrounding the inauguration. She was still too weak and needed to take care of the new baby. Reluctantly, Bill agreed, but he stopped by several times during the campaign, after the election, and before the inauguration to see his wife and lovely baby girl.

Laura was surrounded by loving friends, and she was very reluctant to leave the protection of the Emerson household.

Roy had opened his law practice down in Dansville, a small village in South Tip, which was the home of a number of Spanish-speaking families. Roy needed a secretary who could speak English and Spanish.

Once, during a visit with Bill, Roy asked if it would be possible for Roy to get Mrs. Gomez's daughter from Puerto Vallarta a visa to come to Dansville and be Roy's secretary. Working with the Immigration Service, Bill arranged for Mrs. Gomez's daughter to get a J-1 visa as a researcher in American law—the visa would be good for two years, with a possible extension for another year.

Soon, Mrs. Gomez's daughter, Evita, arrived at the Terre Haute airport, was picked up by Roy, and moved into the Emerson household. She got along well with everyone in this big house; Laura liked her very much. Evita began to teach the Spanish language to the kids, who were eager learners. Every day Evita went with Roy to Dansville, where she worked with Roy's clients, most of whom, in the early years, were Spanish-speakers.

The first group of clients, who were agricultural workers, came in complaining about their treatment by the growers—low wages, bad housing, and being charged for everything from water to food for themselves and their family members (contrary to the growers' agreement with the agricultural broker who had brought the workers from Mexico).

Roy had not done well in his administrative law course at Indiana University, but he knew enough to file a complaint against the growers with the US Department of Agriculture representatives in Indianapolis. Soon, a delegation was sent up from Indianapolis to talk to Roy's clients and to confront the growers. Evita acted as an interpreter, and the agriculture delegation's visit produced a marked change in the way the growers treated their seasonal Mexican agricultural workers.

Roy had scored a victory in his first case without even having to go into litigation. He felt pretty good about that, but the workers could pay him very little. He accepted the small fee in full satisfaction of their monetary obligation to Roy.

Roy was paying for his office and for Evita's salary out of his VA checks and his Indiana military monies. In the early days, more went into Evita's pocket than into Roy's pocket. Fees from clients were very small and hard to come by.

Roy's next big case made local and national news. The Tip County prosecutor, Luke Ayers, and the Tip County sheriff, Bill Adams, were right-wing Republicans and long-time office holders in their respective positions. Roy didn't really care whether someone was a Republican, Democrat, or minor party member. What irritated Roy was when the elected person seemed disinterested in the people, particularly the little people, like his clients, or was beholden for election and reelection to pressure groups and moneyed people. Roy personally did not like Luke Ayers and Bill Adams, and the feeling was mutual. If Roy had decided to utilize the political muscle he had available to him but refused to use—because of the great respect, admiration, and, indeed, love that Roy had for Laura and Bill Rice (who now was the vice president of the United States of America, with Laura and the baby still guests in the Emerson household)—the following criminal prosecution would have been dropped immediately.]

Luke Ayers and Bill Adams were beholden to the growers, who would repeatedly contribute heavily to their campaign funds and assure their reelection. The growers were infuriated at Roy for turning the US Department of Agriculture inspectors against the growers to get the illegal treatment of the Mexican agricultural workers stopped.

The growers, gathering together, decided to discipline this "pissant James Elroy 'Roy' Emerson," as they put it, and to keep Roy off the backs of the growers and let them get away with anything the growers wanted to do, in respect to the poor agricultural workers.

The Mexican men, who worked long hours in the growers' fields (frequently with the women laboring alongside of their men and with their children helping out in the picking), had very little money or opportunities for recreation. The bars and restaurants in Dansville were not cordial at all to the migrant workers and their families; in fact, the owners of the bars and restaurants were downright rude to these poor people—a situation that made Roy very angry.

Roy had tended many wounded and dying Chicano American marines in Happy Valley and on Hill 861-A—men who gave their bodies and frequently died in order to answer the call of their then-president to fight the North Vietnamese forces and the Viet Cong. Roy would never, ever forget the sacrifices of these brave men. So Roy disliked the growers, who became prosperous, while other Chicano American marines were being wounded and dying at the behest of their then-president.

On Friday evenings, the men had a habit of buying e inexpensive beer at a market and sharing it among their fellows while they bet on certain fighting chickens (armed with metal spurs) in a field near their encampment. It was not a practice that Roy appreciated because he felt bad for the chickens—after all, he and his sister, Emily, had grown up as trailer trash in the farming part of South Tip and valued a meal of chicken; chickens were not to be arbitrarily destroyed.

However, this practice had been going on Friday nights for a long time and, although it was a bad practice, everyone in the county knew that these impoverished Mexican male agricultural workers got some little pleasure in the form of gambling and fellowship, although a few chickens would be left dead after the contests.

At the request of the growers and to discipline Roy and the workers for causing troubles for the growers with the US Department of Agriculture, the growers pressured Luke and Bill to raid one of these Friday evening gatherings, arrest the men who could be caught, and prosecute them to the letter of the law. Indiana law at that time provided for large fines and/or two years' imprisonment upon conviction of cock fighting.

With complaints and warrants already typed by Luke's staff and placed into Bill's hands (with names and addresses to be filled in later when the arrests were made), a flying phalanx of deputies descended upon the field near the workers' housing complex and grabbed ten workers and a couple of dead chickens that had been killed in the cock fighting.

All ten of the men were dragged away (over the tearful protests of their wives and children) to the Tippecanoe County Jail in Decatur and brought before the district court judge, Albert Evans (a rock-ribbed Republican who was, however, a very good legal scholar) and charged on the complaints and warrants with conducting cock fighting in South Tip.

The charge was, as stated above, a two-year misdemeanor, within the jurisdiction of the district court judge, who scheduled a jury trial for two weeks after the arraignment (i.e., the appearance before the judge to read the charges, take pleas, and set a bond), at which Roy appeared (at the request of the men's families), entered a plea of not guilty, and established bond at one hundred dollars per defendant.

None of the families could come up with the cash bonds, so the men were forced to stay in jail until the day for the jury trial.

Behind the scenes, Roy was working hard on the case and enlisting the support of an expert witness (a poultry scientist) from Western Indiana University and the research staff of a national organization for legal defense of Chicano peoples.

When the day established for the jury trial arrived, the little district courthouse was crowded with the growers or their representatives, members of the defendants' families, and even a contingent of local press from Decatur and Terre Haute. Since the sentence could be over one year if the defendants were convicted, the jury had to include twelve citizens and two alternates.

Roy did the best he could with his challenges (i.e., removal of unwanted jurors) to ensure that the men got a fair jury, representing a cross-section of the Tip County community; however, Roy looked at the jurors as a hanging jury, and he expected the worst for the men if the jury were to get the case to consider.

Roy's strategy was to convince the judge to take the case away from the jury and to direct a verdict of not guilty; this was a formidable task, given the pressure on the court from the publicity and the growers.

In order not to tarnish his image among the Tip County voters and avoid the charge that he was a racist, Luke, expecting the case to be a shoe-in for conviction, sent his young, pretty assistant prosecutor to handle the prosecution. She was quite lovely and attracted the attention of the judge, jurors, and spectators immediately (except for Roy, who had a couple of tricks up his sleeves).

The young assistant prosecutor did a nice job, for an inexperienced prosecutor, in presenting the proofs for the prosecution—witnesses who described the arrests, the field where the cock fighting was going on, and a couple of bagged but dead birds and several of the metal spurs used in the cock fight.

Roy made no objections to any of the prosecutor's testimony, much to the distress of his ten clients and their families (whom the judge had to threaten with contempt of court if they did not quiet down when the prosecutor's proofs were finished).

Roy waived his opening statement to the jury—again, much to the disgust of the defendants and their families who raised a murmur in the courtroom that had to be gaveled down by the judge.

Roy called just one witness—a gentleman sitting with a briefcase in the last row of the benches in the district courtroom.

Roy intoned, "The defense calls Dr. Manfred Van Field." There was surprise on the prosecutor's side of the courtroom as Dr. Van Field walked from the back row through the swinging door separating spectators from participants in the trial and strode purposefully up to the witness stand, where he was sworn in by the court clerk. Dr. Van Field seated himself comfortably, adjusted the microphone in front of him, and placed his briefcase on the little table before the witness chair.

Roy asked the witness, "Would you please state your name, address, and occupation."

"I am Dr. Manfred Van Field, professor of poultry science at Western Indiana University. I live in Terre Haute near the university campus with my wife and two children. I have been teaching at Western Indiana for fifteen years."

Under the prodding of Sheriff Adams, the young, pretty assistant prosecutor jumped up and objected to the appearance of Dr. Van Field. The judge asked her the basis for her objection. She hemmed and hawed but could not postulate a basis for the objection under the Indiana Rules of Evidence. The judge overruled her objection and listened carefully to Roy's interrogation of Dr. Van Field.

"Doctor, would you state your educational background?"

Objection by the assistant prosecutor; overruled by the judge, who was studying the doctor carefully.

"I grew up on a farm in this county. My father fought with the German army in the Netherlands in World War II and was captured and brought to the United States as a prisoner of war. He had been a farmer. After the armistice, he was allowed to stay in the USA because of his hard work for farmers in South Tippecanoe County. He married my mother, an American citizen, and he became an American citizen. My parents had two children: me and my sister, who is also a professor at Western Indiana University."

Objection by the assistant prosecutor was again overruled by the judge, who gave the young woman a dirty look.

"After I completed high school, I entered the United States Marines and fought for two tours of duty in Vietnam."

"Would you indicate the awards you received for your combat in Vietnam?"

Objection; but the judge said that awards were irrelevant. The judge told Roy to get on with it, meaning the doctor's testimony, and upheld the assistant prosecutor's objection.

"I attended Western Indiana University on a scholarship and the GI Bill and earned a degree in agriculture with highest honors. I was selected for a fellowship and completed my master's degree in agriculture at Western Indiana. Then I was awarded a fellowship in the poultry science department at Michigan State University up in East Lansing, Michigan. I went up to East Lansing and stayed there for four years, writing my dissertation on poultry diseases, receiving my PhD degree after three years of study and completed a postdoctoral fellowship in the US Department of Agriculture Poultry Laboratory on Mount Hope Road nearby Michigan State for one year. I began my teaching career at Western Indiana after completing my postdoctoral fellowship, and I have been advanced through the years to the academic position of full professor. I have published numerous articles on poultry science in professional journals and have been an expert witness in a number of lawsuits in various courts throughout the state of Indiana and in other states in respect to poultry diseases and money damages for loss of flocks of poultry. I have been a consultant internationally for the US Department of Agriculture and have advised the governments of China and South Korea, where the people eat a lot of poultry products. I have a paper in my briefcase, which is called a curriculum vitae, cataloging my education and my publications, which I can show to this court and to the prosecuting attorney."

Dr. Van Field brought out from his briefcase a large sheaf of papers containing his curriculum vitae. He handed it up to the judge, who glanced at it and turned it over to the assistant prosecutor.

She and Sheriff Bill Adams were studying the sheaf of papers carefully when Roy said, "I ask the court to rule that Dr. Van Field is an expert witness, allowed under the Indiana Rules of Evidence, to give opinions on matters before the court in this case."

The assistant prosecutor hesitated but finally objected to Dr. Van Field's being classified as an expert, but the judge quickly overruled her objection and ruled that Dr. Van Field was *indeed* an expert witness on matters pertaining to poultry science.

"Dr. Van Field, please describe the sexes of poultry."

There was laughter among the jurors and throughout the courtroom, except from the defendants and their family members. Dr. Van Field went through a detailed presentation of the nature of poultry, their scientific names, physical characteristics, and the difference physiologically between male and female chickens. Again, there was more laughter among the jurors, all of whom thought they knew about the differences in sexes of poultry and how eggs were laid.

Then Roy asked the leave of the court to have Dr. Van Field exit the witness stand, go to the table where the assistant prosecutor's exhibits were sitting (namely, the dead birds and the metal spurs), and examine the evidence. The assistant prosecutor's objection was quickly overruled. Dr. Van Field went to the table, carefully examined the dead birds, looked briefly at the metal spurs, and reseated himself on the witness chair.

"Have you had sufficient opportunity to examine all the dead birds that are evidence in this case?"

"Yes, Mr. Emerson, I have completed my examination of the exhibits."

"Please tell the court and the jury your findings."

"All of the dead birds—the exhibits—are females, called hens, and not males, called roosters."

The assistant prosecutor's face became red, and the sheriff showed agitation. The jurors reared up in their seats to hear what Dr. Van Field was going to say in addition to his previous testimony.

"Doctor, please describe the anatomical difference between poultry males and females as that difference would pertain to this case."

Objection; overruled. The judge was listening carefully to the witness.

"I could go into a long anatomical definition, but I think it sufficient to say that poultry females, 'hens,' lay eggs and poultry males, 'roosters,' impregnate the females so that they will lay eggs.

It's somewhat the same with human being males and females, if you get what I mean."

A look of puzzlement came over the jurors. The judge was picking up the drift of Roy's case.

"Doctor, in your work with poultry, would you be familiar with the law respecting cock fighting?"

"Objection!" said the assistant prosecutor. "This witness is not a lawyer; the determination of the law is for this court."

The judge replied, "No, I'll give Mr. Emerson a little latitude with this witness on this topic, recognizing it is for the court to decide the meaning of the law that the defendants are accused of violating. Go ahead, Mr. Emerson."

"For a number of years I have been an agricultural consultant to the Indiana Legislature and the governor of Indiana. I have testified many times before State Senate and House Agricultural Committees. I am very familiar with the law concerning so-called cock fighting. As a matter of fact, the state senator from Tippecanoe County and I drafted the statute that now appears in the law books—word for word. So I know what I believe the statute says and how it applies."

The judge was leaning over the bench and looking carefully at the witness. The assistant prosecutor's objection to this testimony and motion to strike the testimony was overruled and denied.

Roy went on. "Would you explain for the court and the jury the meaning of the words *cock fighting* in the statute as you and the state senator wrote it?"

"Objection! Mr. Emerson is asking the witness for a legal opinion."

The judge overruled the objection, noting that the witness said he wrote the law along with the county's state senator. "Go ahead, Dr. Van Field."

"Mr. Emerson and Judge Evans, if you will look carefully at the wording of the statute, it prohibits cock fighting between male poultry *only*. Although I think the law should be changed to cover a case like this one, the law does not apply cock fighting to conflicts between female poultry."

"Would you describe, once again, the sex of the exhibits on the table below your witness chair?"

"All of the poultry exhibits are females; none is a male."

"No further questions!"

The pretty assistant prosecutor fumbled and bumbled around, trying to cross-examine Dr. Van Field, but her efforts produced laughter in the courtroom from all but the defendants and their families when she persistently asked for his definition of cock fighting. Her questioning just reinforced the fact that the birds that had done the fighting were hens and not roosters.

The reason for the selection of hens and not roosters by these poor male agricultural workers was that roosters were not plentiful but hens were plentiful, even though they were valued by the immigrant community for laying eggs.

Roy rested the case for the defense, and Dr. Van Field was excused from the witness stand.

Roy told the judge he had a motion to make and asked that the jurors be excused for legal argument. The judge told the jurors to step out briefly and go to the jury assembly room.

When they exited, Roy presented a brief oral argument asking the judge to dismiss the charges against the men because the testimony of Dr. Van Field was convincing beyond a reasonable doubt that the men had *not been* cock fighting, as defined in the Indiana Criminal Law.

Roy handed to the judge and to the assistant prosecutor a detailed memorandum of the law, examining the wording of the statute and citing *every* case from Indiana and other states of the United States where a statute such as Indiana's was interpreted to involve *only* fighting between *male* poultry.

The judge asked the assistant prosecuting attorney for her response, but she had none other than to ask for a recess. However, the judge said this case had gone on long enough, and he directed the bailiff to the jurors bring back.

Upon the jurors' return to the jury box, the judge thanked them for their jury service and for taking time away from their work and their families to engage in a function that is important to American democracy. However, the judge said he was convinced, by the testimony and after reading the law, that the statute applied only to fighting between male and not female poultry. Therefore, the defendants were not guilty.

The judge then said, as a matter of law, he was directing a judgment of acquittal. The jurors nodded their approval and slowly filed out, looking at Roy with smiles on their faces.

Roy had Evita, who had attended the trial as his interpreter, tell the defendants and their families that the men were free to go home. He urged them, however, to stop any more cock fighting, lest they be arrested again by Sheriff Adams and prosecuted by the office of Luke Ayers.

The defendants and their families hugged and kissed Roy and Evita and said, "Sí, Sí!"

Roy and Evita left the courtroom, went back to their office, and finished a couple of low-cost wills for impoverished clients.

The case was written up by the county newspaper and by the Terre Haute newspaper under the headline "A Cock-Less Cock Fight Doth Not Make for Criminal Cock Fighting."

Prosecutor Ayers and Sheriff Adams were terribly embarrassed by the result of the trial; they became the talk of coffee-shop joking, and both of them determined to get Roy Emerson somehow or somewhere. The growers were furious, but the cock fighting stopped.

No one from the prosecutor's side of the case ever thought to ask Dr. Van Field how he knew Roy or how it came to pass that he was involved in the case. The doctor and Roy were friends, and both were members of the Terre Haute Marine Corps League (Roy as an honorary member, being a lowly navy medic in Vietnam), and the doctor gave his testimony without any compensation from Roy or from his clients (whom Dr. Van Field knew to be poor people without much money).

Now, one would have thought that after the loss of the case and the humorous publicity surrounding the dismissal as it affected the prosecutor, his assistant, the sheriff, and the growers, they would have left well enough alone. Instead, Prosecuting Attorney Luke Ayers was determined to get that damned Roy Emerson, and the assistant prosecutor was assigned to file a brief on appeal to the next higher court, the Circuit Court of Tippecanoe County.

Through tears, the assistant prosecutor urged that the case be forgotten, but the prosecuting attorney got red in the face and ordered her to proceed with the appeal.

The circuit judge was a woman named Lindsey Owens. She was one, tough cookie. An honors graduate of an Ivy League law school, she had been an Indiana Supreme Court law clerk, had practiced law in Tip County, and had been elected and reelected several times. She was a very brilliant and fair judge. She received a weak brief from the prosecutor's office, seeking to overrule Judge Albert Evans's ruling in dismissing the case.

Roy filed an extensive brief and asked for oral argument, which was granted with fifteen minutes for each side.

When the time came for the oral argument, the circuit courtroom was filled with the defendants, their family members, representatives of the growers, the sheriff, the prosecuting attorney, and representatives of the media, including a couple of reporters from the national magazines. It was portrayed as a battle between David (in the form of Roy Emerson) and Goliath (in the form of the state of Indiana). The pretty assistant prosecutor tried with her best efforts to get the circuit judge to give a broad interpretation to the term *cock fighting* in the statute, so that the statute criminalized male *and* female poultry conflict.

There was a brief exchange between Judge Lindsey Owens and the pretty assistant prosecuting attorney over the meaning of cock fighting, with Judge Owens assuring the assistant prosecutor, "I really do understand the meaning of the word *cock*" (being the mother of two children).

Roy took very little time on his oral argument, basically quoting from Dr. Van Field's testimony as recorded in the transcript (i.e., question-and-answer writing taken down by the court reporter).

The judge complimented Roy on the extensive and informative brief he had filed. Roy gave credit where credit was due—to state and national legal research facilities dealing with Chicano affairs and *not* just to him.

Within two weeks, the judge issued a very detailed opinion affirming the decision of District Court Judge Albert Evans and dismissing the assistant prosecuting attorney's appeal.

There were more stories about the case in local, state, and national media, including news magazines, all of which embarrassed Prosecutor Ayers, Sheriff Adams, and the growers. The prosecutor, sheriff, and growers were not to be dissuaded from proceeding foolishly with another appeal—this time to the Indiana Court of Appeals.

The poor pretty assistant prosecutor was ordered to file a further appeal. Surprisingly, the Indiana Court of Appeals granted leave (i.e., discretionary review) to the assistant prosecutor to pursue the appeal and set a briefing schedule and date for oral argument. The assistant prosecutor did her best to prepare a brief upholding her interpretation of the statute, and Roy presented a brief that updated the cited cases and clearly showed a trend in the law to strike down such statutes as Indiana's, pertaining to cock fighting as being unconstitutionally vague and deceptive.

At oral argument of the case before three judges (two men and a woman) of the Indiana Court of Appeals, the judges peppered the assistant prosecutor with questions as to why the statute was not deceptively vague and, therefore, unconstitutional under the Indiana Constitution. The assistant prosecutor had no answer to these questions. Roy rested on his brief and made no oral argument.

The Indiana Court of Appeals issued an opinion in which it

affirmed the circuit court judge and the district court judge but for different reasons. The Court of Appeals declared the statute unconstitutional under the Indiana Constitution as being unduly vague and deceptive. This opinion was referenced in the local, state, and national media, which had continued to follow the case.

The only retaliation the growers could take against Roy was to insist that the agricultural workers' broker *not* let the same agricultural workers involved in the case return to the growers' South Tip farms in the next growing season.

Roy began to feel sorry for the assistant prosecuting attorney, who was ordered to pursue an appeal to the Indiana Supreme Court, which denied "leave to appeal because it was not persuaded that a substantial question of state law was presented for the court's review."

The assistant prosecuting attorney was made to file a further appeal in the nature of a *writ of certiorari* (for discretionary review) to the US Supreme Court, which denied the writ, giving no reasons for the high court's ruling. The various appeals by the assistant prosecuting attorney were followed by the media, who gave the denials a good bit of publicity.

Roy became a hero in the Mexican community in South Tip. Roy told Evita he did not deserve the honor.

Prosecuting Attorney Ayers fired the pretty assistant prosecuting attorney for failure to win the cock fighting case. Her successor was a very attractive and voluptuous older woman attorney, who was divorced. Roy would continue to do battle with these two persons in his criminal and civil practice.

19

SOME UNUSUAL HAPPENINGS

You'll remember that Bill was elected as the new vice president of the United States, and Bill's dear friend, the president, was reelected by a substantial margin of popular and electoral college votes. However, the campaign, inauguration and inaugural proceedings took the wind out of the president's sails, and as his new administration began, the president had a gray look.

Without being a pest, Bill encouraged the president to get a thorough checkup at Bethesda Naval Hospital and take some time away for a rest. The president refused because of the problems for the United States around the world. Prior to the State of the Union address and during a contentious White House press conference (the question-answer period was particularly taxing for the president), the president collapsed at the podium and was out cold.

Pandemonium broke out in the conference room. The White House physician was summoned. He pronounced that the president had probably had a heart attack and needed to be rushed immediately to Bethesda Naval Hospital so that he would survive the coronary.

Bill Rice was not in Washington during this press conference and, truthfully, he was not even watching it on his air force plane as he was winging his way to Los Angeles to discuss federal financial help for the state of California and the extremely high unemployment rate in the Southern California area. Bill was relaxing in his suite on the plane when he felt the jet go into an extreme turn and thought the plane was now heading back eastward.

Bill's aide came into his suite and advised him of the situation with the president. Immediately, Bill indicated that the meetings in California had to be canceled in the interest of natural security. A phone call needed to be placed to the Bethesda Naval Hospital to advise that Vice President Bill Rice was on his way to the hospital, and the aide was asked to try to locate the president's wife so that Bill could express his concerns and his best wishes for a speedy recovery for the president.

While Bill was still en route back to Andrews Air Force Base, the attorney general was already researching the issue of presidential succession under Section 4 of Twenty-Fifth Amendment of the US Constitution.

Upon the vice president's landing at Andrews, he was met by the presidential Secret Service detail and the presidential armored limousine and was whisked immediately to Bethesda Naval Hospital to see the status of the president and the First Lady. Upon arriving at the hospital, Bill was met at the main entrance by the rear admiral, who was the medical director of the hospital.

Bill and his aide were taken into a private conference room and shown MRI pictures of the president's chest, including his heart, and told that the president's condition was grave. The president had experienced a massive coronary that would require some surgery and a long period of rest.

Bill replied without any delay that he would probably become "acting president" under the Constitution, but the president was, had been, and would continue to be the elected primary executive of the nation. Bill might be installed as "acting president," but he would seek to visit or to call the president daily as his healing progressed and he proceeded to restored health so that he could resume his executive duties.

Bill assured the admiral and the group of doctors and presidential staff gathered around the room, "I have no intention of usurping the office of the elected president of the United States." Having finished this meeting, the admiral took the vice-president up to the coronary Intensive Care Unit (ICU), where Bill found the First Lady in the waiting room. Bill embraced her, and together they cried for the condition of the president.

Drying her eyes, the First Lady said, "You will make a wonderful president."

Immediately, Bill responded, "Your wonderful husband is the elected president of all the people. You will stay in the White House, and I will never set foot in the president's office. My job is to keep things together until our wonderful president recovers his health and is well enough to resume his executive responsibilities."

Bill asked the admiral if he and the First Lady could enter the ICU and see the president. The admiral looked at his cardiologists, and they indicated that under the circumstances a short visit would be okay. Just the two went into the ICU with the doctors and nursing staff and found the president on a respirator and just partially awake.

The First Lady and Bill went over to the prone president, embraced him, and kissed him fondly.

Bill whispered into the president's ear, "You are and will remain the president of the nation. Just get well soon and come back to us soon. I'll do my best to keep your chair warm. But the chair is yours, and we hope you can return to us who love and respect you as quickly as you feel better."

After the meeting, Bill gave his first order as acting president to the presidential aides who were clustered around in the ICU waiting room: "Take care of the president and the First Lady, and meet any of their needs. I will be an interim replacement, only if the doctors say the president cannot function just now, and when he is better, he is going to resume his office. I have no desire to be an unelected president of the United States."

Leaving the ICU, Bill asked his media representatives to schedule a prime-time address to the nation, which was placed on the agenda for that night at eight o'clock. Bill gave a very brief report to the people, advising them of the president's collapse at the press conference, his hospitalization at Bethesda Naval Medical Center, and Bill's and the First Lady's fondest hope for a swift recovery for the president.

Bill asked the nation to pray for a swift recovery of the president.

The Emersons, Laura, and little Louise (in Laura's arms) watched the address on their television, and Laura commented that she thought Bill looked tired. She said she hoped he would do a good job as acting president. Doctors from Bethesda Naval Hospital, together with key members of the president's staff and Bill, attended a joint Congressional Committee Meeting on emergency presidential succession. The doctors told the Congress and Bill that the president was gravely ill, would be hospitalized for a long time, and would need a long period of recovery.

Asked bluntly by the congressional panel if the president was so disabled that he could not carry out the functions of his office, the doctors replied in the affirmative.

The congressional panel recessed briefly and came back into the conference room to announce that Section 4 of the Twenty-Fifth Amendment should be implemented immediately.

While Bill was still in the Congressional Conference Room, the Chief Justice of the United States Supreme Court was summoned. He recessed a court hearing, came across the Capitol Plaza, and swore Bill in as the acting president of the United States, under the provisions of the Twenty-Fifth Amendment of the Constitution. Bill later told Roy, Margaret Mary, and Laura that an *uncomfortable feeling* came over him as he took the oath of office of acting president.

Now, an interesting dilemma was presented for Bill. His wife, recovering from a difficult pregnancy, and his newborn baby daughter were living with the Emersons in Decatur, Indiana, in Tip County. Until she felt better and the baby was stronger, Laura put her foot down and told Bill that she refused to come back to Washington. The health of the new baby was too important to jeopardize; also,

Laura's and the child's doctors were located in Terre Haute, and she had no intention of changing doctors at the present time.

Therefore, a presidential Secret Service detail was dispatched to guard the acting First Lady and Bill and Laura's daughter. There was a house available for sale across the street from the Emersons' big home. The Secret Service rented it for an entire year and moved in a squad of seven agents, six Secret Service guards, and a supervisor of the detail. Margaret Mary, Roy, and Laura invited them to live with the Emersons, but the supervisor refused; they needed a large house where they could set up certain essential electronic equipment.

So the Secret Service detail moved into the house across from the Emerson homestead. There were six agents—an older woman, a younger woman, two Caucasian male agents, an African American agent, and a Latino agent, supervised by a massive African American man.

Laura and the Emersons could never remember all of the agents' names, so they were called Agents A, B, C, D, E, and F, and the supervisor was named Agent G. All had military training, were smartly dressed, were in great physical condition, and were thoroughly devoted to their jobs of protecting the acting president, the acting First Lady, and their daughter, Louise.

The agents and their supervisor became very dear friends of Laura and the Emerson family. The children were particularly taken by the appearance of the agents; each child adopted an agent as her or his favorite.

On one occasion, Mrs. Bucher, Margaret Mary, and Laura (who was feeling better) spent hours in the kitchen and prepared a huge meal for the entire family and for all the agents. When invited to dinner, the agents refused to attend, but Mrs. Bucher threatened the supervisor, saying if the agents did not sit down with the family for a specially prepared dinner, she would march tomorrow into the newspaper office in Terre Haute and tell the press about Laura's and the baby's presence in the Emerson household, guarded by a large Secret Service detail.

Looking at this stubborn older woman who was resolute about having the squad to dinner, the supervisor backed down, with a side agreement with Mrs. Bucher that he would be standing on guard at the front door, and one of the detail members (having drawn straws) would guard the back door during the dinner.

A huge meal was served to all. Little Louise sat in a high chair, the youngest Emerson daughter was in a booster chair, and the rest of the family members were spread around a large dining room table, with the members of the Secret Service staff, and Evita Gomez also joining the group. She could not take her eyes off the handsome Latino Secret Service agent. From time to time he would glance over at Evita, who was a beautiful young Latina.

Laura offered a prayer of thanksgiving for the life of the president and for strength to be given to her husband to carry out temporarily the difficult duties of the office. Margaret Mary offered a prayer for Laura, baby Louise, and for the Secret Service detail that was committed to the protection of Laura and the baby. Everyone had a good dinner; the Secret Service agents turned down wine and after-dinner liqueurs.

Roy invited the agents attending the dinner to sit and visit with him in the living room, but they refused and returned to duty.

The supervisor and back-door guard were given dinner and nonalcoholic drinks where they were standing. They thanked Laura, who delivered the food, and Margaret Mary, who delivered the drinks, for their kindness and thoughtfulness.

Evita made a special trip to the station of the handsome Latino agent to give him a piece of cake, which she had made herself, and a cup of coffee. He thanked her for the dessert; her smile began to melt his cold and iron exterior. She was a lovely young woman, and the agent was quite taken with her.

(These two beautiful people would fall deeply in love after the agent's assignment at the Emersons. They later would marry, and Evita would become a United States citizen. The couple would go on to have several children and live in the Washington, DC, area.)

Bill was a sensitive acting president. He signed all correspondence and legislative bills as "Bill Rice, acting president." Bill would not move into the White House; he would not go into the Oval Office; he replaced none of the president's staff members or cabinet officers.

The Secret Service made Bill move into Blair House, across Pennsylvania Avenue from the White House, for security purposes, it being easier for the Secret Service to provide protection for the acting president in and around Lafayette Square. Bill refused to use the Oval Office; he worked out of the vice president's office in the White House and the Executive Office Building, right next to the White House.

The time came to deliver the State of the Union address to the Congress. Bill asked the president's staff to write the address. Bill went over the draft with the president himself, who was now able to sit up in his hospital bed, and advised that the address would be delivered to the nation in the name of the president. That is exactly what Bill did. He advised the assemblage in the House of Representatives' chamber that he was delivering the address approved by the elected president of the United States of America as his *surrogate.*

The address was well written and well received. At the conclusion of the address, Bill was given a standing ovation by the attendees, including members of the opposition political party.

Bill handled each crisis as it came up day by day, visiting or telephoning the president frequently and seeing to it at cabinet meetings and conferences that everyone understood it was the president's decision that Bill was carrying out. Bill did not communicate much with Laura and the baby because he did not want to give away her location and have the media descend upon the Emerson household.

Within eleven months, the president was feeling well enough to resume his duties. There was a ceremony in the president's Oval Office (which Bill had not occupied even once during the president's absence), whereby Bill signed a document resigning the office of acting president of the United States of America.

After Bill put his signature on this document, emotion overtook him. He hugged and kissed the president and told him how happy he was to have the chief back in his office. There was a famous picture of the two men embracing in all the national newspapers, the international press, and all manner of news magazines.

Laura was so pleased about Bill's performance during the president's absence that she cried over the picture in the Terre Haute newspaper, called him, and told him how much she loved and missed him. He asked her to come home to the vice presidential mansion up on Massachusetts Avenue, next to the British embassy and near the Vatican Legation, and Laura promised to return within two months.

Those two months passed quickly, and a tearful farewell occurred between Laura, the baby, and all the Emersons, particularly Mrs. Bucher. Mrs. Bucher cried for a whole day after Laura and the baby departed. Georgie asked to stay behind with the Emersons, and his mother allowed him to remain in Decatur.

20
ROY'S CAMPAIGN

With the removal of the Secret Service detail, quiet returned to the Emerson household. Roy had been busy with his law practice every day during Laura's presence in the Emerson home.

A case came into his office from an African American family in South Tip. Apparently, their nineteen-year-old son had been arrested for shoplifting. He had migraine headaches. He could not make bond, and he was lodged in the Tippecanoe County Jail in Decatur.

Two of the evening jail deputies, who had a terrible reputation (known to Sheriff Adams to act sadistically toward the prisoners), were asked by the young man for tablets to ease his headaches. The two deputies entered the jail cell and beat him senseless with rubber truncheons. The young man suffered a fractured skull and brain injury.

Roy sued the deputies in federal court for a violation of the young man's civil rights. After months of contention between the lawyers for the deputies and Roy, a structured settlement was arranged, meaning that some money was paid to Roy and the family up front of the settlement period, and there was a long period of payments to the boy and his family, along with lifetime medical insurance, medical care, and the payment of all of the boy's medical and pharmacy bills. Roy donated the small fee that he received to the boy's family.

Roy's office began to pull in a lot of small clients. One class of clients was divorcing mothers whose husbands worked in the steel and auto assembly factories of Tip and Monroe Counties. The divorcing families didn't have a lot of monetary assets, and their houses, cars, and snowmobiles were heavily encumbered with debt.

New Indiana Supreme Court Child Support Guidelines would assure the mothers that child support monies would be deducted from the workers' pay and sent directly to the mothers. But after years of marriage, there was very little property to award to a rejected spouse who had labored hard in raising a family and sometimes worked to support the family when their husbands were out of work.

One evening, Roy and Dr. Van Field were attending one of their Marine Corps League meetings in Terre Haute. Manfred introduced Roy to a friend and fellow faculty colleague, Will L. Buckmaster, PhD, of the business school faculty. It turned out that Dr. Will was an actuary—a specialist in mathematical predictions of life expectancies, life insurance premiums, and establishing the present value of pensions and other deferred compensation plans.

Roy was complaining to Manfred and Will that many of his divorcing women clients, married for long, hard years to factory workers, were walking away from divorce proceedings with practically nothing in their pockets for later years, if they were still single and their children had been raised. Will suggested to Roy that he could put a present value on pensions and factory-sponsored compensation plans, and, in Will's opinion, the values of these pensions and plans were as much property as were tables, chairs, cars, and snowmobiles.

As a result of this conversation, Roy began to enlist the assistance and testimony of Dr. Buckmaster in his divorce cases where the departing husband had a pension or other factory-sponsored compensation plan.

The lawyers representing the male spouses cried bloody murder in the courtroom that the wives did not deserve any consideration of the pensions or plans because they had not been working in the factories to earn the pensions or plan benefits. Dr. Will demolished these arguments by pointing out that the insurance industry and the National Association of Actuaries considered such pensions and compensation plans as property, so the same should be divisible in a divorce, just like tables, chairs, cars, and real properties.

The judges bought Roy's arguments, buttressed by Dr. Will's testimony, and began awarding the wives an interest in the husband's pension or deferred compensation plans. The hue and cry about this type of ruling was raised among the attorneys representing husbands and in the union halls around Tip and Monroe Counties. But Bill's rulings were upheld on appeal, and female spouses were given some property to tide them over in the years when their children had grown up, so long as they were still single.

The result of this victory for Roy and the wives was a huge rock thrown through the front window of his law office in Dansville, which occurred after the closure of the office. The rock landed in Evita's chair, and if she had been in the office, she could have suffered a serious injury. After this incident, Roy replaced his front window with more shatter-resistant glass and moved the furniture around so that Evita was not so close to the window. To show the miscreants that he and Evita were not afraid of them, Roy had a bull's-eye painted on his front window below the sign reading Roy Emerson Law Office so that there would be a target for the hoodlums to aim for the next time.

The bull's-eye on Roy's office window became the talk of the café crowd in Dansville and Decatur.

One night a car full of drunken guys drove to Roy's office after closing hours. One of them got out of the car with a whiskey bottle full of gasoline with a make-shift rag fuse—in World War II, this was called Molotov cocktail. The drunk was about to throw this object at the bull's-eye when the next-door neighbor, who had worked late and was closing his store, came out and shouted at the hoodlums, saying he was going to take down their vehicle registration number.

The drunk dropped the flaming Molotov cocktail, got back into the car, and the hoodlums sped off. The neighbor reported the incident to the Dansville police chief, Dan Henderson, who investigated the occurrence and wrote up a report. No one had identified the assailants, so no prosecution could be requested.

But Roy, who was a close personal friend of Dan (likewise, a Marine Corps League member in Terre Haute), got a copy of the police report and placed it in a framed container with the burned-out Molotov cocktail on the office wall as a souvenir.

With the advice of Will at Western Indiana University, Roy started taking a unique approach in divorce cases involving professional people (doctors, dentists, veterinarians, attorneys, and certified public accountants). Many of these men had married their wives when they were undergraduates or graduates or professional school students, and their wives worked (while having the family's children) to help their husbands complete their professional or graduate training.

Will began to testify in such cases, where Roy represented the wives, that the degree earned by these fellows had a distinct property value, and Professor Will Buckmaster, PhD, could predict very accurately as to its present cash value. Thus, Roy began to ask the judges in Monroe and Tip Counties for consideration of these degrees as property in which the wives had contributed substantial value and from which the wives should be awarded appropriate compensation for the present value of these degrees.

The judges accepted Roy's arguments and Dr. Buckmaster's testimony, and appropriate awards were made to the spouses for the value of their contributions to their divorcing husbands' degrees. Now, Roy's name was anathema around the medical society, dental society, Monroe and Tip County Bar Associations, and the Professional Accountants' Council.

There was actually a picket line, consisting of hired pickets, protesting one day outside of Roy's office, saying that Roy was "a dishonest lawyer using gutter tactics to penalize the hard work of husbands in divorce cases." Roy and Evita went out to confront the pickets, and a shouting match started that had to be broken up by Dansville police chief, Dan Henderson.

Dan told Roy and Evita to go back into the office and resume their work, and he advised the pickets that the First Amendment authorized them to protest on public but not private property, so they would have to move across the street and into the park, which is exactly what they did for six hours.

Later, Dan told Roy that the pickets had been paid for by the growers.

Roy laughed and replied, "I must really have gotten their goat."

Roy would *not* take any legal case if he felt he could not face his lovely wife, Margaret Mary; her wonderful mother, Mrs. Bucher; and his own children and tell them the types of cases he was handling. Therefore, he would not take the cases of drug dealers, domestic assailants, child molesters, criminal sexual conduct defendants, draft evaders, or anyone defaming the American flag (as some protesters were wont to do in opposition to America's involvement in foreign wars; Roy's memories of his experiences in Happy Valley and at Khe Sanh were too painful to allow him to represent such persons, although he considered himself a civil libertarian).

There was a wonderful and helpful Roman Catholic priest, Father Pedro Arroyo, who was the pastor of Saint Guadalupe Parish in Dansville. He had grown up in Dansville, entered the seminary after a successful career on the gridiron and classroom at Calvin Coolidge High School, had been ordained by the Diocese of Terre Haute and assigned, first as a prison minister in the federal correctional facilities at Terre Haute and later as pastor of Saint Guadalupe Parish, where he continued his work with offenders—institutionalized, on bond, probation, or on parole.

Saint Guadalupe Parish had a large community building where Father Arroyo held meetings with offenders and did counseling in anger management.

With Father Arroyo's assistance, Roy began to plead young first offenders guilty as charged under a seldom-used Indiana criminal procedure statute, now known as the Speaker-Sessions Youthful Trainee Act (YTA), named for the state senator and House of

Representatives members who put through the law. Under the YTA, the offender would plead guilty; if the judge accepted the status of YTA, the offender could be jailed and then put on probation for up to two years to do public service and get counseling. Invariably, the sentence was to Father Arroyo's counseling center, where the offenders would be fed, worked, and attend counseling sessions.

No work was required at the parish church or grounds, which would be a violation of the First Amendment. Father Arroyo, with Roy's and Dan Henderson's assistance, actually got a vacant boarding house in Dansville and turned it into a shelter for men and women who were sentenced under the YTA and were homeless. Father's housekeeper prepared delicious meals, and Roy, Father Arroyo, and Dan got an alternative education program started with the Dansville schools to allow offenders without high school diplomas to earn their diplomas.

The program was highly successful and was written up in newspapers around the state, particularly in Terre Haute because if the YTA program was successfully completed by the offender, the charge and conviction were wiped clean from his or her record.

People were beginning to pat Roy on the back and urge him to run against Luke Ayers for Tip County prosecuting attorney. Every innovation in criminal sentencing that Roy obtained was invariably opposed by Ayers and his voluptuous assistant prosecuting attorney.

Even when Roy was representing high school kids, caught with a joint of marijuana in their pants or their school lockers (but who were not drug dealers), Roy asked the judges to consider an obscure provision of the Indiana Public Health Code that provided that a judge could consider a plea of guilty to marijuana use or possession (but not manufacture, distribution, or sale), followed by a sentence to a drug rehabilitation program which, when successfully completed, would result in the cancellation of the criminal plea of guilty and would wipe the offender's record clean.

It must be noted that the YTA law and the Public Health Code did authorize the judges, in addition to probation and counseling and/or rehabilitation, to provide a sentence of jail for the offender and to cancel the YTA or special Public Health Code treatment if the offender failed to live up to the strict letter of his or her sentence conditions.

Unfortunately, to the chagrin of Father Arroyo, Roy, and Dan Henderson, a number of the offenders failed in their efforts to comply with the judges' sentencing conditions. The YTA status or Public Health Code treatment was revoked, and the offenders were jailed. Once jailed for failing in such programs, Roy refused to continue his representation of the offenders.

Roy tried some other innovations. He hired an assistant for Evita to handle collection cases for a couple of businesses in Dansville and Decatur. In order to try to protect the credit rating of the debtors, Roy tried (with the assistance of his newly hired helper) to get the debtors to admit the debt and to begin paying the amount in small increments, without taking them to court, getting default judgments against them, or garnishing their meager wages (which in some cases could have resulted in the employers of the debtors, who hated paperwork, firing the debtors).

The big-time collection lawyers and law firms in Terre Haute and Decatur objected to the efforts of this interloper, Roy Emerson, and his minions in the collection practice business.

The judges began to turn down the big collection firms' efforts to get automatic default judgments against small-time debtors (not business debtors) without attempting first to use Roy's approach.

By the beginning of the new election year for county offices, it seemed that everyone was down on Roy except his family, his Marine Corps League buddies, Mrs. Bucher, Evita, his new office helper/accountant, his happy clients, and Dansville police chief Dan Henderson.

Roy got talking to Dan, and they agreed to run as Democrats for county prosecuting attorney and sheriff, respectively. When they announced their candidacies in the county newspaper, Luke Ayers and Bill Adams sneered at them and said they would swamp both candidates. Consequently, no other Democrats or Republican candidates tossed their hats into the ring, and the primary election time passed without any opposition to Luke, Bill, Roy, or Dan. The battle lines were drawn for the general election in November. A good turnout was expected because it was a presidential election year.

One day the Emerson family, Mrs. Bucher, Evita, and the new office assistant had some very important visitors. Air Force Two (the vice president's huge jet aircraft) arrived unexpectedly in the Terre Haute airport, and the Secret Service was sent out in several vehicles to round up the Emersons, Mrs. Bucher, the children, and Roy's office staff.

After about an hour of running around, everyone was located, and the Secret Service sedans sped back to the Terre Haute airport, where the massive Air Force Two was parked.

Roy had a hunch who was aboard, but the others were a little sheepish as they ascended the long flight of stairs up into the aircraft. At the door of the airplane, the Emersons were personally greeted by the vice president's wife, Mrs. Laura Evans Rice. Seeing Laura, the entire group hugged her, cried, kissed her, hugged her some more, and cried some more.

Georgie clung to the legs of his lovely mother.

Bill stood with his staff in the main aisle of the huge plane and watched the greeting. No one wanted to let Laura go, particularly Margaret Mary, Mrs. Bucher, and Georgie "Emerson." The greetings, hugging, crying, and kissing must have lasted for at least ten minutes, and then when the vice president of the United States cleared his throat and invited his guests into his massive quarters.

Laura limped into the large rooms, with Georgie hanging on her leg and Mrs. Bucher and Margaret Mary clutching her tenderly. When everyone was seated, it took all the guests and Laura quite a while to compose themselves.

Bill directed his staff to take the kids, including Georgie, and Mrs. Bucher and Roy's office staff to the galley and give them a good meal and chocolate sundaes. Bill served good scotch to Laura, Roy,

Margaret Mary, and himself. Roy was so moved by the kindness and generosity shown to him by Bill and Laura that he began bawling like a kid. He hugged and kissed Bill and held on to him for a long time. Tears came to Bill's and Laura's eyes, and finally Laura got hold of Roy and led him back to his seat.

A drink of scotch seemed to relax the adults, and everyone began to settle down. Margaret Mary and Roy told Bill and Laura how proud they were of them, but they said they lost parts of their hearts when Laura and her wonderful baby girl left the Emerson household to move to Washington, DC.

The Emerson girls still asked about their little sister. Laura was beaming; she looked at Bill and said, "Go ahead and ask them; you already know my opinion."

Bill said to Roy, "The way I handled my position of acting president when our elected president was convalescing at Bethesda Naval Hospital endeared me to the outgoing president and to the Republican Party regulars. They have offered to stake me through the many state primaries and to see that I become the presidential nominee of the Republican Party in the forthcoming election. Roy and Margaret Mary, I want your *frank opinion* about this generous offer from my president and the party officials."

Roy looked at Margaret Mary, and she at him. Roy spoke first.

"Bill, without any doubt you would make a wonderful president of the United States, even though you are a Republican, and I am the Democratic candidate for Tip County prosecuting attorney. But I look at your gorgeous wife, Laura, your beautiful daughter, whom we had the privilege of getting to know when they were staying with us, and your outstanding and very intelligent son, Georgie, and think in my heart of hearts that they need to be in a stable family relationship—free of political traveling and the pressures of the highest elected office in the land. Personally, I think you would be elected and would make an outstanding president. I have always felt, even as far back as our studies in history and political science at Service, that you were a man for the little people. But Bill, to tell you my true feelings, I really think you should leave Washington and return with your family to Indianapolis and resume your Rice Corporation business, which, I know, went into a blind trust with your other holdings when you became vice president, and spend the rest of your life realizing happiness for yourself, your gorgeous wife, Laura, and your wonderful children. Although it will break the hearts of all the Emersons, particularly of our girls, if Georgie were to leave the Emerson household, I think Georgie *should* live with his mother and adoptive father, whom Georgie talks about all the time and loves very much, as Georgie's youth is slowly slipping away. Well, Bill, that's how I feel. How about you, Margaret Mary? What are your thoughts on this matter?"

Margaret said, "I second everything my husband has said. I would, however, respect any decision that you and Laura reach, and Roy and I would support you all the way. However, I look at Laura and you and your beautiful children, and I think, as a mother and wife, that I would want to spend the rest of my life with them without all the distractions of high office and politics."

Bill looked over at Laura, who said, "That's exactly what I have told him, but I wanted him to hear it from people he really trusts. Nevertheless, irrespective of my feelings, he needs to do what he feels is his duty to this nation, which he has served so well. If he runs, I and the children—and you Emersons—will fully support him."

Bill took a long pull on his scotch, thought for a moment, and then said, "Roy, in your new prosecuting attorney's office, do you have a job for a washed-up Republican politician?"

With that remark, Laura, Margaret Mary, and Roy jumped up and hugged and kissed Bill repeatedly; there were tears all around, even in Bill's eyes.

Bill said, "I think we'll move back into the big house in Indianapolis after the inauguration in January. I am going to donate my nonclassified papers to Service. And I guess, I'll be going back into the furniture business. Roy, do you need a new desk and chair in your office?" Everybody broke out laughing, including Bill.

Roy, always a smart aleck, said, "No, I only buy from Democratic businessmen!"

More hearty laughter, and another round of scotch drinks was poured. By now, the kids, Mrs. Bucher, Evita, and the office assistant were done with their victuals and sundaes. They came to the room where Bill and Laura were sitting and asked if it was time to go.

Roy winked and said, "Yes, it is. I can't waste all my time sitting around talking politics to a damned Republican."

Everyone broke out laughing, although Margaret Mary gave Roy a punch in the ribs because he was cursing around the children. As everyone was leaving the plane, Roy and Margaret Mary hugged and kissed Bill and Laura.

Roy said, "Bill, I'm releasing you from the promise you made years ago to put in a good word for me if I ran for prosecuting attorney. I'll win the office on my own, without any help from the Republicans!"

The Secret Service contingent drove everyone back where he or she needed to be, and Air Force Two took off from the Terre Haute airport. The visit had been so short that the Terre Haute press and the television media did not even have enough time to descend on the plane and try to get an interview.

A call to the Emerson household produced a response of "No comment." The media was nonplussed by the vice presidential visit and the lack of comment from the Emersons or from Vice President Bill Rice's staff, so the visit was not written up or talked about by the media, as there was nothing important to say.

In the months between the primary and general elections, the Ayers-Adams naysayers began a drum roll of criticism of the campaigns of Roy and Dan. Both were called inexperienced and prejudiced against business. Dan lacked a college education, and Roy graduated only with a C from law school (it was really a C+, but Roy didn't make a big fuss over the gaffe). They complained that Roy had frequently represented juvenile and adult criminals, including offenders charged with marijuana use and possession, and they said he was a "fourth-rate practitioner of domestic relations law."

Bill and Dan ignored the jibes without retort, and they concentrated on the need for a change in these two elected county offices.

A very bad thing happened to the Republican prosecuting attorney, his voluptuous assistant, and the Republican Party, four weeks before the county elections. The Republicans had run polls; the Republican presidential candidate (without Bill Rice on the ticket) and all county Republican incumbents were running well ahead of Roy, Dan, and the Democratic candidates.

However, one night Luke Ayers went off the road in his huge black Lincoln Continental, struck a tree at a very high speed, and killed himself and his voluptuous female passenger. Luke was married with two children. The passenger, Luke's assistant prosecuting attorney, was divorced with two children. The rumor mill got going that some sex play had been occurring when Luke lost control of the car, and alcohol was a factor in the crash and in the deaths of both persons. Each had suffered a broken neck, even though the air bags on the vehicle deployed properly on the heavy impact with the large tree.

The current sheriff's report, photographs, and the autopsy protocol were kept a deep and dark secret. The county newspaper and the Terre Haute newspaper and various television stations demanded a copy of the report, photographs, and autopsy protocol under the Indiana Freedom of Information Act (FOIA), which would authorize the disclosure because no criminal prosecution was forthcoming.

Sheriff Bill Adams turned down flat the requests of the media for the materials, and they promptly filed a circuit court lawsuit in both Monroe and Tippecanoe Counties to force disclosure. Emergency hearings were scheduled, and both courts mandated that the sheriff turn over the requested materials under FOIA because none of the exceptions to disclosure in the FOIA appeared applicable.

Sheriff Bill Adams declined to take an appeal, and the materials were duly turned over.

On the day of the delivery of the materials to the media, Roy and Dan Henderson made personal visits to the editors of the newspapers and the station managers of various radio and television stations, asking them *not* to release the materials they had just received.

After the election, Roy and Dan guessed, the media could do what they wanted with the materials, but they asked the media moguls to remember that Luke had a wife and two children, and the voluptuous assistant prosecutor had two children; their feelings need to be spared. Although Roy and Dan thought the materials would fatally damage Republican candidates and office holders if released, they said they wanted to win the election fair and square, and not based upon sensational publication of death pictures and autopsy findings (which were probably adverse to Luke and his passenger).

Reluctantly, the media people said they would wait until after the election, but no long-lasting promises of withholding publication were made to Roy and Dan.

The Republicans made a mad scramble to put up a write-in candidate for county prosecuting attorney—an overweight, not-too-intelligent a lawyer from Decatur, whom many people thought was a drunk. He did practically no campaigning while Roy and Dan were canvassing Tip County, north and south, every day of the weeks prior to the election.

Sheriff Bill Adams appeared in a bad light because of the finding by the two circuit courts that he had violated FOIA. The newspapers retracted all endorsements of candidates for prosecutor and sheriff. The unions had already endorsed Luke, as had the growers' association. The chambers of commerce had made no endorsements.

On election day, Roy, Margaret Mary, and Dan voted early and went to their respective offices and carried out their daily tasks. Evita couldn't vote, nor could Mrs. Bucher, a legal resident of Wisconsin. However, the office assistant in the Emerson law office did vote because she lived in South Tip.

That night, everybody was invited over to the Emersons for a big dinner whipped up by Mrs. Bucher, even with freshly baked pies. She had been working practically nonstop in the kitchen for two days to make a feast. The election returns for county offices came in pretty quickly because of the small number of precincts, but the presidential and congressional election results took precedence.

By about one in the morning it was apparent that Roy, who had fallen asleep with some of the kids in his arms, and Dan, who was awake, had won election to their offices by slim majorities. Bill Adams had a few more votes than Dan, but their opponents appeared on the television and gave concession speeches; there would be no recount. Roy was sleeping so soundly in his easy chair, holding onto the kids, that Dan decided not to wake him. Dan went over to the couch and curled up.

The next morning, when everyone was awake, the Terre Haute paper arrived with partial general election results, showing Roy and Dan to be leading in those precincts that had reported in by press time. However, a call to the Tip County Clerk's Office indicated that Roy and Bill had won their elections.

Mrs. Bucher laid out a big breakfast spread for all. Some of the neighbors came in to congratulate Roy and Dan, and they were invited to the free feed.

Dan asked Roy whom he would hire as his assistant prosecuting attorney. Winking at Dan but being eyed by Margaret Mary, Roy said—surprisingly—that he was going to ask that pretty woman former assistant prosecuting attorney to rejoin the office staff.

Margaret Mary looked over at Roy and said, "Just make sure, Roy Emerson, that when you have your hands on your *briefs* that you're not taking off your underpants. Such a pretty girl as that young lawyer deserves a hunk like Dan Henderson and not some old fogey like you, Roy Emerson." Everybody broke out laughing.

Roy did call the young woman lawyer, and she was surprised but said she would be honored to return as assistant prosecuting attorney. Roy told her to get right over to the Emerson household and meet everybody. In about an hour, she arrived and was introduced by Roy all around.

Dan Henderson was particularly taken by her appearance, and she by him—he was introduced as the new county sheriff.

(I am jumping ahead a little bit in my story, but Betsy Mullins, the new assistant prosecuting attorney, fell for Dan, and he for her. They started dating and were married in a year. She continued to work in the office until she got big with her and Dan's first child.)

Since there was no county prosecuting attorney, the judges appointed Roy as the interim prosecutor, and he was sworn in.

Bill Adams continued as county sheriff until the first of the year, when both Roy and Dan were sworn in as permanent elected office holders.

Before January, Roy had to close his office or find someone to whom he could turn it over. Father Arroyo knew a young Chicano lawyer just coming out of law school. Roy met with the new lawyer and Father Arroyo and then turned over the office, lock, stock, and barrel, to the young lawyer for a low price, to be paid to Roy over a period of years. Unfortunately, for the young Chicano attorney, who really had a crush on Evita, Evita was in love with the Latino Secret Service man who had guarded the Emerson house when Laura and the Rice/Emerson baby lived there.

Soon, Evita left the law office for Washington, DC, and there she married the Secret Service agent and settled down to become an American citizen and raise a family. Father Arroyo found another beautiful, bilingual Latina for the office as a secretary. Soon, she and the young lawyer were dating, and in a year they were married in Father Arroyo's parish church.

It seemed like everything was going along just peachy keen, but it turned out that it was not!

21

ELECTED COUNTY OFFICIALS

Before the election and on the day that the courts decreed that Sheriff Bill Adams must release the accident files, photographs, and autopsy protocol to the media, Bill had delivered a copy of the same file to the prosecutor's office, anticipating that Bill would be reelected and the write-in Republican would be elected as county prosecutor.

In the turmoil around the office when Roy was elected, and the Republican write-in candidate was defeated, Bill was still in a state of shock that the voters had turned him out of office. Consequently, Bill waited too long to retrieve the accident files, photographs, and autopsy protocol from Luke's former office, which was now occupied by Interim Prosecuting Attorney Roy Emerson. Roy found the file on his desk and put it in a safe place, to look it over with Dan when both had been sworn in as permanent prosecutor and county sheriff.

A spy sent over by Bill Adams before he went out of office to retrieve the errant files could not find them. The former prosecutor's secretary could not find them either—the reason being that Roy had taken them home and kept them in a box beneath his bed.

The only thing that appeared before the election in the media about the horrible accident was a description of the accident and a photograph of the vehicle wrapped around a huge tree. The story lacked details; the television and radio stations rebroadcast the sketchy description of the accident, essentially drawn from the newspaper reports.

The week of their swearing-in, Roy asked Dan to come over to the Emerson household, have dinner with Roy and the family, and discuss a very pressing matter with Roy. Mrs. Bucher and Margaret Mary fixed a fabulous dinner, with homemade cake, and a fine meal was had by all. Dan was a beer drinker. After dinner, Roy and Dan insisted that they help the ladies dry and put away the dishes, pots, and pans. Dan sipped on a beer, and Roy had a little glass of scotch on the rocks as they worked in the kitchen.

By the time everything had been cleaned up and put away, it was bedtime for Margaret Mary, Mrs. Bucher, and the children. Roy walked upstairs to kiss his mother-in-law, wife, and daughters good night, and he retrieved the box from under his bed and came back down into the living room where Dan was seated.

Roy offered Dan another beer, but Dan said he preferred coffee instead. Roy brewed a pot of coffee for both of them. When each had a steaming cup of coffee, Roy opened his box and, sitting beside Dan on the couch, the two men looked carefully over the accident reports, photographs, and autopsy protocol.

Indeed, the reports showed hanky-panky had been going on in the automobile, probably leading to the crash. The photographs showed Luke's bloody body with his pants and his briefs down around his knees. The voluptuous assistant prosecutor had no top on at all, even no brassiere. The examination by the forensic lab disclosed semen stains on Luke's pants, underpants, and the seat of the car and some semen stains on the assistant prosecutor's skirt.

Blood analysis on both bodies revealed that Luke had three times the allowed legal limit of alcohol in his system for a driver, and the assistant prosecutor had twice the allowed legal limit of alcohol in her system.

If this material were to be disclosed in the media, it would be devastating for Luke's wife (a bit of a naive lady, who thought her husband could do no wrong) and Luke's teenage son and daughter and the assistant prosecutor's two older teenage daughters. A delicate matter was presented for Roy and Dan: how to balance full disclosure of public facts as required by FOIA with the desire to protect the delicate sensibilities of survivors of a terrible automobile accident that should never have occurred?

Both men decided to make another personal trip to the media moguls and see what could be withheld from the public newspapers and airways.

Neither Roy's nor Dan's pleas to the media received a favorable reception from the editors or producers. So Roy took off on a different track; he was going to try to find out where the two decedents had been drinking and inform their family members that they had the right to litigate their wrongful death claims under the Indiana Dramshop Act, which provides civil liability for sales or furnishing of alcohol to obviously intoxicated persons.

At that time there would be a story for the media to follow, and perhaps, some of the materials now in their hands under FOIA could be worked into the story—hopefully, in good taste. After some deliberation, it was agreed that the Dramshop approach was the way to play the story.

Roy and Dan could tell from the sheriff's reports and the autopsy blood results that Luke and the lady had been drinking heavily before the accident. No alcohol had been found in the wrecked vehicle. Therefore, they must have been drinking in a bar or in the prosecutor's office. Yet there was no alcohol found in the prosecutor's office when Roy began to occupy the same. The conclusion was that both had to have been drinking in a bar.

Asking around, Dan learned of Luke's favorite watering hole and went in to talk to the server and bartender there about the last night of Luke's and the lady's drinking. Yes, the bar staff admitted, both were loaded when they left the bar; however, the staff continued to serve them alcohol (but no food) because, after all, they were the prosecuting attorney and his assistant.

"Why shouldn't we have continued to serve them?" they asked. "If we had cut them off, what would they have done about our liquor license since we always seem to have some problems with the Indiana Liquor Control Commission?"

Roy and Dan went out to Luke's home and asked to speak privately to his wife. She insisted that both children be present. Without sharing with them the sheriff's reports, photographs, and autopsy protocol, Roy and Dan indicated that there was extensive evidence they believed in the case to authorize the widow, on her own behalf and the children's, to sue the bar where both had been drinking and had gotten drunk for civil damages.

They emphasized that Mrs. Ayers owed it to herself and her children to get compensation for this tragic death. Mrs. Ayers asked about the children of the assistant prosecutor. Dan and Roy indicated they were bound for their house where they were staying with their grandmother. Mrs. Ayers said she and the children would think about the suggestion.

Dan and Roy went over to the assistant prosecutor's house and asked to meet with the grandmother, who insisted that the children be present for the discussion. Essentially, both men repeated the same story and suggestion that they had given to Mrs. Ayers. The grandmother said she would talk to the children and think about the matter.

Within a few days, Mrs. Ayers came into the office to pick up her husband's belongings; she arrived with the grandmother of the children of the deceased assistant prosecuting attorney to pick up her belongings. Both told Roy they had decided to take the suggestion he and Dan had given them and to look into suing the bar. Roy gave both women a referral to a fine law firm in Terre Haute that specialized in plaintiffs' Dramshop Act cases.

The ladies picked up all the belongings and thanked Roy for the referral.

In a couple of weeks, Roy was contacted by a partner in the referred law firm in Terre Haute, indicating that his staff had talked to both ladies and wondered whether there was a case there. Roy said there *was* a case there.

Litigation was initiated against the bar, and the law firm subpoenaed the materials from Roy's office. Roy turned over a complete copy of everything, including the photographs, keeping the originals for his closed file on the tragedy. After a couple of years of litigation, the insurance lawyers for the bar owner paid up monies under a structured settlement for Luke Ayers's family and for the assistant prosecutor's two children.

The lawsuit was covered in the media, but none of the gory details or photographs of the decedents or from the autopsy protocol were reported.

Within two months after Roy's swearing-in, one night Mrs. Bucher received a distress call from her husband in Milwaukee, saying that she needed to come back home right away. She sensed something bad had happened to him; he was older than she was. Margaret Mary and Roy got her a flight out of Terre Haute. After she arrived in Milwaukee and had seen Margaret Mary's father, she called the Emersons and announced that Mr. Bucher had a very malignant form of prostate and colon cancer and had been receiving radiation and chemotherapy, which did not appear to be doing any good in shrinking the spreading tumors.

Roy and Margaret Mary told her to winterize the house in Milwaukee and bring her husband immediately down to live with the Emersons. Margaret Mary would get him medical treatment at her hospital in Terre Haute.

In a few days the Buchers arrived at the airport and were picked up by Margaret Mary and Roy. Mr. Bucher looked terrible; he was gray and feverish. They took him to the Emerson home immediately, and Margaret Mary and Mrs. Bucher put him to bed. The next day Roy drove him over to Terre Haute Hospital for treatment, but the diagnosis was terrible, given the spread of the cancer cells into various organs of his body. He was given six months to live, if that.

All of the Emersons did their best to make Mr. Bucher's last days as pleasant and pain-free as possible, but he lived for only five months. He was buried next to Roy's parents in the cemetery in Decatur. This plot would become *the* burial plot for Mrs. Bucher and for Roy and Margaret Mary.

The next thing that bothered Roy and Dan was the sheer volume of backed-up criminal cases in the local courts. Roy and Dan met with the judges and agreed that there would be a major effort to move these cases through the court system. Roy and Betsy Mullins worked nights and weekends on these cases. Margaret Mary or Mrs. Bucher would bring dinner for Roy, and Dan would bring dinner for Betsy.

Finally, Betsy, who lived in South Tip was so exhausted from daily driving back and forth that Margaret Mary asked her to move into the Emerson household. There was plenty of room, with an extra bedroom and bath where Laura had stayed with the baby. Mr. Bucher had sadly passed away by the time an exhausted Betsy Mullins accepted the invitation and moved in with Roy's family.

Dan tried to spend as much time as he could with Betsy. Sometimes, though, when he would come over for a late-night summer with Betsy, she would fall asleep right after dinner, and Dan would practically have to carry her up to the bedroom. Her immune system got so worn down that she contracted a flu that kept her in bed for a week and really drained her energy. However, when the flu had run its course, tired or not, Betsy returned to work in the courts with Roy.

Efforts by Roy to get the county commissioners to appropriate funds for another assistant prosecutor to work with Betsy and Roy to clean up the backlog of cases and keep the new cases moving more quickly through the system were turned down—supposedly for financial reasons but really because the growers, who had a lot of say on the County Commission, couldn't stand Roy and wanted to see him fail.

So Roy enlisted the help of some of his Marine Corps League buddies from Western Indiana University, which had a paralegal program. A number of very fine paralegal students were assigned for credit but without pay to Roy's office, and they did masterful things to help Roy and Betsy with the caseload.

Unexpectedly, one day Betsy Mullins, who was an honors

graduate of the Valparaiso University Law School, located in northwestern Indiana, received a call from the school's director of clinical programs, asking if her office could use some interns (young law students who lived in the Monroe and Tip Counties area). Betsy talked to Roy, who was enthusiastic about the offer and directed Betsy to return the call and ask the director to send down as many student interns as he could; the Tip County prosecuting attorney's office was swamped with cases and needed help.

Pretty soon, three lovely young female law students appeared at Betsy and Roy's office, indicating they were from Valparaiso and wanted to pitch in to help the staff with their cases. Two of the girls lived in Terre Haute, and one was from Decatur. Roy and Betsy gave them a gracious welcome, immediately took them over to the judges' chambers, and had them sworn in under an Indiana Court rule as "prosecutorial assistants," which would allow them to appear in the courts and to handle cases without any compensation from the county.

They were given credit for clinical training by Valparaiso for up to a year's work in the prosecuting attorney's office. The young ladies came from upper-middle-class homes; they could stay with their families or find an apartment for themselves, and all of them owned an automobile which would facilitate transportation from their homes or shared apartment to the office.

Eventually, the girls moved in with the family of the Valparaiso student from Decatur, and they were welcomed by the students' parents, just as if they were their daughters. Frequently, the Valparaiso interns would eat and actually sleep at the Emersons' house, with Mrs. Bucher hovering around them, feeding them, and talking to them, just like a mother hen.

The situation was like the rearrival of Laura and her baby to Mrs. Bucher, who was thrilled with the appearance of the girls. Likewise, the Emersons were kind to and frequently entertained the paralegal students from Western Indiana University in Terre Haute. With the application of these added hands to the heavy Tip County prosecutorial caseload, the pile of unprocessed case files continued to go down, and eventually, the office reached a point where it was *somewhat* current.

However, a steady stream of paralegal students and law student interns was requested by Roy and Betsy so that Roy would not have to go begging to the grower-dominated County Commission for appropriations for a new assistant prosecuting attorney. As a matter of fact, several of the Valparaiso students who interned in Roy and Betsy's office asked to stay on as voluntary prosecutors after they passed the bar examination. Their assistance was welcomed, much to the chagrin of the growers and their dominated county commissioners, who could not get a financial stranglehold on Roy and his office.

22

FLASHBACK: ROY E. DONS HIS WAR HELMET

On the Sunday before Thanksgiving, Roy insisted that his entire office (including Betsy Mullins and the secretaries), Roy's dear friend, Sheriff Dan Henderson, *plus* all the paralegal volunteers and the Valparaiso interns and their parents or significant others come to the Emerson household for a huge pre-Thanksgiving dinner.

Mrs. Bucher, Margaret Mary, and some hired household help worked like beavers in the kitchen to bake two turkeys, two hams, plenty of sweet potatoes, salads, side dishes, pies, and wonderful rolls (following Mrs. Bucher's secret recipe that Margaret Mary herself did not know). Roy stayed on the front porch and greeted all the guests. He sat in a rocking chair on the porch (having worked a long day with Betsy Mullins on the preceding Saturday) and fell asleep while reading the first part of the Terre Haute newspaper.

The house that the Secret Service detail had rented during Laura's stay in the Emerson household was still for sale, but the dismal economy in Decatur kept the house on the market for a long time—unoccupied—until two young women rented the house. They had moved into the house two weeks earlier, but apparently there were two men accompanying them, and they always went out to shop after dark.

Roy generally was not a busybody, but he thought their shopping pattern rather odd. On this particular day, after Roy had greeted all his guests and was about to nod off again over his newspaper, he noticed that the neighbors had parked their car facing the wrong way down the street, which was John Tyler Avenue. A young Decatur police office on routine patrol stopped his vehicle on Roy's side of the street, waved to Roy, and walked up to the door of the renters' home to ask them to repark their vehicle on Roy's side of Tyler Avenue facing the right way. There were a few steps from the sidewalk to the lawn of the house and a walkway up the lawn to the steps leading to the front door. It was seemingly quiet in the house—no television, radio, or people in the windows.

Suddenly, a fusillade of shots cut down the police officer as he approached the house. Hit by several bullets, he fell back onto the top of the steps and was bleeding profusely. Roy could hear the yells and curses inside the house after the young officer was gunned down.

Roy's viewing this atrocity snapped his mind; he flashed back to his days as a navy medic assigned to the marines in Happy Valley and Hill 861-A at Khe Sanh. Margaret Mary had been after Roy for years to get treatment at the VA hospital in Terre Haute for post-traumatic stress disorder, but he always refused, preferring instead to talk to his Marine Corps League buddies about his experiences (and theirs) in the Vietnam Conflict.

Dan Henderson heard the gunfire, went to Roy's front window, saw the officer down, and made a call to the Decatur Police Department and to 911.

Roy bolted from his front porch rocker into his house and down into the basement. In a flash;, he emerged wearing his old, battered Red Cross medical helmet and twin medical bags on his chest. He must have gotten his Marine Corps League buddies to help him to assemble his twin medical bags (like the ones he wore in Vietnam), which he hid from Margaret Mary in the basement with his medical helmet.

Roy came flying back up the steps of his home and in a bound was down his own front steps. Amid a fusillade of bullets, he crawled over to the hoodlums' automobile, which provided some protection from their intensive firing.

Sirens could be heard in the distance, and soon three Decatur Police Department automobiles arrived at the scene. The firing had died down from the rented house. Although Roy was yelling at the officers to be careful in approaching the house, they came from their vehicles with guns drawn, walked up the steps, and got on the lawn walkway, where a heavy exchange of gunfire between the officers and the assailants in the rented house occurred, felling all three officers with serious injuries.

Medical vehicles had not yet arrived. Dan Henderson was madly calling his sheriff's deputies for backup to the Decatur Police Department at the Tyler Avenue rented home location. More sirens could be heard in the distance.

Margaret Mary was out on the front porch, yelling at the top of her lungs for Roy to come back home.

He turned around and responded to Margaret Mary, "My marines are down! I've heard the call 'medic, medic,' and I have to go to them!"

He crawled forward amid a fusillade of bullets that pierced the assailants' automobile but sailed over Roy's head. Roy crawled up the stairs, grabbed the feet of the downed first-to-arrive policeman, dragged him down the steps, and brought him behind the assailants' automobile.

Giving him a quick examination, Roy took out a blood expander from his medical kits and hung one of them up from the passenger's side of the vehicle and began to run an IV into the vein of the seriously wounded officer.

Roy didn't stop there; he crawled back to the steps and grabbed the boots of the next downed officer, a woman. He slithered her down the steps from the sidewalk to the lawn and brought her badly injured body to the passenger's side of the assailants' vehicle, examined her quickly, and strung up a second blood expander with an IV from the side of the vehicle and into the injured officer's arm.

Getting to the other two downed officers without getting shot down was a formidable task for Roy.

The media had arrived on the scene and was actively taking photographs and video footage of the goings on amid shots aimed from the rented house at the photographers, reporters, and camera-persons.

About that time an armored vehicle containing the SWAT squad from the Tip County Sheriff's Department arrived on the scene.

The driver and commander, occupying the front seat of the sealed SWAT vehicle, saw that they could not get up the street because of the assailants' and Roy's parked automobiles, so the driver maneuvered the armored vehicle onto Roy's front lawn and was about to discharge the SWAT members with their shields and high-powered weapons when two rocket-propelled grenades were fired at the front and side of the SWAT vehicle, exploding with a terrific concussion. All the bulletproof glass was broken out of the front windows of the vehicle, seriously cutting and injuring the driver and the SWAT commander.

The second rocket-propelled grenade hit the middle of the SWAT vehicle with such force that upon its explosion, the vehicle was tossed over on its passenger side and the tires caught on fire, along with leaking diesel fuel from the engine and diesel fuel tank. The vehicle was blazing steadily when the rear-door was opened, and the SWAT team members stumbled out, injured and disoriented.

While all the rocket firing was going on, Roy ran up the steps, onto the lawn of the assailants' house, picked up the body of the third downed Decatur police office, and carried him in a marine medic over his shoulders to safety behind the assailants' automobile.

There was a photograph made of Roy, with blood all over his body, carrying this seriously injured officer on his shoulders over to the safety of the assailants' automobile. Arriving there, Roy set up with surgical tape a third blood expander and put it into the vein of the injured officer with an IV tube.

By this time Margaret Mary had gathered up all the bandages,

Band-Aids, and medicines from the house, along with all the fresh towels, and she ran in a crouched position to the car where the injured officers were receiving IV blood expanders.

She tried, without success, to get hold of Roy and turn him away from the fusillade of shots from the rented house, but she got only a piece of his flying shirt. Roy crawled back to the steps and, in a leap, jumped up the steps, went over to the downed officer closer to the front door of the house, picked him up in a marine medic's carry, and started running toward the steps leading down to the sidewalk.

A load of buckshot from a sawed-off shotgun protruding from the rented home hit Roy in the lower back and buttocks. He nearly fell down but completed his trip to the other side of the assailants' rented automobile. Examining the young officer, he found that he had died. Roy cradled him in his arms and rocked him back and forth and cried over his body.

There was a fierce exchange of gunfire between the officers, including Sheriff Dan Henderson, and the assailants in the house.

An FBI fog vehicle arrived to dispense tear gas and caustic gasses into the rented house. Finding the street blocked, the vehicle went up onto the broad lawns of the houses fronting the other side of Tyler Avenue and slowly crawled toward the rented house. At the house, the assailants were pouring automatic rifle fire into the fog vehicle. There were cracks in the armored glass on the front window, driver's side, and passenger's side of the vehicle but no penetration of bullets was accomplished.

The assailants had only two rocket-propelled grenades, and these had been expended against the SWAT team vehicle. The fog vehicle, which had tubes protruding from an armored extension on each side, poured caustic and tear gasses through the broken-out front windows of the rented house into the entire premises at a terrific rate.

Soon, two of the assailants—a young woman and an escaped inmate of the federal penitentiary—emerged from the house, first throwing out their weapons before emerging, coughing heavily from the gases, with their hands up.

Dan and the FBI agents ran as fast as they could to the front door and handcuffed the two survivors.

Entering the premises with cloths over their mouths, they found the other two assailants—a woman and a man, lying dead on the floor of the front room near the broken-out windows.

Roy was cradling in his arms the dead Decatur police officer. Margaret Mary was trying to comfort him, but Roy kept uttering, "Lieutenant, I lost my marine. I don't deserve those medals." He said this over and over again.

Finally, Dan Henderson, an FBI supervisor, the Decatur City Chief of Police, and two paramedics came to Roy and pried the body out of his arms and got him up. Promptly, Roy collapsed, bleeding from the lower back and buttocks where he had been struck by the buckshot.

Over and over, Roy kept saying, "Let me go to the other men. They're down; they need me as a medic."

Roy couldn't walk; he was placed on a gurney from which he tried mightily to get off and return to his duties with the wounded SWAT team members. It was not until he was given a sedative that he calmed down and finally passed out. Margaret Mary was allowed to ride in the paramedic vehicle with the treating paramedics to the hospital. She begged them to take him to the Terre Haute VA Medical Center, saying, "He's a decorated navy/marine medic from the Vietnam Conflict and would want to be treated there."

The paramedics agreed and drove Roy to the emergency room of the VA Medical Center. The paramedic vehicle was followed by media, and Roy's removal (unconscious) on a gurney was duly recorded by photographers and video cameras.

Roy had been seriously injured, and he would need surgery and extensive rehabilitation to regain the ability to walk. Roy was unconscious for several days. As Roy's wife and a skilled nurse, Margaret Mary followed the progress of the treatment and Roy's convalescence very closely.

It took hours to clean up the debris from this shoot-out. A

huge crane had to be brought into Roy's front lawn to remove the destroyed SWAT vehicle. The forensic team spent hours investigating the shooting. Three of the downed Decatur police officers survived this onslaught with Roy's ministrations and rescue. The fourth officer, whom Roy knew was dead and whom he cradled in his arms, was pronounced dead at the scene of the shoot-out.

The chief United States marshal and the supervisor of the FBI field office in Terre Haute had the two surviving shooters (one of whom was an escaped federal convict) lodged in a federal correctional facility for action by the federal grand jury on serious charges, including murder of a law enforcement officer, when the grand jury could be convened, and Roy was well enough to testify.

This would take several weeks, during which the federal magistrate judge set bond for the two assailants at an astronomical amount. The woman began to talk to the FBI and the marshal's service and agreed to testify against the male prisoner. Her boyfriend had been killed in the fusillade of firing by the police.

Mrs. Bucher, Betsy Mullins, Roy's office assistants and staff, and the Emerson children were nearly traumatized by the events they witnessed looking out the front windows of the Emerson house.

However, Mrs. Bucher said to all, including the children, "Let's go and help the police."

Out they walked and talked to all the officers, inviting them to come into the house to use the facilities and to eat the food that Mrs. Bucher, Mary Margaret, and the domestic help had been working on for days. Gradually, the supervisors of the officers permitted them to enter the Emerson house, and they used the facilities and consumed the victuals and lemonade while they spend hours working over the crime scene.

The incidents of that day were on the local, state, and national media. The lead picture was the photograph of Roy carrying the fourth seriously wounded (and now dead) police officer on his shoulders in a marine/navy medic carry. The newspaper headlines read in Terre Haute and on Terre Haute television and radio:

"Flashback: Roy E. Dons his Battle Helmet!" The battered Red Cross helmet that Roy had worn during this holocaust and that he had brought back from Vietnam was clearly visible in the photographs and on the videotapes.

This picture of Roy's act of carrying the wounded policeman was on the front cover of all of America's national magazines for the next week, with the headline "Civilian Hero."

Since it was nearing the end of the calendar year, one national magazine named Roy (shown in this picture) as the Man of the Year, with extensive photographs of the Emerson household, Roy's medals, a story about his exploits in Vietnam, and in the shoot-out encounter and pictures of him in the VA Medical Center.

As soon as Roy could get into a wheelchair, Margaret Mary pushed him to the grand jury room in the United States District Court in Terre Haute. When he entered the jury room as a witness, the grand jury foreman stood up, as did the representative of the US Attorney's Office and the other grand jury men and women, and clapped for Roy.

He was still pretty well beaten up and was a little woozy. But he told the story of what his own eyes had seen of the events of that Sunday and of his rescue of the officers and the slain police officer. He said he could *not see* the faces of the assailants, but he sure felt the effects of the buckshot into his lower back and buttocks, from which he was still suffering.

At the end of his testimony, when Margaret Mary entered the grand jury room to wheel out her husband, the assistant US attorney asked her to wait awhile and tell the grand jury what she had witnessed, including her ministrations to the injured officers. Margaret Mary spent about an hour on the witness stand in the grand jury room, but unlike Roy, she had seen the two assailants throw their weapons out of the rented house and come out to surrender with their hands up. She could identify them by sight.

The grand jury foreperson thanked Margaret Mary and Roy

for her testimony, and everyone stoop up in the grand jury room as Margaret Mary went to leave.

While Roy was in the hospital and was finally able to sit up, one day (unexpectedly) a huge delegation of dignitaries arrived, including the mayor of Decatur, the chief of police, the United States congressman, the supervisor of the FBI field office, the United States marshal (a very nice woman) and the warden of the Terre Haute prison (from whom both assailants escaped while being aided by the two women). Margaret Mary showed up with the chiefs of the United States Navy's and the United States Marines' recruiting offices in Terre Haute. The secretary of the navy in Washington, DC, at the request of a US congressman, permitted Margaret Mary to dress in her navy uniform and wear her Bronze Star medal.

There was a huge contingent of media there, with photographers and television camera persons. Roy's entire ward was filled.

Unknown to Roy, the United States Department of the Navy and the commandant of the Marine Corps had authorized a high medal for a civilian who renders extraordinary service to the nation. The congressman was bearing this medal and presented it to Margaret Mary to pin onto her husband's hospital gown.

After she had pinned on the medal and passionately embraced her husband, Roy, spoke up. "Friends, forgive what I am about to say, because I do not wish to seem ungrateful for this wonderful medal. However, I do not really deserve this medal, as I did not deserve all the medals I received in Vietnam and which are in a framed plaque on the wall of my living room at the Emerson household in Decatur. This medal should be given to the family of the dead police officer; it was he, not me, who gave the greatest sacrifice to his city and to his nation. Please remove this medal and give it to his family."

The United States marshal and the United States attorney (also a woman) lost their composure and hugged and kissed Margaret Mary and Roy, telling both of them that Roy was a hero and deserved this medal. Another medal and compensation were being given to the injured Decatur police officers and to the family of the deceased police officer, who was married and had two children.

Tears came to Roy's eyes; he lowered his head and bawled like a baby, saying over and over again, "I could not save my marine, Lieutenant, I'm afraid I lost my marine."

The doctors asked the crowd, including Margaret Mary, to leave. Roy needed rest. The dignitaries and assembled media removed themselves from the hospital ward as Margaret Mary kissed her husband passionately and said, "Come home soon. The children really miss you, as does my mother!"

A lawyer was deputized by the United States attorney to be delegated to the Tip County Prosecuting Attorney's Office to help out Betsy Mullins and the paralegals and legal intern volunteers with cases while Roy was incapacitated. Betsy told the United States attorney how helpful this person was, who was an experienced prosecutor and former assistant United States attorney herself.

The United States marshal made a special task of frequently visiting the Emerson household whenever she was in Decatur and during the remainder of her term in office. To her, Roy Emerson had gone above and beyond the call of duty and, if she had been his commander in the military (she had served in the US Air Force as an officer in Special Operations), she would have put Roy in for a Congressional Medal of Honor in connection with his actions during this dangerous shoot-out.

Margaret Mary, Mrs. Bucher, and the Emerson children grew to love and respect this United States marshal and would embrace her fondly whenever she paid a visit to the Emerson household.

While Roy was still convalescing and after his picture and story had appeared in the national magazine as Man of the Year, a steady parade of political operatives made their way to his hospital room or to his home to ask him to run for every political office in Indiana, from US senator to US congressman, to governor, to state senator or state representative, either as a Democrat or a Republican.

Roy's standard response was, "Not me. I belong in the Tip

County Prosecuting Attorney's Office and at home with my family and my dear friend, Sheriff Dan Henderson, not in another political office. Why don't you call my friend Bill Rice in Indianapolis, and ask him if he wants to run?"

Invariably, the response was, "We did; he said no and told us to ask his friend, Roy Emerson."

Roy's standard response was, "Well, you did as Bill Rice recommended, but the answer is still no."

Roy was discharged to his home in Decatur on crutches. He could go into the office for a couple of hours each day (which his doctors had reluctantly allowed and which was heavily policed by Margaret Mary). Later, he got off his crutches and was able to walk—a bit shakily—with a cane. He walked with a cane for the remainder of his life.

If he overdid it with his working, Margaret Mary, his children, and Mrs. Bucher threatened to take away his cane and hide it.

Eventually, the wonderful woman assigned to his office by the US attorney was no longer needed, as Roy was anxious to return to the courtroom.

As far as the surviving assailants were concerned, the woman testified against the man but got a long prison sentence. The man was found guilty of murder, among other charges, and got the death penalty. His appeals were pending for years after the shoot-out, but he spent his time on death row in Terre Haute until his sentence of death was finally approved and carried out. Roy refused to attend his execution. Roy really did not believe in the death penalty. In many ways, Roy Emerson was a liberal.

23

MORE GOINGS-ON

Roy knew that his assistant, Betsy Mullins, was in love with his friend, Sheriff Dan Henderson, and would soon leave to marry him. So Roy lobbied the county commissioners for the addition of a third assistant prosecuting attorney. When the dignitaries who had appeared in the hospital ward when Roy was bedridden showed up with Roy at the Finance Committee meeting (with Roy wearing the medal that had been awarded to him by the secretary of the navy and the commandant of the Marine Corps), the Finance Committee members' support by the growers was overwhelmed, and they approved an added appropriate on a unanimous vote. The County Commission approved the additional monies, and Roy bade Betsy a fond adieu and hired two of the three Valparaiso interns as new assistant prosecuting attorneys.

However, there was still a lot of work to do in the office.

As mentioned, Father Pedro Arroyo and Roy were close personal friends. One day Father Arroyo arrived at Roy's office and poured out his heart about the activities of a Latino gang in South Tip County in Dansville, which was recruiting young members and terrifying the community.

Father's efforts to enlist the community against the gang were to no avail. Roy called Sheriff Dan Henderson and asked if he might join the meeting over a lunch; Dan got free of some of his paperwork, came to the lunch shop that Roy and his assistants attended each day (and now had Father Arroyo as a guest), and learned firsthand from Father Arroyo about the gang problems in South Tip.

All of the attendees decided to do something about these problems. But what to do? Vigorous law enforcement and prosecution only seemed to steel the recruitment of other young Latino youth to the gang. Roy decided to turn to his Marine Corps League buddies at Western Indiana, who recommended a sociology professor who had written her dissertation at New York University concerning gangs.

The professor, Elizabeth Anne Wilkins, PhD, advised that she would conduct a series of seminars for Roy, Dan, Roy's prosecutorial assistants, and Father Arroyo—at no charge—if they could come to her classroom on several Saturday afternoons at Western Indiana University. Other law enforcement personnel were also invited and did attend, such as the police chiefs of Dansville, Decatur, and Terre Haute. The seminars and lectures were enlightening.

The doctor gave the attendees a sheaf of materials to read about gangs. The reading was rough-going because it was sociological in nature with many graphs and statistical studies. The result was that vigorous law enforcement against gangs only chips away at the edges of the gangs; it is necessary to get inside the gangs and work from there to peel away the members and discourage others from joining.

But how to do this? The literature was somewhat inconclusive as to the best way to accomplish this end, but the most effective way seemed to be a mentoring approach, one that Father Arroyo had tried to set up, and working with parents and other community leaders to give alternatives to gang members such as jobs and other community project assignments.

As Dr. Wilkins told Roy, "You could prosecute the hell out of the gang members and their leaders day after day, but others would rise up to take their places and keep the gang going. The gang has to be destroyed, and the literature and my teaching suggests different ways to accomplish this task."

All of the attendee's thanked the doctor, and at the end of

the sessions all the attendees took the doctor out for a fine dinner and drinks (somebody other than the doctor drove her home after dinner).

Now the hard work arrived at Roy's door. It was necessary to get started on what Roy called gang warfare. Gangs were also getting started in Decatur and Terre Haute, much to the dismay of the law enforcement officials in both cities.

The first thing Roy, his assistants, and Sheriff Dan Henderson did was to schedule a few meetings with purported gang members at Father Arroyo's community center just to exchange ideas and grievances without any fear of prosecution. A few turned up, and the gang leaders and members launched into a bitter denunciation of Tip County law enforcement and the Tip County legal system, particularly the juvenile court system. Roy and Father Arroyo listened in silence; they agreed to look into the complaints and to meet the gang leaders and members once again to discuss their findings.

The first thing that "Roy E.'s task force," as it began to be called, found was harsh conditions for inmates, particularly tattooed gang members, in the Tip County Juvenile Home. The recommendation to the county commissioners was to appropriate some money to have Dr. Wilkins come over to the Juvenile Home and teach the staff more humane ways to handle obstreperous inmates, particularly gang members.

For the next meeting at Father Arroyo's, Roy convinced all the Tip County judges to attend, where they heard from the gang leaders and their members about the setting of excessive bonds at arraignments (which the members' poor families could not meet), resulting in long confinement in the Tip County Jail with hardened criminals and harsh sentencing that would not utilize probation or the YTA procedure for gang leaders and their members.

The judges were peculiarly silent during the verbal tirade by the gang leaders and their members against the judicial system and its workings in actual practice. The judges decided to try to implement the gang members' suggestions for a year to see how things worked.

Also, the judges asked to and did confer with Dr. Wilkins about a new approach to setting bonds and sentencing alternatives to jail.

One of the suggestions she made to the judges was to utilize sentences to the Tip County Jail, rather than to the State of Indiana Correctional Facilities, so that the gang members could have more direct contact with their friends and families. Also, she advised the judges to use treatment programs, instead of incarceration for members who were drug addicted or alcoholic.

Gradually, the talking with the gang leaders and members and the changes they suggested began to bear fruit, at least in Dansville, and the gang there slowly disintegrated. But not in Decatur.

Now, one would think that Man of the Year Roy Emerson would relax a bit, leave public office, and join a law firm doing corporate work and make big money so that he could take Margaret Mary to the country club and afford private schools for their kids. But Roy had no intention of doing such a thing; there was still a lot to be accomplished in the prosecutor's office, and his assistants were not seasoned enough to take over the top job.

Also, Roy was still worried about the gang problems in Decatur. So Roy, the Man of the Year, announced for reelection. He had no opponents; no one wanted to see the picture of Roy carrying that dying police officer on his shoulders in a political brochure.

The Republicans were particularly careful to stay away from Roy Emerson. Any criticism of him would produce a terrible backlash against the Republican Party. Once, Roy called the Rice residence from home, with Margaret Mary on the extension phone. Laura answered; Roy told her he was calling to urge Bill Rice to run for Indiana state governor.

Laura told Roy, pleasantly, "Go to hell. I see little enough of him now with his business interests. Also, we live in a bigger house here in Indianapolis than we would live in at the governor's so-called mansion."

Margaret Mary, from the other line, said to Laura, "Also, I told Roy to go to hell, but he said he had already been there, being in Happy Valley, on Hill 861-A, and being married to me."

Everybody started laughing and told each other how much they loved each other and really missed seeing each other. Laura invited them to come down and stay with the Rices in Indianapolis. Margaret Mary invited Laura, Bill, Georgie, and the baby to come back up to Decatur. "Spend a full week with the Emerson girls and with my mother, who cried for a full day, Laura, when you and the baby left our household."

Laura said she would get Bill's okay to do that—and a couple of weeks later, Bill's executive jet landed at the Terre Haute airport, and a limousine rented by Roy and Margaret Mary picked up Laura and Georgie and the baby.

Upon Laura's arrival at the household, pandemonium broke out. It took almost an hour to get Mrs. Bucher to let go of Laura, Georgie, and baby Louise and to stop crying. The Emerson girls, even the littlest ones, hugged and kissed Georgie, making him get red in the face. Laura positively melted in Margaret Mary's arms and hugged and kissed Roy tenderly. Laura told the Emersons how proud she, Bill, and the entire state were of Roy and Margaret Mary.

Roy repeated his typical phrase, "Like Bill Rice said for his elected president, I am only a *surrogate* in receiving medals for my dead marines and for that wonderful dead Decatur police officer I could not save."

"The Rice Furniture Company is establishing a college scholarship fund for the decedent's children," Laura said.

The deceased officer's family was called during Laura's visit and invited over for dinner. Although they were a little shy, they came over, all dressed up, and were embraced by Laura, Roy, and Margaret Mary and treated to a wonderful dinner. After dinner, Laura presented to the widow with a receipt for large scholarship contributions to an account at Regions Bank in Indianapolis for the children of her deceased husband. Also, Laura presented a $100,000 certified check to the widow, in memory of her husband, for her and the children's housing and related expenses.

There was bawling, love, and kisses in the Emerson household for at least an hour after this presentation. The widow and the children could hardly stop hugging Laura when the time came for them to leave. They told her they would never forget the kindness of the Rice family. Laura assured them that Bill Rice was pleased to try to help out.

When the week was up, Mrs. Bucher refused to let Laura, Georgie, and the baby leave. She stole Laura's bags from her bedroom and hid them in the basement. Margaret Mary was embarrassed over her mother's actions, and the Emerson kids were sent on a search party and found the bags in the basement.

Then Mrs. Bucher really lost it, and she threatened to go out to the Terre Haute airport and to flatten the tires on Bill's executive jet.

Finally, Laura gave in and agreed to extend her stay—but *only* for another week. She called her husband and reported a kidnapping (which Bill should call in to the FBI) of her and the Rice children by Mrs. Bucher and the Emersons. Bill laughed and told Laura and the kids to stay as long as they desired. Georgie could miss as much school as Laura wanted.

Finally, Mrs. Bucher, Margaret Mary, and Roy persuaded Laura to leave Georgie behind when she returned to Indianapolis. They said he was part of their family already, and they would educate him in public schools of Decatur with their girls. They loved Georgie as if he were their own son and Mrs. Bucher's grandson.

Laura called Bill and got his okay, advising him that this was the only way she could get free of the kidnapping at the Emerson household. Bill laughed and told her to do what her heart told her to do. Georgie wanted to stay behind; the Emerson girls pleaded with Laura to let him stay. Margaret Mary and Mrs. Bucher assured Laura that he was a member of their family and would be treated as such. Roy piped up and said he would keep Georgie out of the juvenile home, whereupon Margaret Mary gave him a good poke in the ribs.

Laura let Georgie stay behind. Roy's rented limousine took everyone back to the executive part of the Terre Haute airport and, amid tears and hugging, Laura and the baby left in Bill's jet to return to Indianapolis. On the way back to Decatur, the Emerson girls held on tightly to Georgie.

Roy, Margaret Mary, and Mrs. Bucher were very pleased that Georgie stayed behind as a newly reinstalled member of the Emerson household. Roy and Margaret Mary promptly enrolled Georgie in the girls' school, where he did exceptionally well as a student and as an athlete. All of Georgie's class schedules, student activities, class photographs, grades, and awards were mailed promptly to the Rices in Indianapolis. Also, Georgie was becoming an accomplished soccer player.

Georgie told Roy, "I want to be a navy medic like you when I grow up."

Roy told Georgie, "When you're older, I'll take you to Annapolis, Maryland, where I hope you'll enroll as a midshipman in the US naval academy."

(Georgie eventually did get a congressional appointment to the naval academy, where he excelled in soccer, leadership, and grades and made a career of the United States Navy.)

Georgie spent the remainder of the growth years with the Emersons, having frequent visits with his parents in Indianapolis, Terre Haute, or Decatur.

Laura, the former escort counseled by Mrs. Bucher, became the social queen of Indianapolis society and retained her beauty until the day of her death.

A few years later, Bill passed away of a fatal heart attack, and eligible males began to court Laura. She never remarried, but she moved herself and the baby up to Decatur into the now-repaired house across the street from the Emersons. She and the baby were loved and cherished by Georgie, the Emersons, Mrs. Bucher (until her death from a heart attack a few years later), and the Emerson girls for the remainder of her life. Laura always remarked to her suitors (although she continued to date), "One really good husband is enough for me for a lifetime!"

24

ROY'S SECOND TERM AS TIP COUNTY PROSECUTOR

After being sworn in by the judges for a second term, Roy's injuries and his limp really began to bother him, and he decided to make this four-year term his last in public office. Like a good manager, he announced this intention to his staff and began to groom his assistants for his succession in four years.

As a result, he allowed them to handle some of the more publicized cases in the courts of Tip County, and Roy began to fade into the background. This did not mean that he sat in his office shuffling papers, but he tried to do some of the more mundane tasks of a prosecutor than to be constantly in circuit court, trying serious felony cases.

Also, he refused to accept interviews from the media about his past exploits; he referred all media inquiries, particularly about cases, to his assistants, who began to see their names in the newspapers and their images on the television screens and hear their names on radio shows. Also, the assistants were Roy's surrogates at speaking engagements and on television and radio call-in shows about criminal law.

Roy decided to spend his final four years in office trying to do something about the gang activity and warfare in Decatur. He would try to coordinate his efforts with the Monroe County prosecutor in Terre Haute, where there was a branch of the Decatur gang. The gang in Decatur was well armed and well financed through the vast income from its drug-dealing activities. Roy felt that the only way to strike at the Decatur gang was to prosecute successfully the gang's leaders, thereby hoping to peel off the peripheral gang members as the leaders went down like tenpins in a bowling activity.

To accomplish successful prosecutions, a task force was set up with the Monroe County prosecuting attorney and the federal Drug Enforcement Agency (DEA). Informants would have to give the prosecutors information on the gang's activities and be ready to testify in court, which was a very dangerous occupation, given the gang's proclivity to extract retribution from the informants *and* their family members.

Wiretapping and eavesdropping authorizing orders, as well as search warrants, were obtained from the federal and state court judges. Gradually, over several years' time, the leaders of the Decatur–Terre Haute gangs were taken down by law enforcement efforts and forced to plead guilty to reduced charges in the federal and state courts. A number of the leaders were given probation in order to become wired informants on their fellow gang members.

This approach proved to be successful in taking down some of the new leaders of the gang. As the leaders went to the federal and state penitentiaries and as the money supply of the gang began to dry up because of the seizure of money, drugs, and firearms, lesser members of the gang began to drop off.

Overall, the efforts of Roy and his fellow law enforcement professionals were proving successful, but only slowly. Progress had to be measured on a case-by-case basis, and, as mentioned, it took a considerable period to finalize a number of these prosecutions.

By the end of Roy's second term, he was physically tired, and he felt that he had accomplished all that he could as the Tip County prosecuting attorney. Democratic Party officials begged Roy to run for a third term or to declare for some other office as a Democratic candidate. Roy flatly refused. Roy told his two assistants that they should run for his office and that he would remain silent until one of them won as primary election if they ran on the same political party side of the ballot.

If they did run under the same party banner, whether Republican or Democratic, Roy would endorse the primary election winner for election to his position in the general election. His two assistant prosecutors ran as Republicans, and the one who won the primary election was endorsed by Roy and won the general election. Her transition into Roy's office was made easy by Roy and by her past experience in the office. Roy promised his successor (by the way, the unsuccessful candidate was *not* discharged by the newly sworn-in prosecuting attorney—the two women were really close personal friends).

25

ROY'S FINAL WORK ASSIGNMENT

After Roy's retirement from the prosecutor's office, numerous law firms and lawyers approached him, asking him to join them in their practice at substantial salaries. He turned all down flat.

Under Laura's prodding (Bill Rice had passed on, and Laura was living with the growing Rice daughter in the house across Tyler Avenue from the Emerson household), the chief operating officer of the Rice Furniture Company approached Roy and offered him the position of general counsel of the company at a substantial salary with very liberal benefits and a large expense account.

Roy thanked him for the offer but said the job would require substantial time away from his friends and family, so he turned down the lucrative offer.

Finally, Roy was approached by the dean of Arts and Sciences at Western Indiana University at Terre Haute and asked to join the faculty in the sociology department. Since Roy did not have advanced degrees, though, he would be hired as a lecturer but with tenure.

Roy said he would come to teach there but only under two conditions: (1) Western Indiana would have to find a teaching position for his experienced wife, Mary Margaret Bucher Emerson, RN, who had a bachelor's degree in nursing, and (2) Western Indiana would have to find a teaching position for a positively gorgeous woman, Laura Evans Rice, who could teach fashion design.

After some hemming and hawing, the dean finally found places as lecturers with tenure for all three people. Roy twisted Margaret Mary's and Laura's arms to go to work with him at Western Indiana University. Finally, they agreed, and all began their positions as lecturers at the university in Terre Haute.

Eventually, Western Indiana had expansion courses offered in Decatur, which were taught by Laura, Margaret Mary, and Roy. After ten years of teaching, all three lecturers retired from Western Indiana.

Roy spent the final years of his life doing a little writing and research on coping with gangs. He died peacefully in his bed of a heart attack, brought on by his many wounds, surrounded by his family and by Laura.

Roy was buried in the cemetery next to his parents with a headstone that had the name of Margaret Mary engraved therein, her date of birth chiseled thereon but date of death left vacant.

Margaret Mary would live to see her children and Laura's educated and successfully on their way in life.

Margaret Mary would pass away before Laura, who remained a beauty until her final moment of her life.

When Laura died, she was buried next to her husband in Indianapolis.

Thus ends the story of James Elroy "Roy" Emerson, the *famous* Tip County prosecuting attorney. Margaret Mary donated all the funds given to her at the time of Roy's funeral, matched by gifts from Laura and other friends of the Emersons and of the Rices, to Western Indiana University in Roy's name in the Western Indiana University's Department of Sociology.

Printed in the United States
By Bookmasters